OUR ETHEL

OUR ETHEL

Phil Batman

The Book Guild Ltd

First published in Great Britain in 2023 by
The Book Guild Ltd
Unit E2 Airfield Business Park,
Harrison Road, Market Harborough,
Leicestershire. LE16 7UL
Tel: 0116 2792299
www.bookguild.co.uk
Email: info@bookguild.co.uk
Twitter: @bookguild

This work is entirely fictitious and bears no resemblance to any persons living or dead.

Typeset in 11pt Minion Pro

Printed and bound in Great Britain by 4edge Limited

ISBN 978 1915603 838

British Library Cataloguing in Publication Data.
A catalogue record for this book is available from the British Library.

For my Nan

PART I

York, Thursday 12th February 1953

One

Dr Lawson turned his Daimler up onto the ramp to the loading bay at the Public Mortuary and came to a stop in front of the sign on the double doors that read 'Strictly no parking, twenty-four-hour access'. He knew that George would be assisting him with post-mortems for the next hour or so and wouldn't need to get the van out to collect any more customers. It was a bright frosty morning and his mood always got a lift from his days at the Public. The work was easy; it was fun; few people wanted to do it; it paid well; and it didn't really matter if he got things wrong. His patients couldn't complain. They were all dead anyway.

He opened the boot, pushed his clubs to one side, and cursed under his breath and winced in pain as his arm took the weight of his briefcase. The loading bay doors were padlocked so he let himself in through the side door. The smell of fried bacon greeted him as he made his way slowly upstairs to the office.

'Morning, Doc,' George shouted down as he heard the door open. 'Just two for you today, a big feller and a little feller. Hardly worth your while getting changed. You'll be on the first tee by eleven.'

'Piss off,' he called back. 'How many times do I have to tell you? I leave no stone unturned.'

The doctor took the chair at the side of the desk, picked up the *Daily Mirror* off the end, and turned to the sport on the back page.

'You've taken the Marilyn Monroe calendar down, George? You've not chucked it out, have you?'

'No, it's in the drawer. Dr Randall complained. You want it?'

'I know what she needs.'

'Dr Randall or Miss Monroe?'

'Both. But I'm too old for all that malarkey. Put the kettle on, George.'

'You're in your prime, Dr Lawson. But I'm getting too old for this malarkey, though.'

George dropped a pair of scissors down onto some papers with a soft thud, raised his bulk up from behind his desk, and went through to the gas hob in the next room. Dr Lawson leaned forward to open the cupboard and inspect the homemade wine. He rocked a large bucket full of dark red liquid and some bubbles left the sides and burst onto the surface.

'Hey, George,' he called through to the kitchen. 'This is coming on a treat. Is it bramble again? Can't wait for me first tipple.'

'It is. I've had the berries in the freezer downstairs. Me and the missus picked them last September. I reckon the heat coming up from the back of the fridges gets the brew going like a train. Any road, Doc, I'm knackered. I'm serious. I'm getting too old for this game. The big feller died on the toilet on the top floor and they found him at eleven last night. I got the call at one this morning, and we didn't get him down the stairs and back here till gone four. I'm dog-tired. I've not been back home to bed. Joey the budgie had fallen off his perch too, run out of water, but his cat was still alive. These dead pets are really getting to me.'

'Did you manage to rehome the cat?' asked the doctor. He put his finger into the juice then sucked it.

'Yes, thank God. The old lady next door took him in. She'd not seen hide nor hair of the old boy for over a week, then she stuck her nose through his letterbox and picked up the smell. That bit might not be in your report.'

'You'll never retire, George,' said the doctor. 'You'd drink yourself to death within a week, then you'd be straight back in here. We'll put you in lucky fridge number 7.'

He called through to the little room along the corridor with the table and the typewriter. 'You got any reports for me yet, Beryl?'

Beryl, a police constable turned coroner's officer, pulled her second typed report from the drum and brought them both along for the pathologist.

'Two quick ones for you today, Doc. You'll be out of here and on the fairway quicker than you can say Jack Robinson.'

'Don't you start. Tell me the tales. I'll have a read of 'em when I've a bit more time.'

George reappeared from the kitchen with three cups of tea on saucers on a little wooden tray and put it down on his desk.

'Start with Harry Moorhouse then. Sixty-eight-year-old man. Retired solicitor. Widowed about ten years ago, and then pulled up the drawbridge and kept himself to himself. Nice man by all accounts. His next-door neighbour says she's been keeping an eye on him, but she'd not seen him for a week and his milk was collecting on the doorstep. She spoke with her daughter yesterday afternoon, and they got in touch with us in the evening. We found him dead on the toilet.'

'Top floor, narrow staircase, eighteen stone,' interrupted George.

Beryl wanted to be away early too. She carried on. 'The house is a bit of a mess, single bloke, but I've seen worse. Poor health. No break-in. Niece down south, neighbour thinks, but we've not traced her yet. Your second customer, Doctor, is a cot death.'

'Oh, Beryl, don't do this to me. You know I hate 'em. I can never find owt. Leave it for Dr Randall tomorrow. Tell her it came in after I'd left.'

'No, Doc, we can't do that,' she told him. 'It needs sorting today, please. Mum needs to know as soon as I can tell her that it wasn't her fault. I told her this morning I'd go back this afternoon when you'd had a look at him.'

'Well, at least they're quick jobs, I suppose.'

'Thank you, Doctor. William Slater. He's just four days old. Mother is Ethel Slater. I've had a chat with her this morning, and there's summat fishy about this case I don't like. Can't put me finger on it. Maybe it's just that she's all alone. It's not easy talking to her either 'cause she's boss-eyed, and you don't know which one to look at. Seventeen years old. Won't say who the father is.'

'Perhaps she didn't catch his name,' said George.

Beryl and the doctor both ignored George now. He had heard too many cot death stories before. He thought they were all the same and he didn't like them. Nobody did. He picked up his scissors and his cup from his desk and disappeared back into the kitchen.

'She lives with her mum and dad in St Paul's Terrace. It's one of those mucky little streets down by the railway station. Gave birth alone by all accounts. The GP saw the baby the day he was born and he wasn't worried. Mum reckons she found him dead in her bed this morning with a bit of blood on his top lip. A neighbour got a phone call to the ambulance and they brought him straight here.'

'Woke up to find him dead beside her?' asked the doctor.

'No, she'd gone downstairs to answer the door then nipped over the street. Says she found him dead when she came back up.'

'Is the mother as upset as you'd expect? Owt else I should know?'

'Broken family, I reckon. Mum's as you'd want, bit worse if anything. Hysterical. Couldn't get her words out. House is full of clutter, pram, nappies, baby stuff, the usual. But it's not a wipe-your-feet-on-the-way-out type of place. Ethel looks after her mum, or tries to. She's got summat serious wrong with her, bed downstairs, sort of paralysed, I think. Her dad Dennis has had a few scrapes with the police. Short fuse. He's well known. Petty stuff, but no serious violence. That we've ever found out about anyway.'

'He's a bit too young for a cot death, Beryl. It's peritonitis and vomited up blood. I've seen it before.'

'I knew I could rely on you, Doctor. You never let me down. I want to do me best for Mum.'

PC Jackson needed to flatter Dr Lawson to make him feel important, even though she knew he could make the occasional embarrassing mistake. And he could erupt if he was challenged. Whether he wrote down cot death or peritonitis on the death certificate would make no difference to a mother. All Ethel Slater needed to hear was that there was nothing she'd done wrong.

The doctor heard George running water into the sink through the wall. He'd rounded up the breadcrumbs from the board and herded them into a coconut shell feeder with the flat edge of his hand, and added the chopped bacon rind and the scrapings of fat from the frying pan. He'd hang it back up for the blue tits outside in the loading bay yard after the doctor had left for the day.

'Come on, shift your bones, George, let's get 'em fettled,' the doctor called through to the kitchen. 'We'll have a look at Harry's pulmonary artery, and the bit of blood come up from William's twisted gut, then Bob's your uncle.'

It was too nice a morning to waste, and Dr Lawson had arranged to meet in the clubhouse at a quarter to eleven.

*

George and the doctor made their way down the stairs, the soles of their shoes sticking to the carpet slightly with the lift from each step. George carried on straight at the bottom and into the viewing room to sprinkle some food into the top of the goldfish tank, and Dr Lawson doubled back along the passage and into the fridge room. A couple of trolleys had been pushed up against a bank of six metal doors built the full length of the wall from floor to ceiling. He turned into the changing room, hung his jacket behind the toilet door, kicked off his shoes and pulled on a pair of rubber boots, and put on an apron and gloves.

He could see the two white porcelain slabs through the hatch, both with a deep sink at the end full of steaming water overflowing onto the tiled floor. One was vacant and awaiting Harry, and spread-eagled in the centre of the other was William Slater. Stretched beside him and much the same size was a soft brown furry little companion with his knitted speckled waistcoat, leather patches for paws, and black buttons for eyes with red rims.

The pathologist stopped to stare at the two of them, alone and lost on the slab.

'Jesus Christ,' he said to himself. 'Dead budgies in cages upset George, but teddy bears on slabs really get to me.'

George wheeled Harry Moorhouse in on a trolley and stationed it alongside the slab. Taking Harry's left wrist and left ankle in each hand, he lugged him across onto it. Then lifting the back of the head off the porcelain with his left hand, George slid a wooden block under the corpse's shoulders with his right. It lay back in a graceful arc.

'Heart and lungs do you? No need for the top off?' asked George.

'Fine.'

George wielded his knife and launched it through a full circle, catching the handle in his palm. Always his opening piece, a juggler's party trick. Then, with the ease of a fishmonger filleting a mackerel, he slit round the neck and down the centre of the chest, slid up through the ribs along the sides of the breastbone, cut through the windpipe and the back of the tongue, heaved the heart and lungs up and out of the chest, and sliced them off at the diaphragm. He dropped the organs onto a chopping board under Dr Lawson's nose. With the weight of the lungs suspended from the heart, the doctor made one cut through the connection and found the glistening clot in the pulmonary artery.

'Pulmonary embolus, just like I said,' he told George.

'Never go for a crap if you've got chest pain,' advised George. The doctor had heard this line many times before and he didn't react. He glanced up at the clock instead. Going well, he thought, ahead of time.

'Let Beryl have the teddy bear, George, will you?' he said. 'Mum will want it back. And I'll do this little mite myself.'

He held his fingers in the hot water in the sink for a minute or so. It eased the arthritis. He didn't like little cases like this one. They bothered him. Life wasn't fair. He squeezed out the water from a sponge and positioned it on the porcelain, then laid the baby on his back on top of it, allowing his head to tilt back. The eyes looked up at the pathologist, clear and unseeing, and he closed each eyelid gently with his index finger. He couldn't allow the baby to be a witness to his own evisceration.

Tiny organs would require delicate instruments and a steady hand. Dr Lawson took his rolled canvas sleeve of baby tools from the shelf and unfurled its contents of fine probes, fresh scalpel blades, curved scissors, and a bone saw. He would start with the belly, he thought, and expose the twisted gut. His scalpel traced a sinuous line in the skin from the throat, down the centre of the chest, skirting round the navel and into each groin, piercing the point of the blade into the abdominal cavity in its travel. No spurt of blood as expected, but also no hiss of gas escaping from the belly. No twisted loop of intestine. Ominous and worrying signs that took him by surprise. He opened the stomach. There was no blood in it, but just a little thin, watery milk. This abdomen was normal, as pristine and dry as the day it was born. Dr Lawson stepped back and held his hands under the running hot water as he looked over at his case and gathered his thoughts. This was not going to plan, not what he wanted. Twenty minutes had passed on the clock since he last looked. Baby William Slater had ceased to be a person now in the care of a teddy bear. He had become a problem to be solved.

'I don't like the look of this at all, not one little bit,' he told George.

George was stitching Harry back up.

'Why not?'

'I think the bleeding must have come up from the lungs and onto his face. I'm thinking this little chap might have been suffocated.'

'Smothered?'

'Mm. Maybe.'

'I'll leave you to it,' said George. 'I'll go warn Beryl.'

For the next couple of hours Dr Lawson became a study in concentration, no longer the butt of ceaseless banter and well-rehearsed jokes. He neglected to look up at the clock on the wall again, and his sporty pals drove off from the first tee in his absence. Dark red fresh blood had flooded the baby's lungs and washed up into his windpipe as the doctor had feared. Every organ in the chest and abdomen was now released from its moorings and laid out for inspection on the slab, their surfaces, vessels, tubes, and chambers squeezed, probed, teased apart, and scrutinised.

Last came William's brain. The doctor had often lost interest before he reached this stage, but this case had gripped his attention. And he knew he could be criticised down the line, certainly by a lawyer and even by a judge, if he left this particular stone unturned. He ran a blade over the top of the scalp from ear to ear and turned back the skin. He paused to tease a bruise from the skull, the shape of a hen's egg, a beautiful speckled pattern of browns and red. And then he ran his scissors along the membranes joining the bones and eased them apart like a poppy opening its petals for the sun.

He put his instruments down and stopped.

'Oh, fuck,' he said under his breath. 'George,' he bellowed upstairs, 'get Beryl down here.'

Beryl appeared at the doorway, then clasped her hands behind her back and watched her feet as she picked her way carefully across the film of water on the floor.

'We need some close-ups of all this, PC Jackson,' he told her. 'And your gaffer to see it too.'

She'd dispensed with wearing an apron, and her cheery smile had been replaced with a frown.

'You've got your witness box face on, Dr Lawson. I just knew this one would go belly up,' she said, keeping her hands behind her back and leaning forward to inspect his findings.

He took up a probe and laid its point against a crack in the skull.

'This fracture is beneath this scalp bruise, Constable, and take a good squint at this.'

He held open the petals of the skull bones with his splayed-out fingers. William's brain was covered with a thick layer of fresh red blood.

'Get all this photographed, Beryl. He's taken a right battering this morning and been smothered.'

'No! I don't believe it!'

'You'd better. And not for the first time either. She's whacked this little scrap at least once more before this morning.'

'Shit!'

The doctor played his probe over the red then the brown areas of the bruise.

'You and the boss get over to St Paul's Terrace. You've got to fix on one of Mum's eyeballs and ask her some very difficult questions. She's murdered this baby. There's no two ways about it.'

Two

Ethel answered the knock at her front door, opened it an inch or two, peered through the gap, then flung it back and snatched the teddy bear out of Beryl Jackson's hand. She dropped it in an instant onto the step, howled, and buried her face in her hands where nobody could see her.

'Please,' she managed to whisper through her tears and her fingers. 'Where is he? Please give me my baby back.'

PC Jackson's first job was to get Ethel's story out of her and report it back to the coroner, a retired small-time solicitor in town who investigated suspicious deaths. She dealt with the lost and bewildered Ethel Slaters of this world all too often, and always did her best to find some words of comfort for them, whatever they had done. She knew a kind word could often get to the truth. She had a child of her own, and realised the mother was usually as much a victim as her dead baby. She could barely imagine what these Ethels had gone through.

She had arrived at the house today with Sergeant Thornton in her wake, a burly, hard-bitten, craggy-faced man who'd never been blessed with any of her compassion. His stock in trade was violence, and he despised the criminal underclass. He took this as a golden opportunity to solve two nasty little crimes in just one visit to the same family.

Ethel Slater was stricken. Time had meant nothing since the ambulance had taken her baby away that morning. She hadn't left the house; she'd wandered from room to room; she hadn't dressed; she hadn't eaten. Charlie Songhirst, a good neighbour, had gone with the baby in the ambulance to the mortuary, and his wife Olive rallied and came over the road to help Ethel's invalid mother. And Ethel's father had told his daughter she'd get what she deserved.

The coroner's officer picked up the bear from the pavement and stretched out her hands onto Ethel's shoulders. She eased her back over the step, and Sergeant Thornton followed. They edged past a pram and an open door and into the kitchen. A towering moustached man they both knew of old leant back against the door to the yard and said nothing. Beryl pulled out a chair from the table, took some damp clothes off it, and dropped them onto the floor, then seated herself across from Ethel and gave her back the teddy bear to hug. She'd made up her mind during the journey across town from the mortuary to avoid looking at Ethel's lazy left eye if she could.

'Ethel, my love,' she said, 'I'm Beryl from the coroner. Do you remember I came to see you this morning? I was with the ambulance. And this is my colleague Sergeant Thornton from the police. Shall we put the kettle on?'

Ethel nodded, and Beryl looked back to the sergeant. There was no chair for him so he'd remained standing in the doorway. She could see his shoulders relax as he was given a job to do. He squeezed his bulk between the back of Ethel's chair and the sink, put a cigarette from a packet on the edge of the cooker between his lips, flicked on the gas hob, then bent his head below some cloths hanging from a line to hold the end of it down to the flame.

'You told me earlier today what happened this morning?' Beryl continued. 'I want you to tell me again. Never mind your father. In your own words, just as slow as you like. I need to write it down. The thing is, Ethel, the doctor's had a careful look at William, and there's some injuries you need to explain.'

She would have expected a reaction to this.

But Ethel just stared at her own hands spread on the table.

Her father snatched his packet of cigarettes from the cooker, then hesitated and slid the kettle onto the ring.

'What happened to your baby?'

'He died.'

'How?'

'I found 'im dead.'

'Where?'

'On me bed.'

'Why was he on your bed, Ethel?' said Beryl. 'Doesn't he have a cot?'

'He slept in the drawer, but I must 'ave forgot to put 'im back in it after I'd fed 'im.'

'Why in a drawer?'

'I'd put a little blanket in there, the bottom drawer of the chest in me bedroom, an' I just wedged it open with a spoon.'

'Did you wake up to find him?'

'The postie woke me up.'

'How?' asked Beryl.

'He was bangin' at the front door. The postie had brought me a parcel from Aunt Annie. I went over the street to show Olive and when I came back up William 'ad blood on 'is top lip where I'd been asleep.'

She held the teddy bear into her face and began to cry again.

Beryl took a sip of tea from her cup, then slid Ethel's across the table towards her.

'Have a drink of your tea, love, an' take your time,' said Beryl. 'We're in no rush. Knocking at the front door woke you up; you went down to open it; the postman had brought you a parcel with this teddy bear from your auntie; and when you went back upstairs you found William on your bed with some blood on his face. Is that right, Ethel? I can see this hurts, but we must get it all written down straight for the coroner.'

'Yes,' whispered Ethel.

'Did you pick William up?'

'His eyes were open but he wasn't lookin' an' his face was white an' nothin' was movin' an' I just knew he was dead. I banged on the wall for Mrs Sath next door.'

'Were you asleep when the postman knocked?'

'Yes, I must 'ave been. He said he'd been knockin' for a while. I'd been up wi' Mum in the night, and I think I'd dozed off after I'd 'eard the mail train.'

'Was William born in the hospital in town, Ethel?' asked Beryl.

'No, I 'ad 'im 'ere upstairs.'

'Did a nurse help you? Or a friend?'

'No, by meself.'

'By yourself, Ethel? Nobody at all? Why was that?'

'No, they'd 'ave taken 'im away. Everybody just wanted to take 'im off me an' get 'im adopted.'

'Jesus Christ!' exploded Dennis. 'Women!' He grabbed the door to the yard with one hand, smashed his empty cup into the sink with the other, and bellowed back to the kitchen as he left, 'Ask 'er why she didn't listen to the fuckin' vicar. Ask 'er that.'

Dennis jumped the couple of steps out into the yard and slammed the door behind him. Sergeant Thornton emptied his tea into the sink, pushed his way behind Ethel's chair again, and let himself out after Dennis. PC Jackson let them both go. There were few men she had met during her time in the York police force she disliked more than Dennis Slater, not even David Thornton. She would have to talk with him again later.

'Ethel,' said Beryl, 'there's just me an' you now. Tell me about William's birth. Was he born in your bed?'

'No, I 'ad 'im standin' up.'

'What? Say that again,' said Beryl.

'The pain were terrible, lyin' on the bed. I was standin' at the foot of me bed leanin' into the frame, an' he came out onto the floor. Then Mrs Sath from next door came round.'

'So you'd asked Mrs Sath to help you have the baby?'

'No, she came round after he was born. I banged on her wall as he was comin' out. I was scared he'd die.'

'Well done, Ethel,' said Beryl. 'I've written all this

down. We'll see what the coroner has to say. One last thing, though, love. Do you want me to tell the father?'

'No need. Mrs Sath's told 'im. William were 'er Eddie's.'

*

The sergeant followed Dennis out into the yard. He was holding open the hatch in a pigeon loft, and a couple of birds were pecking mechanically at the corn in the palm of his outstretched hand.

'Ey up, lad,' said the sergeant. 'It's always a pleasure to see you, Slater. I've been meaning to have a word with you for a while.'

'Fuck off, Thornton,' Dennis said without taking his eyes off his pigeons.

Sergeant Thornton leant over the back gate and looked up and down a snicket at the bikes, the bins and the rubbish. He took a long slow drag from his cigarette, then turned round to watch Dennis gently stroking the top of a pigeon's head.

'Did you sleep at home last night, Dennis?'

'Nowt to do wi' you where I was.'

'You're wrong there, Dennis. Where were you?'

'Out.'

'Shaggin' somebody's wife?'

'Fishin' down the brick pond.'

The policeman took a step back into the yard and pulled open the lavatory door across the flags. The wooden seat was down on the pan, a rusty pipe led up the bricks behind it to a cistern, and there were some old newspapers and cigarette butts scattered on the concrete floor.

'Where do you keep the rod an' line, Dennis?'

Dennis ignored the question and bent to take more grain from the bucket. Sergeant Thornton raised a foot to kick the seed out of his hand, then grabbed his neck by the collar.

'And the brick you put through Sid Waggett's window in town, Dennis? Practisin' your castin' off, were you?' he snapped.

'Nowt to do wi' me, Sarge, scout's honour.'

Dennis raised his arm outside the sergeant's, brought his fingers into a salute at the temple, and smiled into his teeth.

Then spat at his chin.

'Dirty bastard!'

Thornton's head jerked back.

He tightened the twist on Dennis's shirt and blew smoke into his face.

'Course it was fuckin' you. That brick had your name written all over it. But you're in deep shit now, lad. We need you inside the house for your side of the story.'

Keeping a grip on his arm, Sergeant Thornton laughed and shoved Dennis back through the door into the kitchen.

*

The sergeant knew he had to take the line of questioning out of Constable Jackson's hands. Just a few more lies from the mouths of Dennis and his daughter would crack this murder investigation.

He stood with his back to the yard door and took in the features of the kitchen. The cooker stood in one corner with a kettle and a pan of nappies in brown water on the rings; a couple of cloths and a pair of pants hung from a string over the cooker stretching from the top of the window frame; the curtain over the window to the yard was tied into a knot in the middle to lift it up from the porcelain sink below; and the plaster on the walls and ceiling was peeling with patches of black mould. There were no blood spatters on any surface, no signs of recent violence. Just squalor.

'Beryl, love,' he said, 'I'll take over. Where's the wrapping from the parcel?' he asked Ethel.

'I lit Mum's fire with it,' Ethel replied.

She didn't look up.

'Did you hear the postman, Dennis?' he asked.

'I was out, overnight fishin',' Dennis replied. 'Remember?'

Ethel flashed a look across to her father.

'You're an evil cunt, Slater,' he told him. 'Now, what's this about the fuckin' vicar, then?'

'He said he knew someone who could get rid of it for 'er; that's all I know.'

Thornton had heard as much as he needed. Women's talk and cups of tea and bits of paper with pencil scribbles were alright as far as they went, but it was some hard evidence he wanted now. He turned and took a step out of the kitchen, then peered behind the front room door. There was a fire burning in the grate, a couple of walking sticks resting on a chair, and an old woman laid flat out in a bed and staring at the ceiling above her. Her eyes are open. She's alive, he thought, just. He pushed past the pram draped with wet clothes in the hallway and kicked a pair of boots and a shopping bag to one side as he climbed the stairs.

The back room at the top of the stairs was in darkness. He pulled the curtain to one side and peered down at the pigeon loft and the open lavatory door and the baby vests and nappies hanging on the line in the yard. His attention was caught by a crow perched on the rim of the bucket of corn on the flags. He watched it hop onto a fence of railway sleepers then launch itself into a lazy flap away over the rooftops. The sergeant placed two eyes with his fingertip in the grime on the windowpane, then a dot for a nose and a smile from ear to ear. There was a mattress with a blanket and a sheet thrown onto the floor, a wooden chair draped with some clothes and a blood-spattered apron, and an empty whiskey bottle toppled over on the boards. He let the curtain fall back into place, lit a cigarette, and flicked the match onto the mattress.

He took the few steps into the bedroom at the front of the house. An unmade bed behind the door was pushed up into the corner. There was a rickety old painted chest of drawers and a rug under the window in front of him, a picture hanging on the wall to his right, Ethel's handbag on the floor, and nothing else. The bottom drawer had been wedged open with its edge resting on the floorboard. He ruffled his hands through the knitted blanket, a bib, a nappy, and a woollen pompom hat inside it, then pulled open the drawers above and tossed out baby cardigans and leggings and Ethel's knickers, skirt, blouse, and a pinny onto the floor. He knocked the drawers back into the cabinet with his knee then picked up the mirror from the top, took his cigarette from between his lips, wiped his chin, forced a smile, and inspected his teeth for a moment. He shook the contents of Ethel's handbag onto the bed and picked them over: a crumpled handkerchief; a comb; a powder compact; a lipstick; a couple of humbugs; a scruffy faded photograph of a baby elephant on a sea of dandelion heads, with a couple of happy kids astride its back; and a few pennies, which fell onto the floor and rolled under the bed.

He bent to kneel in the gap between the end of the bed and the chest of drawers, and retrieved the pennies together with a flimsy shoebox from the dust and fluff underneath. He leant back on his haunches on the rug, put his hands around the small of his back, stretched his shoulders backwards, and groaned. He emptied a blanket and a baby's pink bonnet from the box on top of Ethel's belongings on the bed. Not much of a murder weapon in that little lot, he thought. What he really wanted was a heavy object. The mirror didn't have any damage to it, and if she'd hit the baby with the picture, she would have smashed the glass.

There must be a clue in the house he'd missed, some blood on a weapon, somewhere. He ran his fingers through his greasy hair. Perhaps the old woman's room downstairs. It's worth a look, he guessed. Maybe find a streak of blood or a little bit of scalp skin on the whiskey bottle. Easing himself to his feet and grabbing the foot of the bed to take his weight, his shoe rucked up the rug and slipped along the floorboards.

'Bingo!'

Here was his crime scene, a pool of dried blood on the floor as big as a plate, hidden from prying eyes. And above it was his murder weapon, a blunt instrument. A wall. A wall with a long crack in the plaster. Shit, he thought. Slater's daughter could swing for this. She's thrown the poor little bugger at the wall.

He turned the lock in the front door at the foot of the stairs on his way back to the kitchen and dropped the key with Ethel's pennies into his pocket.

'Beryl,' he said, 'we won't be needing your coroner anymore, love, but keep your pencil and paper handy.

'Ethel Slater,' he said. He stood in front of the stove and looked down at her swivelling cross eyes. She watched his lips move and smelt his foul breath and heard words coming out but knew somehow and somewhere deep in her brain that she must be dreaming. 'I am arresting you on suspicion of the murder of William Slater on the morning of 12th February 1953 contrary to common law. You are not obliged to say anything unless you wish to do so, and anything you do say will be taken down in writing and may be used in evidence.'

Three

Inspector Harrison arrived at the police station in York in the late afternoon. He'd received the telephone call from Sergeant Thornton several hours before, but he'd been far too busy with an assault and drowning in a lock in the Leeds canal to attend sooner. No matter. The suspect wasn't going anywhere. She could wait. And Inspector Harrison was a lot more comfortable spending the night in a warm police station drinking free cups of tea than in his bedsit with only the gas fire for company since his wife had left him. He enjoyed murders.

The sergeant had given the inspector enough detail to whet his appetite over the telephone.

'She's plonked in the cell,' he said. 'We brought her in at dinnertime, so she's had plenty of time to stew. Plus, she's simple. I reckon she'll sing like a canary.'

'Give me the cause of death first off, Sergeant, then you can tell me the tale.'

'Doc Lawson did the PM. It's a four-day-old baby, and

he says it died early this morning. Still warm and floppy. Have a read of this. Mind you, it's just his summary, Inspector. Doc wants to get his fancy microscope out and look at a bruise in more detail. But he says his conclusion won't change and you'll get his typed report with all the whistles and bells when he's got a bit more time.'

The sergeant turned round a sheet of paper on the counter between them and slid it under the inspector's nose.

'So,' he said. 'Looks like she's hit him once when he was born, and finished the job this morning. Two bruises, fractured skull, bleed over the brain. Blunt instrument, severe force, he reckons. And smothered. Bugger me, a real belt and braces job, ey? Have you had a good look round the house?'

'I have.'

'And?'

'She's done it in her bedroom. She's flung him at the wall. Twice. There's a pool of blood on the floor she's tried to cover over with a mucky little rug, and a thumping big crack in the plaster on the wall, where he bounced.'

'Have you got it all photographed yet?'

'Tomorrow morning. I've got the key.'

'Smart work, Sergeant. I would think that should wrap things up. Is there owt else I should know?'

'Well, there's a couple of loose ends, I suppose. There's her father, Dennis Slater, kicking around the house, and her mother living in the room downstairs. And a nosey old woman next door. She's heard the whole thing start to finish. I went round there this aft, had a bit of a chat, made a few notes, good coppering. She reckons her son is the father.'

'But you don't believe her?'

'Yes, I do actually. I had Dennis down for that part, but I've gone off that idea. I've known him for years. He likes to throw his weight around when he's in drink, and he's spent a few nights in the cell here. Good with his fists. He's not as big as he thinks he is, but he's an arrogant, good-looking bastard and he likes to shag around. He was at it out somewhere in town last night. Anything with a pulse is fair game and I wouldn't put his own daughter past him. He wants taking off the streets and locking up. He's a nasty piece of work.'

'Is the girl a prostitute?'

'Hardly. She'd have a job drumming up business. You can judge for yourself when you have a look at her. She's not got form anyway.'

'And the nosey parker?'

'Our star witness. A Mrs Sathersthwaite at number 15 next door. Stuck-up old cow really. She had me take my shoes off before she'd let me in the house. Her son Edward is the father, and he runs his own garage business in Preston. Her husband was some big noise in the railway. She sleeps through the other side of the wall from Ethel, and she heard all the kerfuffle when the baby was being born, and being killed.'

'What kerfuffle?'

'It sounds to me like all hell broke loose. She thought the wall was coming through.'

'So the Slaters are dog-rough then?'

'They all are down there, to be fair. Dennis knocks his missus about, and the old woman thinks the violence got worse after the baby was born.'

'Do you know why she did it, Sarge?'

'Yep, revenge. The old bag's son had dropped Ethel like a hot potato, I reckon.'

'Housey-housey, full house. Crime scene, witness, motive. If we can get a confession out of her, we'll have it all stitched up in a day.'

'You'll be in bed by midnight, Inspector.'

Inspector Harrison handed the piece of paper back to the sergeant, glanced at his watch, then eyed the chair and the fire crackling in the hearth.

'Shall we let the dog see the rabbit, Inspector?'

'Let's have a brew first, David. I've been stood on a towpath all afternoon.'

'I'll bring her up from the cell and put her in the interview room.'

'Grand idea. And tell her the inspector has arrived and is reading through what the doctors have found.'

He took his *Daily Mail*, his packet of cigarettes and his matches from his coat pocket, and settled down in the chair.

Sleepy York, he thought. Little domestic jobs like this one didn't really excite him. The canal in Leeds was a lot more interesting, but there wasn't much he could do with that case yet until the body surfaced downstream or got trapped in lock gates. At least Ethel Slater was a quick result, and that looked good with the chief inspector.

*

The interview room was no bigger than Ethel's bedroom at home. There were two stiff chairs on either side of a small wooden table, with a lamp and a heavy clear glass ashtray containing a few old butts, a filing cabinet, a tall coat stand, and a small barred window high on the wall above the door. The loud tick of a clock was designed to impress the slow passage of time.

Ethel sat facing a wall. The inspector pushed open the door and hung his overcoat and trilby on the stand without looking towards her, then moved round to take his chair opposite her and switch on the lamp.

Ethel shielded her eyes from the glare.

He studied her face carefully as he lit another cigarette, and then leaned back.

'I'm Inspector Harrison,' he said. 'I'm here to ask you some questions about how your baby died. Do you understand that?'

Ethel nodded.

'Can I call you Ethel, love?'

'Yes,' she said. 'But I need to go 'ome first or can you telephone Olive to see to me mum, please?'

'Who's Olive when she's at home?'

'She lives over the street.'

'We'll take you home in a car, Ethel, just as soon as you've told me the truth.'

The inspector could see that Ethel had been crying. Dried tears stuck some strands of hair over her cheek that had fallen down from her scarf, her eyelids looked thin and red, and her breath was rancid. One eye was staring at his hand poised over the sheet of paper on the desk between them, but the other seemed to have veered away to the lamp. She really wasn't what he thought a woman should look like.

He tapped the end of his cigarette into the ashtray and leaned into her.

'Give me a clue, Ethel,' he said. 'Which eye works?'

She lifted her hand to her right eye and looked at his yellow fingers and grubby nails.

'I'm going to ask you some questions about the baby, Ethel, and write down the answers. It won't take long. Then when we're done, all I want you to do is read through it and sign the piece of paper with your name. Alright?'

Ethel didn't answer again.

'I can read it out to you, then, and you can sign it,' he said.

Ethel sniffed and looked at the table.

'Look, Ethel, you can stay silent if you want, but we can get you out of here and back home a lot quicker if you speak to me and not just sit there. And I'll let you into a few secrets before we start proper. You're in big trouble. Get that straight. I've spoken with the doctor and I've seen the body, and he's got massive injuries. A lot. Serious injuries. That's killed him. There's only you could have caused them, Ethel. You know that, don't you? You've hit him twice, haven't you?'

'No, that's not true,' said Ethel. 'I've never 'urt 'im.'

'Then who?'

'Nobody. Nobody's 'it 'im.'

'That can't be right, can it, love? Think about it. There was only you in the house last night. Is that right?'

'Mum was downstairs, an' Dad came in late.'

'But your dad was out all night, Ethel, wasn't he?'

'I 'eard the yard door gone midnight.'

Any lingering suspicion the inspector might have had

that Ethel was innocent vanished with her answer. She was trying to put even her own father in the frame.

He leant back on his chair and watched her eyes.

'Let's go back right to the beginning of all this. Could the baby's father have done it? Do you know who he is, by the way?'

'Yes, it's Eddie Sath next door.'

'Good girl, that's the spirit,' said the inspector. 'Get it off your chest.'

He wrote 'father next door' on his sheet of paper, then lit another cigarette from the stub of the old one and balanced it on the edge of the ashtray. Trails of smoke curled up over them both.

'Has Eddie been alone with the baby? What was he called, by the way?'

'William. No, Eddie went away.'

'Then how about your father? He lives in the same house, doesn't he?'

'Yes, but he's wanted nowt to do wi' me or the baby since I told 'im.'

'So he's not been with William alone, just the two of them?'

Ethel shook her head.

'Well, Ethel,' he said, 'I was bang on the nail the first time, wasn't I? William has been battered round the head this morning, and there's nobody else but you could have done it. Right?'

The inspector took a long, deep drag from his cigarette and watched Ethel sag as his words hit home. He took his time to write down that this was an unwanted bastard child and mother had been abandoned by the father of the child and her own father. There had been no contact with either of them since the baby was born.

They had arrived at a crossroads now, and he had a crucial decision to make. If he played down her crime, he would tell her she'd get a caution if she confessed. Go down the other route, and he could threaten her with the death sentence unless she confessed here and now.

He could see that Ethel was shivering.

He had made up his mind. Fear of God had never let him down.

'Come on, love, tell me what happened this morning, right from the start, in your own words. Slow as you like, so I can write it down.'

'I don't know what 'appened, I keep telling you. I found 'im dead in my bed.'

'Where did you sleep?'

'In bed. He was laid next to me.'

'Thrown onto the bed?'

'I don't know. I think he was just where I must 'ave left him.'

'So, let's get this right, you wake up in the morning, nice and warm and dozy, sun streaming in through the window, and there lying next to you is your baby, William, dead, with these terrible injuries. A mystery. Who's gone and done that while I've been asleep, you thinks to yourself? You expect the judge to believe that, Ethel?'

Ethel watched his fingers roll the ash at the tip of his cigarette around the lip of the tray.

'Had you been up with him during the night?'

'I don't think so. I think he went to sleep there after I'd fed 'im last thing.'

'Oops, you're telling me another fib already, Ethel. Babies don't go for hours all night without milk, from what I've heard, do they? Sounds to me like you've been awake during the night. Did he cry a lot?'

'Mrs Sath would take 'im out if he cried a lot.'

'Who's Mrs Sath?'

'Eddie's mum, she's Granny Sath.'

'Right, the old woman next door. So, you wakes up this morning and find the baby next to you with these fatal injuries, right? Then what did you do, Ethel?'

'No, I'd gone down to the front door. The postie had brung a parcel from Auntie Annie in Rochdale, and I found 'im when I got back upstairs.'

'Just stop there a minute, Ethel. You've told me another lie, haven't you? You told me not five minutes since that you woke up next to him dead. I wrote it down, and now you're telling me he's dead when you come back upstairs. Which is it, Ethel? We need to be clear if I'm going to help you.'

'Back upstairs.'

'Before we go any further, there's summat else I'm obliged to tell you. Which is how the law works. From what you've told me so far, you're going to prison then get sent for a trial in a court in Leeds, Ethel. With a judge and a jury and lawyers and all the rest of it. In a few months' time. And if the judge thinks you've murdered your baby and hears you telling this pack of lies, he'll sentence you to hang. But if you tell him the truth, what we're going to write down here and you sign, he'll be more lenient with you. Do you know what I mean by lenient?'

Hang was the only word that Ethel had heard. Her hand jerked up to her mouth.

'I think you are very, very tired, love. I think you've not got any sleep in a long time, and it's all catching up with you. You're not thinking straight. You're confused, I can see that. I'll tell you what I think has happened, and we can tell the judge this, and he'll understand. William has been crying a lot during the night, and in the morning you've come back upstairs and he's still crying and you've seen your mum is left downstairs and your dad doesn't care about anybody and Eddie's left everything to you. You're all alone and you've had enough. And summat snaps and you grab him and throw him at the wall. Isn't that the truth of it, Ethel?'

'Do you know the judge?' said Ethel. 'Can you talk to him?'

'He's a nice man, but you don't want to get on the wrong side of him with a half-baked tale full of lies, do you?'

'But I can't 'ave 'it 'im, no way. I can't 'ave. I went to show Olive the teddy then I found 'im on the bed. He was white as a sheet an' cold an' he 'ad some blood under his nose. I knew he'd gone. An' I shouted an' banged for Mrs Sath. An' that's the truth of it. I'll never forget it. I can't get it out of me 'ead.'

The inspector put his pen down and turned his head to look at the clock above the door.

'Look, Ethel,' he said, 'we've been in here a long time, and we both need a rest. I'm on your side. Just remember that. I'm going to write down what we know has happened this morning and during the night, then I'm going to leave you a spell to think on things while I have another talk with the doctor.'

Inspector Harrison had no doubt she was guilty. An illegitimate baby born alone in a small, dingy bedroom in a seedy backstreet terrace. No father on the scene. Unwanted child. Abandoned mother. Massive injuries with a fractured skull. He was just saving everybody's time. He knew from years of experience that juries liked an early confession from someone they knew was guilty. It made their task so much easier than wading through hours of pointless evidence about lowlife people. It was his duty to get one and he was halfway there with Ethel. Sometimes he just needed to get a suspect to cry, break her, but this one was so ugly when she wept. It was painful to look at her for long. She'd not bothered with lipstick, not even pulled a comb through her hair, made worse with damp red nose and cheeks, quivering lips and rolling boss eyes that looked everywhere and nowhere.

Ethel lifted her collar to bury her face. The inspector ground the stub of his cigarette into the ashtray, made a few notes, wrote down the time, and left Ethel alone.

*

'She's just about there, I reckon,' Inspector Harrison told the sergeant back at the counter. 'Give me another hour and she'll be in the bag. What do we know about the house? I'm just wondering if I need a break to take a look at the scene.'

'There's not much to know,' said the sergeant. 'It's down the far end of St Paul's Terrace, near the shunting yards outside the station. I had a quick look round before we brought her in this morning. Ethel's got the front bedroom. There's a bed and a chest of drawers and no room for much else. The bed hadn't been made and I reckon the baby had to make do sleeping in the bottom drawer. There was a teddy bear and a mirror on top of the drawers, and a shoebox pushed under the bed by the wall. A few bits of clothes and baby things in some drawers. Her dad sleeps in the back bedroom and her mother was put up in the downstairs front room.'

'She's bothered about her mother. Do we know why she's camped downstairs?'

'I reckon she's a cripple. Hobbles around on sticks by the look of it.'

'Steep stairs?'

'Very, and cluttered.'

'What's in the shoebox?'

'Nowt much. Nothing heavy. Bit of string. Baby stuff.'

The inspector drummed his fingers on the counter for a moment then tapped the side of his nose.

'That'll do very nicely, I think,' he said. He picked up his *Daily Mail* from the counter and settled down for a smoke and a read.

*

The inspector found Ethel slumped at the table when he returned to the interview room.

'Ethel, we need to get all this sorted out as soon as we can and get you home where you belong. I've had another chat with the doctor and I've heard from the bobbies that your mother has fallen down the stairs.'

'No!' Ethel erupted. 'She can't 'ave! We brought 'er bed down.'

Her face crashed forward onto the table, the chair legs scraping back and tipping her off onto the floor.

Grabbing her coat sleeve as she lunged for the door, he slammed her back down onto her chair.

'I'm goin' 'ome. You don't understand.'

This was just what the inspector needed.

She had broken.

'Stay there! The sooner you come clean with me, the quicker we get you out of here.'

He watched her shoulders shudder and the tears stream down her cheeks.

'Look, let's get the truth written down that the judge will believe. There's still bits I've got to be clear about, though, Ethel. Were you going to put William's body in the shoebox, then Granny Sath came round?'

'Is she alright? What was she doin'?'

'Trying to get upstairs to look for you and the baby, I should think. She's asking for you.'

'I've got to be with her. I've got to go now. Telephone Olive for me, now. Please?'

'Yes, of course we can. The sergeant will call Olive from the desk, and then we'll both run you home. As soon as we've written down the truth. Was the shoebox for William, Ethel?'

'Yes, it's 'is baby box.'

'You'd hidden it, hadn't you? Under your bed until you needed it?'

''As Dad got Olive to come across?'

'Look, Ethel, we've got to finish this soon. I've written this down. You'd not slept because William was awake crying with colic or something so you'd kept him in bed beside you. Then the postman knocked at the door and you knew you had the whole day alone again and you were so tired you snapped and threw him at the wall.'

'For God's sake, no,' said Ethel. 'I was asleep when the postie knocked.'

'Ethel, I can't just cross things out and write down a different story. The judge will see what you've done and he'll know you're telling lies. We've been through this already. Just think on. We want you home. We don't want your mum going the same way as your baby.'

She burst into tears behind her hands.

'Yes,' she mumbled. 'Is she still at the bottom of the stairs? Can she reach 'er sticks?'

Ethel's good eye fixed on the inspector's piece of paper. She bit on her thumb nail as he wrote down a few more words.

'Mum needs her medicine. She's probably not 'ad it all day now I come to think of it. When did she fall?'

'We're nearly done now, Ethel. The judge will see you were at the end of your tether. Now, can you remember back to when he was born? You were at home, weren't you? He took a thump then too. Who was there to help you?'

'Nobody,' said Ethel. 'I wanted to 'ave 'im by meself.'

'What? By yourself? So you just lay on your bed, no-one else with you in the room, you could have called your mum downstairs, and he just slides out like toothpaste?'

'No. I 'ad 'im standin' up.'

'Ethel, I've never had a baby and I never want owt to do with them, but one thing I do know is that women don't have babies standing up. Just keep asking yourself, what's the judge going to think?'

'He came out onto the floor. Mrs Sath sorted 'im out.'

'Whoa, Ethel! Stop! Stop! First we had you alone standing up giving birth, and now Mrs Sath from next door has popped up. Where's she come from? The judge might call these inconsistencies, love. I call them lies.'

'I banged on her wall and she came round.'

'So, this is the first crash into the wall?'

'Yes. My mum likely won't 'ave 'ad a bite to eat all day. I gave 'er a slice of bread first thing, but Dad won't 'ave thought to see to her since. Can you telephone Olive, now, please?'

'Yes, of course we will. We need to get you home as soon as we can, and you can get the doctor to come round to see if she's broken any bones. First just let me write down here what's happened when you gave birth. I think, in all the pain of you going through labour and the crying and Eddie left you and being on your own is that you've hit his head on the bedroom wall. The judge will put himself in your position. Do you think that's how it was, and you've got yourself in a muddle with everything that's gone on since?'

'I can't really remember. Just write down what you want. I've got to get off.'

The inspector took his time to light another cigarette while Ethel stared at his cupped hands. He finished Ethel's written confession with five short sentences.

'I confess that shortly after giving birth alone to my son William on 8th February, I threw him against my bedroom wall. He was unwanted and I felt I had been abandoned. On 12th February I threw

him against the wall for a second time. I'm sorry,
I didn't mean to kill my baby. I have read over this
statement and it is all the truth.'

'Ethel, I'd ask you now to read through this summary of what you've said and sign the piece of paper with your name at the bottom, please,' said the inspector. 'Just there.'

'I can't read so well.'

'I'll read it out to you then. The last sentence is the really important one, Ethel. It says that you're sorry and that you didn't mean to kill William. That's what the judge needs to know. That's right, isn't it? Now can you manage to put your name at the bottom, here, please?'

He turned the piece of paper round, put his finger below his own words, and held out the pen to Ethel. She shuffled forward. Then, covering her left eye with her hand and leaning her elbow on the table, she took the pen in her right and lowered her face to the page. The inspector smiled down at the top of her head as he watched his pen struggle to spell out the two words of her name, so carefully and deliberately, falling away down the page, each letter separated from its neighbours and slanting in a different direction.

'Good girl,' he said. 'That's the worst of it over.'

He added his own scrawled signature, the date, 13th February 1953, and 1.15am, the time on the clock above the door.

'Thank you, Ethel. You just stay where you are, while I sort a few things out with Sergeant Thornton.'

Inspector Harrison collected his hat and coat from the stand, left her to herself, and took the piece of paper back to the sergeant.

*

'You were right,' he said. 'She's gormless. But she did it alright, no question, and she's coughed. There's stuff in there she won't face up to, but her story's all over the place. And those eyes! It was like talking to a bleedin' frog. Get this typed up in the morning and file the original with her signature in the filing cabinet. Charge her with murder now, and bail her, then you can kick her out. No reason she can't walk home. It's not far.'

'Thank you, Inspector. Suppose it's a change for you to get a nice straightforward job? Is this an early night for you?'

Inspector Harrison looked at his watch and hesitated a moment.

'Look, Thornton,' he said, 'don't get me wrong. You've got a result, and that's what we all want at the end of the day. But I wouldn't be doing my job properly if I didn't say this. You've done it all arse about. And we've been here before, haven't we?'

Sergeant Thornton's face fell.

'You've not followed the fucking procedures. Search warrant, basics, ey?'

Thornton's frame stiffened.

'But I reckon we can cover our tracks, lad. Get her up before the beak first thing. Get a bloody search warrant, and suggest he remands her to Armley. Say she didn't want a solicitor. Then go round and get some statements. Best start with her mother before the old bird falls off her perch. And get someone round to the house and go over it with a fine-tooth comb. Photograph it, 'specially her bedroom wall with next door. And say a prayer while you're at it that she's not had the nous to clean up the crime scene. There might be something wet and sticky on that wall we could use.'

'Thank you, sir.'

The inspector stuffed his newspaper and his pen into his inside pocket.

'One last thing, Sarge,' the inspector asked. 'Any chance of a lift home?'

'I shouldn't really,' the sergeant replied. 'I can't leave the desk unattended.'

'Nobody will know. Nothing ever happens here. It's only the other side of town, and I'm knackered. You'll be there and back in half an hour. I'll have to call a patrol car otherwise.'

'Well, we can't have that. Just let me sort her out first. You've done us proud, Inspector. Very grateful.'

'My pleasure,' said Inspector Harrison. He extended his hand onto Thornton's shoulder. 'But you always say that. I don't see it that way really, though, to be honest. Just doing me job.'

PART II

York, April 1942

Four

Ethel's first childhood memory was the night the bomb dropped onto the house a couple of doors up the street, but her life really began when the circus came to town. What stuck in her mind from both of these days was the noise, and the look on the faces around her. Fear in her mother's eyes at the deafening thump then sickening rumble of the stricken house with Mrs Broadbent still inside it. And the pure delight in Eddie's eyes when the gates that had never opened onto the railway sidings rumbled apart and an elephant walked through.

Ethel and her mother had gone to bed early as soon as darkness fell on the night of the bomb. They were alone at home. Her father was away fighting the enemy, Mum had told her, and they'd not seen him for a long time. She'd helped her mother drag the table into the middle of the kitchen and weigh the tablecloth down with pots and pans and plates. The table would keep the ceiling from falling on top of them, and the tablecloth would keep the dust out of their eyes. Knowing it was there made her mum feel secure, and it doubled up for a hidey-hole during the days for Ethel and Eddie.

Her mother was still awake in the back bedroom when the air-raid siren began to wail. St Paul's Terrace was but yards from the railway station and the warden had warned her that they were a likely target for bombs aimed to destroy the sidings at the end of the street. She prayed it was a false alarm. But then within a few minutes she picked up the faint throb of enemy bombers approaching the city. She shook Ethel from her dreams in her tiny front bedroom and they felt their way down the stairs in the darkness to their kitchen shelter. They held a table leg each for support at first and Ethel cuddled Winifred, her old teddy bear, to keep her safe and warm. Mary had planned they would sing songs to ward off the terror, but instead they just crouched in silence in the inky blackness waiting for the next dull thud in the town. They reached for each other's arms for comfort as the raid grew louder.

Ethel would remember for the rest of her days the seconds Mrs Broadbent's house took the hit. In times of stress later in life, all the detail would play back to her in slow motion. A peal of thunder could set the memory running. The whistle of the bomb in its final descent and the roar of the falling bricks and roof tiles always caused her pain. The walls and floor in the kitchen at home rolled and buckled, and the doors, windows, and blackouts blew out into the night. White plaster snowed down from the ceiling onto their hideaway. She remembered her mother's screams as she fled the safety of the kitchen shelter and ran out into the street. Ethel followed her mother and they were beaten back by the flames and the heat of the inferno and the rubble and blazing furniture where number 9 used to be. The acrid stink of explosive that night and the pitiful shouts for Nellie Broadbent haunted Ethel for evermore.

All of the neighbours came out into the street after the blast to do what they could, except for Eddie and his mother and father. Charlie Songhirst from number 14 helped the firemen tackle the blaze and play hoses into the fire, and his wife Olive took everybody into her house. Ethel looked round the rooms for Eddie but he wasn't there so she joined her mum in the kitchen and sat on her knee. All the adults talked about was Mrs Broadbent. Somebody said she'd be under the kitchen table still and because that was at the back of the house she should be alright. Somebody else asked who would look after her dog and cat and the chickens in the sheds out on the moor road if she wasn't. And Ethel could never understand what Olive meant when she whispered to her mum that it was a shame the bomb hadn't landed on her other side instead of on poor old Nellie. But why, thought Ethel? That was Eddie's house.

The first grey light of dawn revealed the devastation bit by bit. The bomb had taken the front of the house down, and the roof had been blown forward and landed strewn across the road. Ethel could see straight into Mrs Broadbent's bedroom at the back of the house. She could see that the grate in the wall hadn't been damaged, and there was still a vase with some flowers on the mantlepiece. Her bed had been thrown forward and its side overhung the gaping hole above the street. The torn edges of the wallpaper flapped in the wind and the drizzle.

Eddie and his parents emerged from their front door during the morning. Eddie told Ethel that his mum couldn't move or speak in their shelter during the night until his dad could convince her that the raid was over, even after the all-clear had sounded. The walls in their house were still standing, but the ceiling had come down on top of their table, the cupboards and stove had blown off from the wall, and the house stank of gas. They stood together at the end of the terrace on the patch of dandelions growing in front of the wooden gates. Ethel grabbed Eddie's hand and began to cry when she saw the fireman come through the hole from the bombed kitchen carrying a torch in one hand and cradling Ruby, the dead little poodle, in the other. Then they watched in horror as two men picked their way carefully down the slope of rubble to an ambulance with a bundle on a stretcher wrapped from head to toe in a tablecloth. Eddie asked one of the firemen if he could see Mrs Broadbent's face, but he said no, let her rest in peace.

Reverend Pearson visited everybody's house down St Paul's Terrace over the next few days. The war will soon be over, he reassured his flock, and anyway, lightning never strikes twice in the same place. Ethel asked him, please, Father, why did the bomb land on Mrs Broadbent's house, and not Eddie Sathersthwaite's? She couldn't understand the answer that it was God's will. Did that mean Eddie had been saved, she wondered, or spared? Mum told Ethel that what the vicar had said meant that her dad would come home soon. The news made Ethel feel uneasy. The council came over the next week or so and cleared the bricks and slates away from the road. They took the bed from the edge of its precipice and shored up some overhanging bits of the roof with girders. Ethel and Eddie could then get past the bombsite to the patch of weeds and the wooden gates at the end of the terrace without having to climb over the debris. Mrs Broadbent's two sons arrived from down south to salvage any of her things they could find. And although the staircase had gone, Charlie Songhirst managed to climb up to the bedroom for the vase for a keepsake for Olive.

Nobody else did anything to clear the bombsite for years afterwards. It always smelt of damp plaster. Clumps of weeds soon grew up through the cracks in the floors, and then a sycamore tree and bramble bushes. Gnarled roots cracked the concrete open in the yard and a forsythia bush in the corner grew unchecked to the height of the gutters. Eddie and Ethel would scramble up through its branches to the broken windows and into Nellie Broadbent's back bedroom. They could hear the squirrels and the pigeons scrabbling in the eaves, light a fire with a few sticks in the empty grate, and sit on the sodden mattress listening out for the return of the German bombers. Eddie would tell Ethel he'd seen the old lady's headless ghost in the crumbling mouldy wardrobe her sons had left in the corner. And that if you were awake on a moonlit night, you could hear Ruby bark at the exact time the bomb had landed. He told Ethel once that bomb blasts always made mincemeat out of dogs' innards. Tom Shaw from the top end of the terrace sometimes came down to play hide-and-seek in the bombed house and king-of-the-castle on the rubble, but Ethel didn't like him much. He called her frogface behind her back. Eddie didn't. Eddie just looked at her straight in the face and called her our Ethel.

The same families had lived in the houses around this gaping hole for as long as anybody could remember. Ethel only ever went into three of the houses at this end of the terrace, but they all felt exactly the same. Dark and cramped and stuffy kitchens and front rooms opening onto the street by a small, cluttered hallway, and two bedrooms upstairs with a water closet in the yard. Ethel lived with her mother two doors down from the bombsite and they waited for Dennis, her father, to return from the war and shatter the peace again. On their other side were the Sathersthwaites, Eddie and his mum and dad. Ethel and Eddie were the only children who lived in these houses. Mrs Sath had told Eddie that was because Mrs Songhirst, who lived opposite, was barren.

The snickets ran along behind the back yards of these houses, the narrow cobbled shady alleys good for nothing but old bikes, stinking bins, stray cats, brawls, and gossip. Most of the men spent their lives working on the railway nearby, except for Ethel's dad, who ran a butcher's shop in town. The smoke and whistles of the engines from the shunting yard over the gates at the end of the terrace filled the daylight hours, and the air in the street was forever steamy even when the sun was shining. This narrow street was Ethel's childhood world, where time had stood still. Small and mean it might be, but it was safe, and it was home.

Ethel's father was just back home from the war when Eddie lost his. This didn't seem right to Ethel; it was as though they were allowed only one dad between them at any one time. Mrs Sath told Eddie and Ethel that both of their dads had fought a war, but a different one each. She told them she supposed they'd been through their own war in a way, the night Mrs Broadbent was bombed. Eddie couldn't understand why his dad had died when there wasn't even a war to fight. His father spent most of his time on his allotment on the far side of the shunting yards tending his sweet peas and his vegetables, and he didn't come home for his tea one Saturday afternoon. Mrs Sath started to worry when darkness began to fall and Charlie Songhirst offered to go over the railway bridge to find him. He'd died in his deckchair outside his shed. He'd made himself a mug of tea on his stove and left it to stand on his rickety little table. It was untouched and cold when he found him, said Charlie. Bill Sath was cold too. His very last cigarette had burned through to a stick of ash on the upturned bucket. He'd gone peacefully.

*

Dennis Slater walked down St Paul's Terrace and into the hall of the family home without so much as a knock on the door. He carried his left arm in a sling and a knapsack slung over his right shoulder. He'd caught a bullet through the elbow and left the rest of the army to continue the fight in the deserts of North Africa. Ethel knew it was her father come home, as Reverend Pearson had warned, and backed off through the doorway into the kitchen. Mary dropped her dustpan and brush into the hearth, and rushed out from the front room to throw her arms round his neck. He gave his wife a kiss on the cheek and ruffled the hair on the back of her head, threw his bag down onto the kitchen table, and let himself out past Ethel into the back yard to check his pigeon loft had survived the blast. His unexpected homecoming brought back to his wife in an instant all the troubles of their married life. Mary had forgotten for a time that she was not the first, or the only, love of Dennis's life, and that their daughter had been a disappointment to her father, not so much for being born, as for not being a boy.

Dennis picked up his life in much the same place as he'd left it three years before. He noticed but failed to care that his wife had become frail in his absence. She had kept her symptoms to herself while he was at war for fear of frightening Ethel. They had begun one evening as she sat quietly in front of the fire. She realised she was continually waking up time and time again even though she knew she hadn't fallen asleep. A shaking in one hand would soon put a stop to her knitting. It disappeared when she was asleep, and then dizzy spells began. The ringing in her ears never went away. She panicked when her leg gave way and she wet herself on her walk up to the church one afternoon, and felt ashamed when Mrs Pearson, the vicar's wife, had to help her home. A visit to Dr Chisholm was more than she could afford, but Olive from the house opposite persuaded her she had no other option. It was her nerves, the doctor was sure, the stress of her husband's life in danger and the fear of another air raid. He was hopeful that cod liver oil for the vitamins and malt extract for the digestion would do the trick.

*

The vicar and the doctor and their wives came down the terrace for the big surprise party at the wooden gates when all the worry of the war was over. Dennis and Charlie Songhirst had set up a trestle table and benches on the lawn of dandelions. Olive had written out place names on little cards. Everybody Ethel knew in the world was there, and many more besides. Mrs Pearson carried a tray loaded with plates of sandwiches down from the vicarage and Mrs Sath provided boiled eggs, cold ham, a jelly, pots of tea, and a jug of fruit cordial. Ethel thought it must be Christmas Day already, only in the summer and with no turkey dinner. The shunting yards were so quiet and all the neighbours were in such high spirits. Reverend Pearson, at the top of the table, rose to his feet after the plates had been stacked and cupped his ear with his hand. 'Bang on time!' Charlie shouted, and Mary told Ethel and Eddie to get up to Ethel's bedroom and be sharp about it.

Ethel and Eddie could see from her upstairs window that all the adults below had climbed onto the bench lifted on top of the trestle and were wrestling each other to peer over the broken glass on the gates. They stood together to witness a sight they had never seen, a full train pulling countless carriages slow down, blast its whistle, and stop before it reached the railway station. The engine came to a halt at the low platform in the shunting yards and belched its last few whisps of steam. Lorries unloaded from the rear of the train lined up along the roadway at the edge of the siding. And then an army of men pulled open the sides of the carriages. First to be offloaded was an iron cage containing a lion, rolling his huge head and mane from side to side, and then a walking-upright bear muzzled and harnessed with ropes and chains. Bare-chested cowboys wearing broad hats and spurred boots led horses decorated with ribbons and rosettes across the tracks to the gates.

Ethel threw her hands up to her mouth, speechless, and Eddie grabbed her as he stared out of the window, reaching first for the nearest finger and then her full palm. They clattered down the stairs of number 13 to join the party, as the gates they thought were closed forever were wheeled back. First through the gap came an elephant, swinging her trunk and eyes in search of a bun, leading a train of them, trunks twined round tails, then a tottering clown with red nose and jugs full of water, a dwarf with handlebar moustache and bowler hat, a juggler hurling tumbling sticks high into the air, a man perched on stilts. More animals followed: the lumbering bear, a lolloping camel, the lion pacing in his cage, and a line of traction engines and waggons loaded with acrobats on swings, canvases, ropes, and poles. The ringmaster, heavy with medallions, led the brass band and drum majorettes up St Paul's Terrace, smiling, bowing, and doffing his hat to the crowd.

Whistles cheers and whoops of laughter greeted the circus as it made its way up and out of the terrace and through the town to the racecourse. Dennis grabbed Ethel round her waist and Charlie grabbed Eddie, and they lofted them up onto the neck of the last elephant in the line, Olive snapping her camera for posterity. This was the day when memories were made and everything was right in Ethel's little world. The day her father had been kind, the day her mother had been happy, the day Eddie had taken her hand, the long summer day the dandelion lawn had been a sea of yellow. Ethel knew then without thinking she wanted to marry Eddie Sath, and they would live happily ever after. There was nothing could ever be more certain than that.

PART III

York, Summer 1952

Five

Ethel reached the top of the stairs, shuffled her feet round on the step so that she faced back down into the void, and pushed her back into her mother's bedroom door. She was practised at this manoeuvre and careful not to drop the cup and saucer from one hand or the medicine bottle and spoon from the other. She turned her head to one side as she entered the room to check that her mother hadn't stirred yet, then set the bottle upright on the window ledge and the cup of tea on the boards between the bed and the wall. She drew the curtains apart a couple of inches to inspect the day. The sky above Railway Terrace was a clear cloudless blue, but the yard and the snicket and the backs of the houses themselves lay in deep shadow. Her father's bike was leaning against the lavatory wall. Her mum was still sound asleep, comfortable, peaceful, thankfully.

'Mum,' she whispered.

Her mother didn't respond. Ethel bent to take the cup off its saucer and held it between her hands. She blew the steam rising from the tea for a moment before she looked at her mother's face again. Her hair was grey and thin now, and she had an old woman's chin. The skin sagged and a little crop of hair grew at the end of it. She had no teeth and the corners of her gaping mouth blew out a tiny bubble with each breath. Her eyes had sunk, there were dark rings round them, and the skin was stretched thin over her cheeks.

Ethel felt the old fear gnawing at the pit of her stomach again.

She was watching her mother slowly rot.

She perched herself down on the side of the bed and reached under the bedspread to search for her mother's hand. It was small and dry. 'Mum,' she said quietly. 'It's mornin'. I've brought you your medicine and a cuppa. I'd best get to the shop, though, Mum. I'm late again.'

Mary opened her eyes and struggled to focus on her daughter. 'I'm scared, Ethel,' she said.

Ethel tried to stay calm and stood up from the bed. She lifted her mother's head off the pillow onto her own shoulder, slotted her hands into her mother's armpits, and shuffled her up the headboard. Ethel then settled down on the edge of the bed again and lifted her tea onto the blankets. Mary attempted to lift the cup, but it rattled in the saucer and some tea slopped over the sides. She put it down again. They both heard the front room door scrape open downstairs, and then Dennis cough and fart in the kitchen. Cigarette smoke drifted up the stairs. She'd left enough tea in the pot for him.

'I'm frightened of the stairs,' said Mary.

Ethel had dreaded this moment. An admission of defeat; the end was in sight. Her mother had become increasingly unsteady on her feet of late and would move around the house placing an outstretched hand on pieces of furniture. She was bound to fall down the stairs sooner or later.

Ethel snapped her eyelids shut. She couldn't let her mother see the tears trickling down her cheeks, and turned away to open the curtains wide. She heard the lavatory flush below, and saw her father emerge into the yard. The top of his cap and the shoulders of his jacket followed their usual routine. He balanced his cup on the top of the wall and dropped his cigarette butt into it, then took a parcel from under his arm and tossed it into the basket on his bike. Her eyes dried as she watched him take the key from his trouser pocket to open the lock on the loft door, scoop a handful of corn from the bucket to top up the dish for his pigeons, lock up the loft again, pull open the back gate, reverse his bike into the snicket, and pedal off to work.

'Try not to worry yourself, Mum,' said Ethel. 'Olive'll bob over in an hour or so, and she'll 'elp you down the stairs. I can fetch you up some bread an' butter if you can wait till then.'

'You're a good girl, our Ethel,' said her mum. 'Did you make Dad 'is sandwich?'

'You ask me every day, Mum! 'Ave I ever said no? I left it with 'is cap an' bike clips, like I allus do. He's gone now.'

Mary tried a smile.

Ethel put the tea back down onto the boards again, filled up the spoon with thick brown medicine from the bottle, and held the end to her mother's lips. She took a sip and Ethel tipped the rest between her gums. She screwed her eyes up.

'Do you think this is doin' any good, Ethel?'

'Dr Chis says it is. You 'ad a good day yesterday.'

'I'm dyin', Ethel.'

'No, Mum. You can't. I don't want you to.'

They forced another smile at each other. Mary's eyes moistened and misted, and Ethel lifted over the edge of the pillow case to dry them gently. Neither of them really knew what to do next, so Ethel just picked up her mother's hand from the bedspread and looked into her face.

'I don't know what to do for the best either, Mum, but I've 'ad a thought about the stairs. Why don't we get your bed moved down to the front room, and then we'll 'ave no more frettin'? Charlie can shift it on Saturday afternoon.'

'But all me things are in the drawer, Ethel, an' I won't be able to get to 'em,' Mary said. 'An' the table and the cabinet's in the front room, and everybody passin' in the street will see me in bed. And what about your dad? Where'll he go?' She held her hands over her mouth and tried not to cry.

'Stop your worryin', Mum. We'll sort it,' Ethel tried to reassure her. 'The table folds away, and nobody can see through the curtains. It'll be right. An' Charlie'll get a mattress from somewhere up 'ere for Dad. Anyway, I've got to get off to the shop now. I'm probably late already. Mr Waggett'll be givin' me the sack an' then we'd never manage. You stay in your dressing gown, and I'll be back at lunchtime. Olive'll be 'ere in a minute.'

'Well, at least your dad'll be able to look out at 'is blessed pigeons,' Mary said.

'He will that,' said Ethel. 'I've got to go, Mum.'

Ethel gave the back of her mum's hand a reassuring pat and leant forward to kiss her forehead. She dashed back to her own bedroom to collect her handbag and take a quick look in her little mirror on the chest of drawers. She hated this mirror because she hated her face. Old before my time, she thought. And ugly. Fat nose. Crooked front teeth. But of all the things she could find to dislike about herself, the worst was her lazy left eye. Frogface, Eddie's friend used to call her. That still hurt. It gave her view of the world a fuzzy edge, a constant reminder. She brought the mirror up to it quickly, pulled the lower lid down gently with a finger, and looked at it with her right eye. It had wandered away to gaze over her shoulder. She tucked a stray strand of hair behind her ear and put the mirror back onto the top, then hurried down the stairs and back up again with a slice of bread and the butter dish and a knife for her mum.

The cap, sandwich, and bike clips had gone from the kitchen table. She wouldn't have time to bring the cup back in from the yard. Grabbing her coat from the peg in the hallway, she knew she was going to be late opening up the shop yet again. There would be the usual little queue of customers waiting outside on the corner, but most of them understood. Ethel just hoped Mrs Sath from next door wasn't one of them.

She pushed her arms into her coat sleeves as she scurried up St Paul's Terrace and made up her mind to try and call into Dr Chisholm's surgery on the walk home at lunchtime. He would call round to see her mum if she could bring herself to ask him, although there was probably nothing much he could do. But his visits always somehow lifted their spirits. There was nothing anybody could do really, but the thought of life without Mum was unbearable. It wasn't so much the stairs that frightened her, though. Charlie would do something about that. It was everything else.

Six

Dennis leant back against the pillow and was careful to flick his ash into the saucer on the chair next to the bed. He knew Charlie didn't smoke. Olive had closed the curtains and he watched her hoist her skirt up to her waist and pull her jumper back over her head in the shade of her bedroom. She sat on the end of the bed to ease her slippers back onto her feet, then Dennis lunged for her backside as she made for the door.

'Come 'ere,' he said. 'I've not finished with you yet.'

'Leave off, you daft bugger,' Olive replied. 'You get worse.'

'Better,' Dennis said to himself as he fell back onto the pillow and the door swung closed behind her.

'Saucer,' Olive called back as she picked her way down past planks of wood piled up the stairs.

They could forget about their own marriages on afternoons like this. They had come of age when life was easier in their youth at the dance-hall in town, when

Dennis and Olive were slicker at the jive than Charlie and Mary. But Dennis had soon tired of Mary when Ethel was conceived, and Olive had eventually bored of Charlie when they married but she didn't conceive. Their old lust had been rekindled when Dennis reminded Olive that although Charlie might not have needs, most men did, and Olive had replied that this woman did too. He could help her with that if she liked, maybe, and Olive had told him the door to her yard was never locked. No harm could come of it, they both knew that. But forbidden sex snatched with Dennis left Olive racked with guilt laid next to her husband in bed for a time, till her frustrations with him soon bubbled back to the surface again.

Dennis followed Olive down to the kitchen holding his coat and the saucer stubbed with his butts.

'Your Ethel's been round this mornin', she told him as he pushed past her to the yard.

'You don't say.'

'She wants Charlie to help shift Mary's bed downstairs.'

'I thought that was comin', said Dennis. 'Suits me. I've 'ad a gutful of sleepin' in an old chair.'

'An' it gives that old cow Aggie Sath summat to talk about,' Olive said. 'She can watch Mary potterin' around her room through the holes in the curtain.'

'Watch her dyin' in bed, more like,' said Dennis. 'I'll 'elp Charlie shift it.'

*

Charlie was just the man in the terrace to drag an iron bed frame on its side through a narrow bedroom doorway, ease it round a tight corner on the landing, then slide it down a steep flight of rickety stairs. He was a fitter in the carriage works on the railway and he took to angling stiff, heavy furniture through frames in his stride, however tight the fit. And he would do any favour for a friend.

Charlie and Olive walked over the street and through the front door of number 13 just after breakfast and found Ethel and her parents planning the move round the kitchen table. They had come up with a plan. Dennis had said he'd miss the match if needs be. They reckoned it best for Mary to sit with Olive in her back kitchen over the road for an hour, while Ethel tried to sort the front room and the men took the bed to pieces and got the frame down the stairs.

With her mum out of harm's way Ethel raked the ashes from the grate and took them to the bin in the snicket, folded the table away along the wall, lifted the two porcelain dogs carefully onto the bed from the top of the glass cabinet and manhandled it into the window bay, then slid her father's armchair and his little pile of clothes along the boards into the corner. She rolled up the rug then swept the dust out into the hallway. Photographs of Dennis in his khaki shorts and of the circus elephant stood on the mantlepiece. That should do, Ethel thought, the bed should just fit with its foot up to the hearth.

Dennis told Ethel to make herself useful with a kettle then sit in the kitchen and keep out of the way. Barked instructions and squeaks and scrapes of metal on bannister and door frame filled the house for the next half hour or so. Ethel made some tea before the base, mattress, and headboard appeared in the front room and Charlie screwed it all back together. Olive helped Mary back home from across the street. Propping her up on her sticks in the doorway to her new bedroom, Charlie and Olive took an elbow each and helped her sit down on the edge of the bed.

She looked her new room up and down. 'I'll be dead before Christmas,' she said.

'Ger away!' said Charlie. 'You're a tough old bird. You'll see us all out.'

She ignored him and got to her feet carefully, edged down the side of the bed to the hearth using one stick, and picked up the photograph of the elephant from the mantlepiece. She touched its trunk then set it to stand in front of Dennis sat astride the gun turret of a tank.

'Ee Ethel,' she said, 'that was an 'appy day. I've not seen young Eddie much since he's got back.'

'He's still next door, Mum,' Ethel said.

Mary continued her shuffle round the bed and arranged the porcelain spaniels on the cabinet to face in from the window. She opened its two glass doors and tried to wipe the dust off its shelf with her hand.

'Could you bring me clothes an' things down from the drawer, please, Ethel, and put 'em in 'ere? An' I want to ask Olive if she can sew these curtains up a bit.'

She fiddled with the net curtains and tried to cover over some holes with its pleats and folds.

'It's nice to see the steam puffin' over the gates again,' she said, and turned back to Charlie, Olive, and Dennis watching her from the doorway. 'You two get off and enjoy what's left of the afternoon,' she told her neighbours. 'And you can go to your game if you want, Dennis.'

She took the desert scene and the day of the circus down off the mantlepiece. It wasn't the happy laughing children on the elephant or the tank in the desert sand she saw, though, but the loving husband with his arm round his wife and the handsome soldier with bronzed limbs and broad smile.

'He's not a bad man, Ethel,' she said, 'an' he wears a uniform well.'

'He clouts you, Mum.'

Mary put the pictures back up against the clock and paused to collect her thoughts for a moment.

'He doesn't mean to, I don't think, love. An' he did see some terrible things in the war, you know. He can't 'elp 'imself sometimes, Ethel. An' there's this. He's angry, maybe there's bits of me not turned out as he would 'ave wanted.'

*

With her father out of the house for the rest of the day, Ethel left her mother to shift her skirt, cardigans, nightdresses, and pills out from her drawer into the cabinet, and busied herself rinsing out some smalls in the sink. She wrung them out as hard as she could, then dropped them into the bucket near the back door to take out to the yard. She'd heard Eddie tinkering with his bike over the fence and hoped she might catch him. They'd played together as children, and she'd known him for as long as she could remember, but he'd been away with the army in Korea for a while and had only just come home again. He kept himself to himself now. He'd changed, grown up, Ethel supposed, become a man, and she couldn't think what to say to him. But she was sorry he didn't talk to her anymore. She missed him in her own quiet way.

Eddie lived with his widowed mother next door to the Slaters, and their back yards were separated by Dennis's pigeon loft and a chest-high fence made of railway sleepers. Eddie would go to work in the button factory if they had any jobs going, but fishing for carp and perch in the old brick ponds way out on the moor road, and tinkering with his motorbike were his only two real passions. There was nothing he liked better than stripping and tuning the engine of his Triumph, then putting it all back together again, polishing the paintwork, and going for a ride. During the winter months his mother would let him use the front room as a workshop, but he would spend his long summer evenings and weekends with his toolkit, oilcan, and polish outside in the yard.

And then there was also our Ethel over the fence. She was nearly twenty and a couple of years younger than himself. She came out into her yard quite often to hang out some washing, fill the bucket from the coal bunker or go to the lavatory, but she rarely spoke these days. He thought she'd changed too while he'd been away, but not for the better, from a fun playmate on the bombsite into a nurse for her mother and a skivvy for her father. He'd paid for sex a few times with women when he was in the army, but there weren't many opportunities back here. Ethel wasn't pretty, that was for sure. She was plump and she had the curse of her evil eye, but she was simple and she was loving and she should be an easy lay. And, he liked to tell himself, she ought to be grateful.

'Mornin', Ethel.' Eddie was kneeling at the side of his bike and spoke to its front wheel as Ethel opened her back door and emerged onto the step.

She put the bucket down on the flags then ran a cloth down the line to take off some rain drops. Eddie smeared some paste on a valve, stood up and came over to lean on the fence.

'Hello, Ed,' she said, and turned to look at him as she pegged out a sock.

Eddie knew how to look at Ethel, straight at her face and fix on the good eye. He didn't think about it anymore. 'Fancy a spin later on?' he said.

'Do you mean that?'

'Why not? We could go to the brick ponds. I'll show you where I fish.'

She turned to him slowly and shyly. She finished hanging a shirt tail and dropped some pegs back into the bucket. 'Yes, I'd like that. I'll ask me mum. We've got some ham. I could make us a flask.'

'Just like the old times,' Eddie said. 'I'll bob round for you later.'

This news was the tonic for Mary that none of Dr Chis's potions could provide. Oh, a wedding, then a baby on the way! It would give her a reason to live. She managed to find her old dance shoes still in their box and to fetch the butter dish over to Ethel while she sliced the loaf. They wrapped two sandwiches in fancy wax paper and filled the flask with hot tea. Just before dinnertime Eddie wheeled his motorbike out through the gate into the snicket and propped it carefully on its stand, then knocked on the Slater's back door. Ethel opened it. She was ready. She tottered down the step into the yard, wearing some grey knitted slacks, a blue blouse and scarf, an orange woollen pompom hat, and glossy red lipstick. He could see her mother held up by her stick and holding their lunch bag in the hallway behind her. He took Ethel's hand for balance as she threw her leg over the seat. Eddie settled his grip on the handlebars and felt Ethel place her fingers lightly on the shoulders of his leather jacket. She giggled with nerves when he told her to hang on tight.

They rode sedately up the terrace then turned left onto the main road towards town. Eddie brought the bike to a halt at the five-bar gate to the moor and asked Ethel to jump off and swing it open. He told her then to squeeze up as tight behind him as she could and fit her knees into the back of his, then pull her hat down over her ears and clasp her hands together in front of his chest. You mustn't be modest, he told her, we're going to go like greased lightning. He eased open the throttle. He just loved that healthy, throaty roar. They gathered speed along the straight towards the railway bridge, dipped their left knees down towards the track to take its arch at full pelt, then raced past old Nellie Broadbent's chicken sheds heading for the horizon. Hitting the crackle and dust of the cinder track, Eddie lowered his head for the final dash uphill and Ethel buried her face into the back of his neck, a heady mix of leather and Brylcreem in her nostrils and rushing wind in her ears. 'Eddie,' she screamed, 'Eddie, Eddie! Slow down!' He paid her no attention. She had never felt excitement and passion like this in her life.

Eddie closed down the throttle as they reached the pond. Ethel relaxed her grip on his jacket but kept her chin on his shoulder. He turned his bike left and followed the grassy path slowly through the trees to a clearing where a steep drop of a couple of feet fell to the rippling water's edge. A deckchair and a little wooden table that Eddie had rescued from his dad's old allotment stood on the bank.

'Is this it?' Ethel said. She got off the bike then put their sandwiches down onto the table and walked over to the edge to look out over the pond.

'Do you sit there, Eddie, and throw your fishing line into the water?'

'Yeah, sort of,' he said.

'Can I sit in it?'

He nodded, and she giggled.

She settled herself into it and rubbed her hands up and down on the arms, then pretended to throw something out into the water.

'What do you catch?'

'Carp, usually. Sometimes a perch.'

She returned a blank expression.

'What's it taste like?'

'Don't know,' Eddie replied. 'I chuck 'em back. Anyway, I don't like fish.'

Neither of them knew what to say next, so Ethel picked up the parcel, shook out a tartan tablecloth to spread over the grass, and unwrapped their sandwiches onto it. She set two beakers out and poured them each some tea. They settled down at either side of their lunch, and ate watching a couple of moorhens bobbing around near the bank.

'Eddie.' Ethel broke the silence. 'There's summat I've been meanin' to ask you.'

'Go on.'

'Did you really see Nellie Broadbent's ghost in her wardrobe?'

'Yeah.'

'And can you hear Ruby barkin' the same time the bomb dropped?'

'Only when the moon's full.'

'Fool.' She giggled. 'I don't know whether to believe you.' She picked a daisy from the grass and threw it at his face.

She lay back on the grass and looked up at the sky. A patch of blue was framed by the restless branches of the trees, a canopy thick with their summer growth of fresh green leaves. They were out of focus, because they were always out of focus. But she didn't care, because she was with Eddie, and she'd told him once that everything she looked at was always blurred, and he didn't care either. She had not felt so happy since the day the circus came to town.

'Eddie,' she said again after a while.

'What?'

'There's summat else.'

'What?' He'd put his hands behind his head and closed his eyes.

'I daren't say it.'

'Okay.'

She said it anyway.

'You've held my hand twice now. Can I hold yours, please?'

He turned to look at her across the crumpled paper and the empty beakers, then stood up. He took off his jacket then undid the top button of his shirt and stepped across the tablecloth to lay alongside her. He stretched his arm out between them and Ethel snatched his hand up off the grass. They both lay back and closed their eyes again.

The lightest of touches roused Ethel from her doze. Eddie had leant up on one elbow and dipped the tip of his nose onto her cheek, and he was kissing her. Without daring to open her eyes so close to his face, she reached her hand to the back of his head and gave in to the kiss. This was just as in a dream she'd had. She could taste the hint of mustard on his lips. Her head rocked back when she felt his tongue play over her crooked teeth, and she thought she was fainting as his lips came to rest on the lids of her ugly eye.

He lifted the weight of her breast and rolled the nipple.

'No, Eddie,' she whispered. 'Someone might see us.'

'There's never anyone here,' he said, and released the belt at the top of her slacks.

'Eddie, please, we shouldn't, not yet,' she whispered again, but she knew she didn't really mean it.

She arched her back up off the grass to help him slip off her slacks, then sensed his panic as he fumbled with his buttons below. She reached up for him quickly, made way for his knees between hers, then felt a stab of pain as he entered her urgently. It was momentary, it was nothing, then a few gentle rhythmic thrusts of his groin into hers. She felt loved as never before, a fullness and warmth, a growing intensity of pleasure she didn't know could exist, then his quickening hot breath on her neck and his tumble down on top of her.

She reached out to touch his hair as he rolled away to pull up his trousers.

'Eddie,' she said. He sat, hunched, head in hands. 'What's the matter?'

'Nothing.'

'You're cryin'?'

'No, I'm not. It's time we went home.'

'Why? No, come on Eddie, it's alright. We can always come 'ere again if you want.'

'No, your mother will be frettin'.' He tucked his shirt in and buttoned his flies.

'No, she won't, not yet. Eddie, I want us to live in the bombed house one day? Say you do too. Please?'

He reeled round at her stupid words and felt disgust at the sight of her bad eye, then noticed a scuff on the mudguard she must have made with her silly dance shoe at the gate.

'Maybe.'

She held her hand up for him to take.

'Get up,' he said. 'I want to go home.'

Seven

Ethel had been awake for an hour or more when the mail train steamed past the gates. She swung her legs out of bed, pulled on her dressing gown from the back of the door and crept down the stairs. She managed to avoid the creaking step three from the bottom by leaning into the bannister as she passed it, but she needn't have bothered. Her mother was already awake too.

She brought the milk in from the step and took a drink straight from the bottle. That might settle her stomach. She just had time to fill the kettle and light the hob before she felt the rush up her gullet and the raw sting at the back of her throat. She spun round to the sink and retched, thin pale milk with streaks of green bile.

This had happened every morning for a couple of weeks, but she felt sick all day long. She couldn't keep this to herself any longer. She was desperate to tell Eddie. He might even want to get married, but probably not. It was more likely he would want nothing to do with her anymore. He would tell her it was her own fault. The only person she had ever really talked to, properly, was her mum, who would love a new baby to help her live through her own final days. But the shame, the terrible shame. It might kill her, folk peering in at her through the curtains then gossiping in the snicket. She daren't tell her father yet either. He would definitely slap her. He might punch her. He could even kill her. He could take a knife to Eddie. Her mother and father would find out the awful truth soon enough. She could tell Dr Chisholm, or Reverend Pearson. She might have to. They might want her to get rid of the baby or arrange to take it away. Or could she tell Charlie and Olive? They might know what to do, and Olive would save her the pain of telling everybody else in the terrace, whether they wanted to hear it or not. And her father might take the news easier from Olive. Or she could even drown herself in the brick pond or throw herself down the stairs, but then what would happen to her poor mum? Her best plan surely was to get rid of the baby, and quick, but how? And why? This baby is mine, she thought, it will love me, it's all mine and nobody else's.

She heard the creak on the stairs, then a thud as her father dropped his coat, apron, and shoes onto the kitchen table behind her.

''Aven't you made a brew yet?' he said.

She couldn't speak. She crashed the kettle onto the ring, pushed past her father, and ran across the street to Olive's house, her only safe haven. She turned the handle to number 14 and put her shoulder to the door. It opened only a few inches onto the years of junk crammed into the Songhirst's hallway and would go no further.

'Olive,' shouted Ethel through the letterbox, 'are you up yet?'

'Yes, love, come round the back,' Olive bellowed at her from the kitchen.

Ethel ran down the pavement away from the bombed house, across the patch of grass, then back up the snicket to Olive's back yard. The door was open. Olive stood at her kitchen table, winkling the caked mud out of the soles of her husband's boots with a knife. She scooped some of it from the table with one hand into the palm of the other and hurled it across the kitchen at the sink, then wiped the blade on her dressing gown.

'There,' she said. 'Done. Sit down and get your breath back. I 'ave to dubbin these once a week or they crack. Anyway, what's with you going to the front? 'As your mum 'ad a bad night again?'

'No,' said Ethel. 'There's summat I've got to tell you. Where's Charlie?'

'Out an' about. You know what he's like. He's on a late.'

Olive rested a hand on Ethel's shoulder in turning to fill the kettle from the tap.

'This sounds serious, our Ethel. You're upset. There's summat up, I can tell. Mrs Sath been shoutin' the odds again?'

'I'm pregnant.'

Olive put down the box of matches onto the side and gripped the rail on the cooker. Two short words that changed everything. For Ethel and herself. Forever. Eddie Sath sitting on his motorbike sprang into her mind's eye, but then the image of another man lifting her leg off the ground in the snicket. Dennis Slater. He couldn't do that to his own daughter, not even Dennis, could he?

'You sure?'

'Yes. I'm weeks overdue.'

Olive sank onto a chair opposite Ethel and stared into her face.

'How?'

Ethel burst into tears and tried to grab Olive.

Olive froze.

Dare I ask the next question, thought Olive? Please God, the answer would not be *my father*! She had to.

'Who?'

'Eddie Sath.'

No words of comfort or of anything else came into Olive's head. She became aware of Charlie's stupid tuneless whistling from the yard. Raw emotion in her chest was all she felt. Jealousy, guilt, and hatred all rolled into one toxic mess. Why should Ethel, simple Ethel, have a baby without even wanting one, when she had tried and failed for years with Charlie? To the point when they had given up even sharing the same bed and their life together had dried up. And why should that frigid old bitch Mrs Sath, her with the swept floors, scrubbed front step, and polished fender, have the gift of a grandchild just dropped into her lap?

'Help me, Olive,' Ethel pleaded.

'Who knows?'

'Just you.'

Olive knew this news would go up and down the terrace within hours. She could never hold it in. Plain, dumpy Ethel having Eddie Sath's baby!

'What should I do?' sobbed Ethel. 'I don't know where to go.'

'Go tell yer mum,' said Olive. 'She'll have known a long time before today, Ethel, if I know owt about our Mary. There's not many things get past her, and she'll need you now more than ever. You can't keep summat like this a secret. And go see Reverend Pearson if you can. He usually knows what to do.'

Olive couldn't bear to look Ethel in the face again, let alone hug her. She now had her own turmoil to deal with. Turmoil she couldn't share with Ethel. Charlie pulled the door open from the yard.

''Ello, love,' he said. 'I didn't know you were 'ere. Everythin' alright? Yer mum badly?'

'Yes, she is,' said Olive. 'But it's summat and nowt.'

'I'll go feed the chickens, Olive,' he said, and took up his boots and returned to the yard.

'I've got to go as well, Olive,' Ethel said. 'I'm late.'

'Go through the front.'

Olive pushed a rolled carpet away from behind the door and opened it for Ethel.

'Can you see to Mum?' Ethel asked.

'Yes,' said Olive, and she squeezed Ethel's elbow as she looked past her up the terrace. There was nobody about yet. 'And mebbe best tell Eddie, eh? It's 'is an' all.'

*

Olive returned to her kitchen chair. Her own secret, her guilt at what she had been doing with Dennis Slater, gnawed at her mind. That the thought had flicked across her brain that Dennis could have got his own daughter pregnant terrified her. He might be capable of that. And so did the memory of what she was doing with him in the snicket when Ethel found them. He'd received his call-up papers that morning, and pushed a note under her front door. *Got to see you*, he'd scrawled, *meet me in the snicket at seven*. This was dangerous, forbidden. It was exciting. Charlie was in his back yard, only yards away from them. It was passion she'd never felt before. Maybe this was the last time she'd see him. Time was precious. She knew then that she was alive. She'd leant back against the bricks, put her arms round his neck to kiss him goodbye, and found the erection that was meant for her. She'd reached for his top button. He'd eased her onto a ledge, lifted her skirt and a thigh, and taken her standing up. She remembered every detail, then the horror on the little child's face over Dennis's shoulder as she'd opened her eyes to see Ethel pushing her teddy in its pram round the corner.

She was only a baby, Dennis had said, she wouldn't understand sex. Or betrayal, thought Olive. Dennis had fought his war, sure enough, and came back for Olive. He came home for other women too, Olive was under no illusions. He learned tricks from older women, more experienced women. But none with a figure as shapely as hers, Olive knew that as well. He would have her in positions her husband had never even dreamt about, wherever he wanted, when Charlie was safely out of the way. His swarthy good looks, his thick black hair she could run her fingers through, his stiff moustache that would tickle her thighs, and his paper-thin charms saw to that. He knew what to do. But what if it was Charlie's fault they hadn't had kids, not hers? Oh my God, what if it was me and not Ethel fallen pregnant, thought Olive? Alone, with

Dennis's baby growing in my belly, breaking the news to kind, dull old Charlie? It would crush him. Eddie Sath had put a stop to her pleasure, whether she liked it or not.

She got up from her chair, pushed it back to the wall, held a match to the ring, and paused. A much more hopeful thought had risen to the surface and pushed her dark brooding aside. Perhaps Eddie had not stopped all her fun, and dropped a pleasure into her own lap as well as his mother's. Why couldn't this baby be the one that Charlie and her had once so desperately wanted? If Ethel and Eddie wouldn't keep it, then maybe she could.

Ethel ran back across the street in her dressing gown and into her hall. Her mother had hauled herself up and was sitting on the side of her bed.

'Ethel, what's up?' she said. 'Where've you been? Your dad's just slammed the back door.'

'It's nowt to worry about, Mum. Olive's comin' over in a minute. I'm late for the shop. I'll see you at dinnertime.'

She left her mother pushing her stick into the skirting board and trying to stand up, and dashed through to the kitchen. The bike clips, apron, and shoes had gone from the table, but her father had left with no tea in his belly and no sandwich for his lunch. Ethel had no time for tea either, but as she ran up the stairs to her bedroom she heard Eddie's whistling and the rattle of his motorbike as it kicked into life.

She stopped halfway up. Olive was right. She returned slowly to the kitchen and opened the back door. She stood on her step and saw Eddie fetching his fishing gear from the yard into the snicket. They had hardly said hello since their time together on the moor a couple of months before.

He seemed to have lost interest in his bike of late, and in her. Ethel knew he'd been avoiding her, and she had been frightened to knock on his back door in case his mother answered.

She dashed out into the lane and took hold of his wrist on the handlebar.

'Eddie, please,' she said. 'Talk to me. What's up wi' yer?'

'Nowt,' he replied. 'Why? Should there be?'

There was no going back now.

'Eddie, I think I'm havin' a baby.'

His fishing rod fell onto the cobbles. He snatched his hand from under hers.

'What? You're 'avin' me on,' he said. 'You can't be.'

'Well, I am,' said Ethel. 'I'm sure, and it's yours.'

She saw panic in his eyes.

'You're on yer own, Ethel. It's got nowt to do wi' me.'

He turned his back on Ethel, swung his leg over the seat, rolled his bike off its stand, and gathered speed away up the snicket without a backward glance. Her mind had been emptied, washed clean of the happy memories of the day on the elephant and the comfort at the brick pond, and drained of any dreams she might have had of a happy life with Eddie. She was left with only the gatepost for support. Reaching for the open back door of number 13, she sank onto the step, held her head in her hands, and wept.

Eight

'Shit, what now?' Mr Waggett said under his breath.

He'd heard the tinny rattle of his little bell and the sickening crash of his flimsy shop door flung open against the ladder followed by Ethel's scream. He slid his feet off the table, slapped his *Pigeon Press* down, stood up to brush the biscuit crumbs off his paunch, and pushed through the curtain from the back parlour to the front.

He'd tried to tell Ethel never to be idle even if there were no customers waiting to be served. It could give the wrong impression if one came into the shop. Her job till closing time this evening was to top up the sweet jars on the middle shelf and give them a wipe with a damp cloth, then swap round the packets of Omo and Ajax on the bottom shelf with the boxes of Navy Cut cigarettes and Saint Bruno pipe tobacco on the top shelf. He hadn't bothered to explain why to Ethel, and she'd never think to ask him, but his reasoning was that if customers had to look in a different place for something they needed, they might see something they didn't even know they wanted. Ethel had been balanced on the top rung of the step ladders when Mrs Sathersthwaite entered.

Waggett's Grocery and Provisions Stores on the corner of Railway Terrace and Hope Street had been a venue for many fierce arguments and exploding feuds and even the occasional fight over the years. Mr Waggett was a sporting man and he enjoyed these contests, never more so than when Mrs Sath pitched in. She was a small wizened old woman whose thin-lipped mouth hid a fearsome tongue. She arrived for combat today wearing her customary gabardine and dark blue felt hat decorated with its grubby grey knitted rose. Ringlets in curlers always poked out from beneath its brim. Her spectacles sat as usual on the end of her nose and Mr Waggett was glad to see from the fire in her eyes that she was incensed. She would take no nonsense.

'You dirty little cow,' she shouted up the ladder.

Not only was Mrs Sath furious, she was very close to tears, and she had Ethel in her sights. Ethel was a nobody, Mr Waggett had always thought that. It had never crossed his mind she could make anybody so angry.

'Mrs Sathersthwaite!' pleaded Mr Waggett. She took no notice of him. He hesitated behind his counter, not quite sure whether to enjoy this row or try to put a stop to it. He could see that Ethel's arms and legs were shaking as she looked down at her feet and picked her way down the rungs.

'What 'ave you gone an' done?' she bellowed into Ethel's face.

She jabbed a finger into Ethel's overalls with one hand, hurled her handbag onto the counter with the other, then pushed Ethel back against the shelves of tins.

'Your father 'as broken my Eddie's nose.'

Mr Waggett made up his mind to ride this one out. Too risky to wade in; Mrs Sath was a heavyweight; and he was curious by now to know what Ethel and Eddie had done. Backed into the corner of the shop, Ethel stared at the ladder. She couldn't bring herself even to look at Mrs Sath. She realised in a second what must have happened. Olive would have told her mother and then taken pleasure in going next door to tell Mrs Sath her juicy secret. The pair of them hated each other. Mrs Sath would have wasted no time in dragging her son's side of the story out of him. Then she would have planned her attack. Ethel had been worried too that Mrs Sath would come for her alone in the shop and that Mr Waggett didn't need much of an excuse to give her the sack.

'What have you done to my Eddie? Your filthy family has ruined my life. I've 'ad enough of scum like you. You drag the street down an' you breed like rabbits.'

The truth dawned on Mr Waggett.

'You've 'ad your eye on my Eddie all your life, you scheming bitch, so you thought you'd get your 'ooks into 'im, din't you? Well, let me tell you summat for free, you've another thing comin'. We've got standards. My Bill made summat of 'imself. He was a gentleman, and Eddie can do a lot better for 'imself than you. An' don't you be expectin' any money from us neither. Take a long look at yerself in a mirror. Nobody would want you, Ethel Slater, you're a mess.'

Mr Waggett liked a bet, and he often took pity on the underdog. Ethel rarely spoke unless she had to, and she'd not said a word yet. He'd never seen Mrs Sath in such cracking form, but Ethel hadn't even come out of her corner. But he was visibly shocked Ethel could have got herself pregnant.

'Mrs Sathersthwaite,' he said. 'I know this is nowt to do wi' me, but it does take two.'

Mrs Sath took her eyes off Ethel and looked to Mr Waggett behind the counter for a second.

Ethel seized her chance.

'Please, Mrs Sath,' she said. 'It's not like you think. It was all Eddie's idea. We went down the fish ponds on 'is bike. We only went the once.'

'Don't you lie to me. You've led 'im on. We've put up with your rows next door for years. Your father slammin' doors an' shoutin' the odds at all 'ours, his revoltin' pigeons, and the rats. You just wanted a way out. We don't deserve to live with the likes of you next door.'

Ethel had begun to cry.

'Eddie said we'd marry. He said we'd 'ave our own 'ouse. I know we woulda done if this 'adn't 'appened.'

'Over my dead body. Your father 'as barged in an' laid into my Eddie an' he's gone. He's gone to Preston. Took 'is bike an' went this mornin'.'

Mr Waggett turned to the clink of the bell above the door as a paying customer arrived. End of round one was his first thought, but then, oh my God was his second, Mrs Pearson of all people, the vicar's wife! This was not good for business.

'Ladies, please,' he begged. 'Calm down.'

'Whore! Another bastard child in the street,' Mrs Sath shouted into Ethel's face. 'Just like you. You were unwanted. Do you know that?'

'No, he can't 'ave gone,' sobbed Ethel.

Mrs Sath burst into tears too, and lunged forward to launch a slap across Ethel's cheek. Ethel fell back into the shelves and clattered to the floor with some tins. Mr Waggett scurried across from behind the counter to round them up and inspect them for dents, as Mrs Sath snatched her handbag, straightened her hat, and pushed her way out past Mrs Pearson.

Mrs Pearson bent to take Ethel's elbow and help her to her feet.

'Shame on Mrs Sathersthwaite,' she said. 'Whatever you've done, there's no need for that.'

Ethel flattened down her skirt and her hair, then held her fingers to her cheek.

'Tell me what's the matter,' Mrs Pearson said.

'I'm in the family way, Mrs Pearson.'

'I thought as much. Don't worry, love, it's not the end of the world.'

Mrs Pearson took a spotted handkerchief out of the sleeve of her cardigan and gave it to Ethel. Then she slid some tins and packets out of the way with her foot, grabbed Ethel in her arms, and held her face into her shoulder.

'There, there, Ethel. There's worse things that can happen than having a baby. Come up to the vicarage if you want and see Gerald. We'll see what's to be done for the best.'

Ethel said thank you, she would. Mr Waggett tried to change the subject and asked Mrs Pearson if there was anything he could help her with. Sprouts, carrots, and potatoes were all she had come in for, and he told her that today was not the first time this sort of thing had happened in the shop, but it was not a joking matter. Mrs Pearson tried to reassure Ethel that things would look better tomorrow morning.

But they didn't. They looked worse. She made an effort to arrive before Mr Waggett and found '*Stores*' on the window painted over with '*Nokin Shop*'. She got the bucket and soap and the ladders, and did her best to wash it off, but Mr Waggett arrived at the shop on time for once.

'Who did that?' he asked Ethel.

'I don't really know, Mr Waggett,' she replied, but she just knew it must have been Tom Shaw, Eddie's old bombsite playmate. It was his style.

He looked at her bruise.

This was an opportunity to keep Ethel's pay packet out of her father's pocket. Slater's Queenie was the fastest flyer the Short Distance Pigeon Union had seen for years, and she beat his own Boxer every race.

'Well,' he said, 'you're sacked. I've 'ad word from customers that you're late openin' up most mornings, an' I'm tryin' to sell food, not ringside seats. I suggest you go back 'ome an' keep out of Aggie Sath's way. I wish you luck, Ethel. I reckon you're going to need it.'

Nine

Ethel sat on the edge of her bed and tried to think. She had no future so she had no plan. She had fed her mother a bit of porridge, her father was down in the kitchen smoking, and she had asked in her prayers that, please God, Eddie would come back home. There was nothing more she could do.

But then her prayer had been answered. She heard the engine turn the corner at the top then slow down to the bottom of the terrace. She leapt to the window to catch sight of his head before he turned his bike down the side of the houses, and saw a motor car. It travelled up to the gates, then swung right over the grass, and stopped just short of the narrow brick opening to the snicket. It reversed slowly into the opening on the other side, then drove back the way it had arrived and parked outside her house.

She watched Reverend Pearson hesitate behind the wheel. The vicar aimed to pay a call on every house in his parish and offer his blessing at least twice a year if he had the time and energy. He preferred to leave his gleaming Anglia in the garage and travel on foot to these visits. He sometimes saw people who were in trouble at the vestry and even at his own home, but Mrs Pearson had persuaded him that this mission of mercy required a trip in his car.

He paused to admire the top of his bald bespectacled head in the rear-view mirror, then angled it slightly. He watched his finger run round the inside of his dog collar. He thought he might run to a new suit. His shoulders sagged in this one, and appearances mattered. He tossed his trilby with the map onto the back seat, then got out. Ethel felt fear now. She hadn't dared leave the house since Mrs Sath had slapped her and she hadn't been up to the vicarage to see him. She realised that Reverend Pearson must have come to take her to the asylum, and felt some relief that things had finally been taken out of her hands. She picked her handbag up off the floor and came downstairs when she heard his voice in her mother's room below.

Her mother reached for her stick and began to lever herself out of her chair. The vicar told Mary that it was nice to see her out of bed and dressed, but not to stand up on his account. Dennis had no time for the vicar, or God. He escaped to the yard by the back door to talk to his prize racer Queenie and her brood in their loft. Pigeons were the only true loves of his life.

Mary was worried the neighbours might think she had died when they saw Reverend Pearson parking his car outside.

'Reverend,' she said, 'would Marjorie ever come down to see me, please? I'm on me death bed.'

He sat down on the end of the bed and picked up her hand from her lap.

'Of course she will,' he said. 'God gives us the strength and wisdom to smoothly surmount all the challenges life brings us. But I'm here to minister to our Ethel today, Mary.'

'She's expectin', Reverend. There'll be nobody to look out for our Ethel when I'm gone and she's not got the gumption to look after a baby by herself. An' I'm no good to man nor beast these days. I'm scared what'll 'appen to 'er.'

Ethel appeared at her mother's bedroom door before the vicar had time to find any more words.

'Ethel, my dear,' Reverend Pearson began. 'Come in. There's nothing I've got to say that I can't say in front of Mary.'

She remained standing in the doorway. She could shield the bruise on her face easier there than looking straight at the vicar.

'Come on in, my child,' he said again. 'I don't bite.'

'Ethel, please,' said her mum. 'Sit yourself down on the edge of the bed 'ere. It sounds like Reverend Pearson's 'ere to 'elp. An' shut the door behind you. We don't want your father listenin' in on us, do we?'

'Mrs Pearson's told me you're in a spot of bother, Ethel, and we've thought of a way to make things better,' the vicar continued.

Ethel was reassured enough to step into the room. She pulled her dressing gown together around her waist and tightened up the knot in the cord, then perched at the head of the bed next to the vicar. Her eyes were red through crying, and she thought that the bruise on her cheek made her lazy eye look even worse. The vicar reached over to take her hand down from her face.

He looked at the bruise.

'Mrs Sath, I know. You must try and forgive her. She's troubled herself. She'll be worried that her Eddie has brought shame on the family name, and she'll think that he's gone for good. And then there's the shock of a grandchild. She's terribly lonely, Ethel, without her Bill and her Eddie in the house. And we must remember at all times, my dear, that God loves you and will forgive you in His mercy. Forgiveness is a virtue.'

Ethel looked away to the two spaniels returning her stare from the top of the glass cabinet.

'I'd no idea Eddie would go,' said Ethel. 'I wish he'd stayed.'

'I didn't know he'd left, Ethel,' said Mary. 'Where's he gone?'

'He'll 'ave gone to Preston,' said Ethel. 'He's got a pal there, Pete. They were in Korea together. Eddie told me about 'im a few times. He said Pete were like a brother to 'im. They 'ad a laugh and sometimes they'd go fishin' overnight somewhere together. I think he's got a garage or summat like that.'

'He'll come home soon. Mrs Sath will see to that,' said the vicar. 'The army changes men, Ethel. War can harden them. It makes them think differently about death. And about what they want from life. Do you want him back?'

'I don't really know,' replied Ethel. 'I don't know what I want.'

'I allus thought you two'd wed one day, without ever really thinkin' about it,' said Mary. 'I'd 'oped you'd do things the right way round, that's all.'

'We all thought that, Ethel, I don't mind tellin' you,' said Reverend Pearson.

He took hold of his own wedding ring between the thumb and first finger of his right hand and slid it up to the knuckle and back again a couple of times.

He knew what Mary meant, that she had done things the wrong way round herself, but now was not the time to dwell on that. At least Mary and Dennis had done the right thing in the eyes of God, more or less, and got married when they realised that Mary was expecting.

'I remember baptising you all those years ago, and that was a day for rejoicing in the Lord. And we've all watched you two playing and messing about in the street together. You were joined at the hip. I know this might seem like the end of the world to you, but it isn't. Eddie's broken your heart, my dear, but there's always time, and time mends broken hearts.'

Ethel closed her eyes and pressed her handkerchief in to dry them. She left it held there to hide her bruise. She'd not found the words before to talk to her mother. She hadn't dare.

'Mum,' she sobbed, 'I'm more worried about you than anythin' else. I just never thought that owt like this could 'appen. It weren't Eddie's fault and it weren't mine either. It were just the once that Saturday afternoon. Nowt else has gone on, I promise. And I do love Eddie, an' he said he loves me. We would 'ave set up together an' done up the old bombed 'ouse an' taken you in, I know we would.'

'Don't you be frettin' about me, our Ethel,' said Mary. 'Olive will see me right, and then there's your dad.'

But Ethel was still much more anxious about her mother than about herself, not so much the awful shame she would feel about the baby and the wagging tongues and twitching curtains in the terrace, but what her father might do. She could cope with his drinking and shouting, and even a slap in the face from time to time. They were aimed at her more frequently these days but were over and done with soon enough come the next morning. It was his terrifying long silences for days that broke Ethel down, the sulks with no end in sight, and the despair in her mother's eyes after Dennis had hit her. He would leave his wife to fend for herself, when anyone could see that she couldn't. She could barely stand up sometimes. He might even abandon her altogether when there was a baby in the house. And then she had seen with her own eyes what her father liked to do with Olive, and she knew in her heart that her mother knew too.

'That's enough about that for now, Ethel,' Reverend Pearson said, easing himself off the bed. 'Go get your coat. I'm taking you on a short drive to see Sister Ash. She can help.'

'Is she in the mental hospital, Reverend?' Ethel asked.

'Nobody's going to hospital, dear.' The vicar laughed. 'Sister Ash is a nurse, and she's seen all this type of thing before.'

Reverend Pearson reassured Mary that he would have Ethel back in time to make tea. He climbed into his car and leant over to open the passenger door for Ethel, took the roadmap off the back seat, and told her to slip her shoes off before she got in and be careful not to touch any switches on the dashboard. She'd only been driven in a car once before, and in the back, at the funeral of Eddie's father. They smelt of leather inside and they were shiny on the outside. It was a Ford Anglia, the vicar told her as they set off, but she didn't know what that was supposed to mean.

They drove past Waggett's Stores on the corner and Ethel recognised the streets further into the town, but then she was soon lost as they motored out along country lanes and through little villages. Reverend Pearson explained that he was taking her for an interview with Sister Ash at a special home, where she would have the baby. Ethel stared ahead out of the windscreen at nothing when she heard this shattering news. The terrifying thoughts of talking with a stranger who would shout at her for being pregnant, living in a new place, and then giving birth there, all hit her at the same time. They both lapsed into their own uneasy thoughts for the rest of the journey.

They drove for less than an hour and then the vicar brought the car to a gentle stop at a crossroads, where a signpost in the verge pointed in all four directions. He left the engine running and walked over to the post without speaking to Ethel. She watched him in silence as he climbed back into his seat, laid out his map on the steering wheel, turned it upside down, then tapped his finger on a circle he'd drawn in pencil around a big house. He turned right then crawled past the church, where Ethel caught a glimpse through the trees of the path snaking up to the porch, a few stone cottages, and the Blacksmith's Arms public house, before pulling up outside their destination. Reverend Pearson wound down the window and paused to admire the stonework. He told Ethel that it was the old manor house. This didn't mean anything to Ethel either. She just knew she'd never seen such a big, lonely old house in her life.

The words Albany House had been carved into the gatepost. Thick green ivy grew up over the front of the house, around and across some arched windows and a balcony and into the gutters above, and smoke rose skywards from one of the chimneys. The house was in the foothills of the climb onto the moors and it looked down onto the valley below. The vicar led Ethel up the gravel drive but then let her take the lead up a narrow path at the side to save his suit from most of the recent shower dripping off the overhanging privet. He asked the gardener where they might find the matron, and without speaking he pointed his hoe to a door hidden from view.

A girl much thinner but no older than Ethel was polishing the bannisters up the stairwell. She looked down from the top and gave them a hollow smile. Billows of steam hit them in the hallway through the door to the laundry on the left, and the clanging of pans and crockery came from the kitchen on the right. Sister Ash broke off from discussing lunch with the cook.

She was expecting them. 'Come through to the office,' she said.

The office was a few scraps of paper on a table in the corner of a room packed with big black iron prams. She shuffled through the papers and brought one to the top. She read down it slowly as she fiddled with some strands of hair that had fallen out from her bun, then pushed her spectacles back onto her forehead and looked up.

'Afternoon, Reverend,' she said.

'Good afternoon, Sister,' the vicar said. 'We're obliged.'

Her mouth smiled but her eyes didn't.

'So here we have Ethel Slater, do we?' She turned to Ethel. 'I see we've been with the father recently?'

Ethel stood before her in front of the table, unsure of what to do with her hands. She didn't really understand either question.

'Has the cat got your tongue? Did he give you the black eye?'

Ethel flinched.

'No, it was 'is mother.'

'Well, maybe you've asked for it. That's not for us to say. We don't judge here, and may God forgive you. But at least we know who the father is, don't we? Some girls don't tell us, or don't even know. Reverend Pearson has brought you nice and early by the looks of your tummy. We like that. When did you conceive?'

Ethel looked to Reverend Pearson. He crossed his legs then back again and looked at Sister Ash.

'Do you have frequent intercourse with this man?'

Ethel's mind was a blank. She shifted on her feet but still remained silent.

'How far gone are you, do you know?'

'It was one Saturday in June a long time ago, and I've missed twice, I think.'

Sister looked down at a diary on the table and flicked forward through the pages.

'Well, go and see the doctor, Miss Slater. He will examine you and tell you when the baby is due. And we need a certificate from him to say you've not picked up an infection. Are you still seeing this man?'

'No. He's gone to Preston.'

'And do we have his name?'

'It's Eddie Sath,' said Ethel.

'Edward Sathersthwaite,' corrected the vicar.

'That's what we like to hear. Reverend Pearson will bring you to stay here when you've six weeks to go. Your parents can visit you if they want, but we don't encourage it. You will have the baby here, and then you stay a fortnight before you go back home. For now, Monica can show you round the house.'

Ethel found Monica at the top of the stairs to the first floor sweeping dust from the carpet with a stiff wire brush. 'Hello, I'm Moni,' she said. 'You look like a drowned rat. You're wet through.'

'It were the rain drippin' off the 'edge down the side of the 'ouse,' said Ethel. She lifted up her dress sticking onto her thighs.

Monica giggled.

'Never mind. It's thin. You'll soon dry. What's the father like?'

Monica studied Ethel as she gathered her thoughts for a few seconds.

'I don't really know,' Ethel replied. 'He's got thick black hair an' lovely eyes an' a quiff. An' he wears a leather jacket sometimes when he goes out on 'is motorbike. An' skinny trousers. He loves his bike. He's allus polishin' it.'

'Blimey,' Monica said. 'Not like mine. He was a smelly old bloke I used to work for in the mill. He used to grunt like a pig when he came. I hated it. Yours sounds really nice.'

'He is.'

Monica finished polishing the last stair rod and dropped her brush back into the pan.

'Come on, I'll show you round a bit. I've 'ad my baby day before yesterday an' I'm a bit stiff an' sore, but I'll show you my baby box.'

Ethel followed her along a corridor and into a shady room above the kitchen. Five or six cots stood in a line along the middle of the floor.

'Here she is,' whispered Monica. 'Don't wake 'er up.'

Oh, she's just perfect, was Ethel's first thought. She was swaddled in white linen and a few strands of brown hair had slid down from under her pink bonnet onto her temples. Her arms twitched at the shoulders then she yawned. Ethel felt the urge to pick her up but she was sound asleep.

'What's 'er name?' asked Ethel.

'She's not got one yet. Her parents will choose one. I've made this to go out with 'er, though.'

But Monica is her mother, surely, thought Ethel. She didn't like to ask.

Monica lifted a cardboard shoebox out of the end of the cot. She'd lined and covered it in flowery wallpaper, tucked in neatly round the corners and sewn down with thin string. She lifted out some vests with sleeves, a flannelette nightgown, a jacket, several towelling nappies, some bibs, a shawl, and a blanket. Monica picked out a small blue teddy bear leaning back in the corner, waved its arm to say hello to Ethel, and gave it to her to hold. Ethel plonked a kiss on its ear and put it back in the cot next to the baby's head.

'And this,' she said, 'a little letter I've written to 'er, not to be opened until 'er eighteenth birthday. It just says never forget that your mummy loved you and will always love you, no matter what 'appens to you or what anybody says. Knittin' an' makin' all this lot keeps you busy in the afternoons. I'd bring in a box an' some paper and yer sewin' things when you come.'

'I don't see to sew very well,' said Ethel.

'Never mind,' said Monica. She peered at Ethel's eyes and her bruise for a few seconds. 'You've got plenty of other jobs to do in the afternoons. They can really drag. You've got nappies and sheets to wash and veg to peel. Our beds are upstairs. You want to see them?'

Ethel leant on the windowsill in the dormitory and looked out over the river down in the valley below to the hills beyond. She heard the church clock strike three and some crows cawing from the treetops opposite the house, but there was not one person to be seen.

'It's lovely, don't you think?' said Monica. 'So quiet. Can you see the steeple through the trees?'

But it was the bombed house that Ethel wanted to see. Not some trees. And a plume of steam belch up above the gates at the end of the terrace from a passing train. She wanted to see the rag-and-bone man and his horse and cart ambling up the street as she rounded the corner walking back home for lunch. A new stray cat raiding the bins. Queenie and her brood in their loft. Bobbing their heads up and down. She wanted to hear the sparrows lined up chattering to each other on the back fence. A pram clattering along the cobbles down the snicket. Not this stifling peace. The clanking of the wagons in the shunting yards. Her mother calling her from downstairs. Eddie tuning his bike in the back yard. And she needed to see

Eddie's face. To bury her face in the back of his neck on a ride to the fish pond. And to hear his laugh.

She began to sob, and turned from the view to face Monica in the room.

'It soon goes,' Monica said.

'I'm sorry,' Ethel replied, and sniffed.

'There's only one room left you need to see,' Monica said. 'On the floor above 'ere, where you give birth. I 'eard it before I saw it. Matron 'elps you.'

Ethel just wanted to get home.

'Matron's alright really,' said Monica. 'She'll 'ave you sayin' prayers and singin' a hymn in the pram room every morning. An' she'll tell you you've sinned in the eyes of God. But God forgives those that repent, there's no limit on forgiveness, an' stuff like that. But who cares? She sends you to church on Sunday mornin'. You 'ave to sit on the seats at the back, that's the only thing. People stare at you. You get sent back on Sunday evening as well, but I'd go to the Blacksmith's Arms instead. But it does pass, Ethel. It's only a few weeks. And then you can go 'ome, as if nothin' 'as 'appened.'

Ethel thought she would ask Matron if she would let her polish the bannisters rather than going to the church or the pub.

Monica could see out of the window that Reverend Pearson had gone to his car. He'd opened the back door, and was straightening and laying out his jacket along the back seat.

'Looks like they've done talkin', Ethel,' she said. 'If you can follow 'im out the front door, you'll miss the hedge.'

Sister Ash had returned to the back kitchen as Ethel scurried down the steps of Albany House. Forgetting to take her shoes off, she climbed into the passenger seat next to the vicar. He consulted his map spread out over the dashboard. She expected no words of comfort from him, and none came. He turned the car in the road and they set off for home.

Ethel steeled herself after a while to speak to him as she picked up on some familiar streets on the journey. 'Reverend Pearson,' she said, 'I don't think I want to go back there.'

He thumped his fist on the steering wheel and stared ahead but made no reply. He groaned, but then kept his thoughts to himself until he turned off the engine outside the vicarage. 'Ethel,' he said before she climbed out, 'you've no say in the matter. Stop and think about somebody else for once in your life. Your poor mother, she's at her wits' end with all your carrying-on. For God's sake, girl, just do as you're told.'

Ten

Ethel rattled her big black iron pram with its precious cargo of her newborn baby along the cobbles down the snicket. She rounded the corner to be met by Olive's two enormous wide eyes, when the mail train thundered past the gates.

She awoke with a jolt and sat bolt upright, then slumped back onto the pillow. She felt exhausted. Her hair was wet with sweat. Olive's eyes and the snicket and the pram was a nightmare that tormented Ethel time and again since her visit to Sister Ash at Albany House. She would get to sleep in the small hours and be awoken by the same dream a short time later. It had her relive the horror of finding Olive pinned by her father against the bricks, and would then disturb the rest of her day.

There was no need to look at the bedside clock this morning. The mail train left the station at 5.30am and passed the end of St Paul's Terrace at 5.31am. She could hear gentle rain pattering on the window, but there was more than an hour of darkness left before the first glimmer of dawn. The train wouldn't have woken Ethel even at full steam in happy times, but life in the terrace with a baby growing inside her had put a stop to those.

She lay on the bed and the reality of her dream played back through her mind. It was the shock in Olive's eyes that had hit her. Olive was looking down the snicket at her over her father's shoulder, half sitting on a ledge from the wall, her dress bunched up around her waist, her legs splayed apart. And her father was leaning into her, his trousers fallen round his ankles, holding one of her naked thighs up from under a knee. Ethel had hurried back home with teddy in her pram to ask Mum why Dad was holding onto Olive in the snicket, and Mum had said they were sorting out the bins and it was her bed time. She knew that evening that something somehow was wrong, but it was only years later that she realised just how wrong.

Ethel daren't venture out of her bedroom until she was quite sure her father was not in the house. Lying face to the wall took the weight of her belly off her aching back. The world was waking up. She heard the clink of the milk bottle on the front step and the whistles of the early trains leaving the station. The first fingers of daylight were creeping down the curtain before she heard the squeak of the handle on her father's bedroom door. He coughed then the loose stair creaked. She smelt the cigarette smoke and heard the catch on the kitchen cupboard, the drop of the kettle onto the ring, the click of the latch on the back door, and finally the reassuring scrape of the bottom of the lavatory door on the flags in the yard.

Her father had not spoken to her or her mother for nearly three weeks now. His brooding and his seething temper had eventually boiled over one morning on his way to his shop when he opened the back door to find his Queenie laid out on the step, her neck wrung and her feathers plucked. He had cried, Ethel thought for the first time in his life. He'd found the sneck on the loft had been forced with a screwdriver during the night, and the rest of the brood had flown. He knew, he just knew, it was that bastard Waggett that had done it, and he blamed Ethel for getting herself pregnant then getting herself sacked. He'd told Ethel, yet again, that she was a slut, and she should've learned to keep her knees together. Her mother had struggled through to the kitchen in her nightdress and on her sticks to try to break up the fight. She'd told her husband that he didn't have a leg to stand on, and he had snatched off the table the first thing that came to hand and thrown a plate at her head. She had fallen to the floor and Ethel had screamed. His parting words were that he'd had a bellyful of this fucking family.

This baby was a row that would never blow over. Once Ethel was sure her father had pedalled his bike off up the snicket and gone, she swung her legs off the bed, cupped her hands under her belly, and stood up. She stretched and winced at the pain in her back, then knelt on the floorboards to drag out the pot from under the bed. Holding it tight into her chest with one hand, she steadied herself on the bannister with the other and slid both feet onto each step before taking the next as she moved down the stairs. She emptied the stale urine down the sink and opened the letter again in the kitchen while the pot of tea brewed.

Her mother had read it aloud to her many times and she knew the words. It was short, typed, frightening, and to the point. Their landlords, the Railway Company, were sorry to inform Mr and Mrs Slater that because they had defaulted on payment of rent for three months, they would have no option but to evict them at the end of November unless the arrears were paid in full. Mum had told Ethel that she'd saved the money in the jar on the mantlepiece as she always did, but it had gone by the time the rent collector called at the door. They both knew where it had gone, and why, but neither could bring themselves to say it. Father's trouser pocket, for pigeon-racing bets, beer, whiskey, cigarettes, and women.

Ethel took her mum's cup of tea and the letter through to the front room. She drew back the curtains. The grey winter light was enough to wake her mother and Ethel sat well back next to her thighs in the middle of the bed. She tried to straighten her own back and pull the dead weight of her mum up against the headboard, then took the cup off the saucer, blew the steam off the tea for a few seconds, and held it up to her lips. Ethel left the letter out on the bed.

Mary took a sip. 'Has your father gone?' she said. 'Did he take his sandwich?'

'Yes,' said Ethel. 'I 'eard 'im go not 'alf an 'our since.'

Ethel steadied the cup between her mother's hands and tipped it to her lips for a few more sips. Routine like this was everything to Ethel.

'You do know this, our Ethel, don't you?' she said. 'I need you. I couldn't go on livin' if I didn't 'ave you?'

Ethel brought the cup down and placed it on its saucer on the chair. She took her mother's hands in hers. 'Come on, Mum.' She whispered for fear of cracking her voice and starting to cry. 'What a thing to say.'

'We've no money comin' in.'

Her eyes had filmed over.

'There's no chance Mr Waggett will have me back, Mum. I've asked at the button factory an' Rowntrees, but they won't take me on either. It's me eye. I'm still out lookin', though.'

'I've been thinkin', Ethel, and talkin' things over with Olive. I've 'ad to ask somebody,' said Mary.

Ethel dropped her mother's hands back onto the sheet. Olive's name brought the memory of the snicket straight back.

'It breaks me 'eart to say this, Ethel, it really does, but I think you should leave 'ome—'

'Never—'

'…and go stay with our Annie in Rochdale and work behind the bar. She might pay you a few bob.'

'But the baby…?'

'Annie knows all about babies.'

'But you can't fend for yourself, Mum, and Dad won't bother with you.'

'Olive says she'll 'elp out. She'll sleep over in your bed.'

Any scrap of hope that Ethel might have had for a future evaporated with this plan. She knew instinctively that her father would share Olive in her own little bed upstairs, when his crippled wife was in more need of their kindness in the room below. And her mother feared that too.

'Can we think about this first, Mum?' Ethel asked. 'I could ask for a job at the Cross Keys.'

'Our Annie likes to feed folk up, Ethel, and you'll be one less mouth to feed 'ere,' continued Mary.

Ethel picked the letter up off the bed and stuffed it into the pocket in her dressing gown.

'I could post you any wages I get, Mum. There is that. Keep it under your mattress, and we might get to stay put in this 'ouse. Then I could come to live back 'ome again.'

'But maybe not wi' the baby.'

'What?'

Ethel stared at her mother's crumpling face. She'd heard her wrong, surely?

She tried so hard not to start crying, but she couldn't stop herself.

'There's sommat else Olive 'as said to me, Ethel. She wants to bring up your baby for 'erself. She reckons it might save 'er marriage.'

The vision of Olive with her father and her baby was too much to bear.

''Ave you told Dad?'

Mary erupted into tears too. Ethel had watched her mother weep silently so many times in her life, but never before had she seen her break down so utterly. She lunged at her laid on the bed and took her into her arms and squeezed her face into her own shoulder so tight she could cry no more.

'Yes.' Her mum was shaking. 'He said nowt. An' he grabbed me an' threw me against the wall in the kitchen. I'm so scared of what he might do, Ethel. He could kill me. He could even kill you. He could do anythin'.'

Eleven

Ethel spotted Auntie Annie and Uncle Albert waiting together near the barrier as the York train clattered into Rochdale station. The platform was quite crowded as this was the last stop before Manchester, but Ethel picked them out as soon as the train began to slow down: the big blousy woman with a skinny little bald husband. She wound down her window and stuck her head out, and waved madly as her carriage rolled past them and the train ground to a standstill.

She had telephoned Annie from a box in town a couple of days before, and asked her if she could meet the first train into Rochdale on Friday. We'll be there, Annie had replied, don't you worry, and she had already cleared some junk out of the spare bedroom. Ethel knew that her mother had written to her sister in Rochdale. She'd not been there when Olive wrote the words down on a piece of paper, but her mother had read it out to Ethel before she asked her to take it to the post box.

*'Dear Annie, ar Ethels in the family way and Dennis
as teken agenst it. Can she stay at the junction pleese
to sort evrything out? You always know whats for
the best with babies.'*

'Whoa,' shouted Annie as she scuttled along beside the
train. She'd opened the handle on the carriage door before
the train had come to a halt, grabbed Ethel's hand with her
own, and reached onto the ledge to take her little suitcase.
Ethel stepped down from the train into one of Annie's
hugs and a sloppy wet kiss on the cheek.

'Ee, come 'ere, love, let's 'ave a proper look at you,'
Annie said. She stood back a step but kept hold of Ethel's
elbow. 'You're as soft as butter! You allus were. We've been
dyin' to see you.'

Uncle Albert limped along the platform to catch up
with his wife, gave Ethel his practised wink, switched his
stick from his right hand to his left, and picked up the case.

Annie led the way through the queue at the ticket
office to the bus stop outside. They joined the end of the
line of women and didn't have long to wait. They wanted
the number 37, which would take them through the town
and drop them right outside The Junction.

'We'd best go up top,' Annie told Ethel. 'Albert'll want
a smoke.'

She took the case off Albert and asked the conductor if
he wouldn't mind fetching it up after them. She made way
for her husband and gave him a firm push in the small of
his back onto the platform. They let him go first up the
stairs, slowly, using his stick as a third leg. The top deck was
crowded so Albert stayed at the back to catch his breath

and look after the suitcase, while Annie and Ethel found a double seat together towards the front. Ethel squeezed her belly into the gap and cleared some condensation off the window with her coat sleeve. She peered out at the passing streets of Rochdale and saw just the same sight as at home: grannies out shopping, and lucky young mothers pushing a pram with a husband at work who loved them, going about their straightforward lives. The fog and the gloom of a winter's day had barely lifted at all.

Ethel couldn't speak for a while, lost for words, embarrassed, even though there was so much she had to say.

Annie broke the silence.

'How's your mum?'

'Same,' replied Ethel. She thought for a moment. 'Worse. She's a job on sometimes just to get out of 'er bed now.'

'And your new bairn? D'ya know when she's due?' Annie patted the front of Ethel's coat.

'Next March, early on,' said Ethel. 'I went to see Dr Chisholm. Olive came wi' me. He asked me all sorts of things, an' he worked it out an' wrote it down on a bit of paper. He said to take it with me to the 'ome.'

'And what's all this about your dad? I've 'eard tell there's been a row?'

Ethel filled up and couldn't answer for a few seconds. She looked out at the road and then spoke to the window without a glance at Annie.

'He's not speaking to us,' she said. 'Mr Waggett or someone wrung Queenie's neck, 'is best pigeon, and he blamed me for it. He'll never forgive me, Auntie Annie, an' he takes it out on Mother. He's forever 'ittin' 'er. He threw a plate at 'er an' knocked 'er over in the kitchen an' she slipped an' fell back on the lino. He just comes an' goes as he pleases now. An' he's spent the rent.'

Annie shook her head. 'It'll be Eddie Sath's baby, int it?' she asked. ''As he beggared off an' left you?'

'Yes,' said Ethel.

Annie lowered her voice and leaned into Ethel's ear.

'Right,' she said. 'Look at me, lass. You know I'm one for speakin' me mind, so let's get summat settled before we get off this bus. You're with me an' Albert till after Christmas, no question. Your father's neither use nor ornament. You know I've allus thought that. But I've no time for 'im at all since he started cloutin' our Mary. He only ever did please 'imself. An' your mum were pregnant wi' you before they got wed. There's no secret there either. I maybe shouldn't say this about your dad, our Ethel, but I will. He's a wrong 'un. A bad lot. An' put 'im out of your 'ead while you're with us at The Junction, so think on.'

Albert tugged the bell cord at the back of the bus well before the stop and pulled himself to his feet. Ethel got off to stand on the kerb first, while Annie saw to Albert and his stick and the suitcase inching down the stairs. The sign of The Junction swayed gently above a pub door, the cheery signalman waving aloft from the window of his box at the Flying Scotsman as it thunders over his points. '*Albert and Annie Lofthouse, Licensees*' was painted on a board above the door, but anybody who ever picked a fight or swore at a barmaid in that pub was left in no doubt that it was the landlady that called the shots.

'You're ten minutes late openin', Annie,' said an old man smoking his pipe and leaning beside the door.

'We open when I say so, Jack.'

She turned the key in the lock and pushed the door open onto a long, dark corridor. Jack stood well back and watched her rump as she bent to pick up some letters from the mat. He followed her through the door to the left, then watched her waist squeeze through the gap at the end of the bar. She pulled him a pint of mild and set the glass down in front of him. They both stood a moment to admire the milky bubbles swirl around the inside and some foam slide down the outside. Jack was widowed and lived alone, and he longed for a cuddle from Annie. He would always want the landlady to pull him his first pint of the day. It was the way she steadied herself with her left hand around the pump on the bar, then reached up for the glass with her right. He enjoyed her tight dress, her cleavage and her thick red lipstick from a distance. The landlady was always just out of reach. Jack thought Annie was dainty in spite of all the flesh.

'Settle up later,' she told Jack. 'I've a new barmaid to show round. Ethel, this is Jack, my favourite customer. Jack, this is Ethel.'

'Mornin', love. See ya later,' Jack said, and turned to put his cap, his pint, and his pipe onto a little round table behind him.

The embers in the grate seemed to have sucked all the air out of the public bar and left it to stink of last night's smoke. The barmaid served her customer through a little hatch, from which he could turn to pass a drink to anybody in the room. A low, deep bench ran around the wall and a couple of ashtrays and a few beermats had been scattered on the table. The slate on the wall next to the dartboard hadn't been wiped clean since the last match, and there were some tin trophy cups and dead flies on the windowsill.

'The saloon's other side of the corridor,' Annie told Ethel as she wiped off drips from the nozzle with a towel. 'We keep that door shut if we can. It's a bit quieter. There's the cellar door down the end, an' that's all there is to it. Albert calls his cellar the engine room. He still thinks he's on board HMS *Dreadnought*, but that's our Albert for you. We'll start you off in 'ere. You'll be pullin' pints soon like there's no tomorrow.'

'I'll show you the ropes, love,' Jack chipped in. 'There's a knack to it.'

'He will that,' said Annie. 'Bring your bits upstairs for now, though, love. I'll show you where you're sleepin'. It's the same room you allus 'ad as a bairn. It's above the saloon, and it can get rowdy in there of a Saturday night on the piano. But you'll be right. You'll not be in bed before chuckin'-out time any road.'

Ethel picked up her suitcase and followed her auntie's thick ankles up the steep stairs.

'I've shifted things round in 'ere a bit,' Annie told Ethel. 'Will it do you?'

'Yes,' said Ethel. 'It's 'ardly changed since last time I slept in 'ere. It's the same as we've done for Mum really. We've moved 'er bed downstairs at 'ome.'

'So I'd 'eard,' said Annie.

There was a put-up bed and a small wardrobe moved in just for Ethel. But there was also a gas fire, a colourful patchwork rag-rug in front of it, a standard lamp to make up for the lack of daylight, and a wireless. Some faded old street scenes in frames and flying ducks hung from a picture rail, and a portrait of an airman waving to the camera from a cockpit stood alone on the mantelpiece. The room even had wallpaper, pale yellow with Chinese pagodas and spindly weeping willows. This was a cut above St Paul's Terrace. The pub was a house of memories of happy times, when Mother had no worries about the stairs and before Father had hit her for the first time. They'd been for Christmas once or twice when she was a child, her parents sharing the bed and Ethel curled up on the floor. Auntie Annie had given her the spare room, reserved for the odd guest at the pub. Ethel realised that she was a guest of sorts too, but one who would be some use and earn her keep behind the bar, and who would be made welcome.

Ethel opened her suitcase on the bed and unpacked her few things into the wardrobe. She lit the gas fire and turned it down to low just to take the chill off the room, then pulled the curtains back to let in some light and made her way downstairs again. Jack was smoking his pipe behind an empty glass and told Ethel that the barrel had gone off. She would find Annie and Albert down in the cellar.

Ethel found Annie rolling a full keg out from against the cellar wall. 'Are you for marryin' Eddie, Ethel?' she asked. 'Our Mary told me years ago there was nowt more certain.'

Ethel shook her head. 'No, he wants nowt to do wi' me, Auntie. I thought we would 'ave done, but he's left his mother's an' gone to Preston.'

'Well, he's a dirty bastard,' said Albert, siphoning beer from the old barrel into a bucket. He turned in the standing water and shuffled back up the cellar steps to the kitchen.

'Take no notice of 'im, Ethel,' Annie said. 'He means well, but he's never any good wi' babies an' stuff like that. I allus thought you'd set up wi' Eddie. You were as thick as thieves as young 'uns. Do you want to keep it or get it adopted?'

'I want to keep it, Auntie Annie. But God knows how, and God knows where. They took me to an 'ome to 'ave the baby but I couldn't go back there.'

'We'll sort summat out, sweet'art,' said Annie, 'don't you worry. You can stay 'ere for a while, but I can't be doin' with you havin' it 'ere. I've enough on with Albert. And our Mary will need you back 'ome. Who knows about it?'

'Everybody. I told Olive, so she told everybody. Mrs Sath soon got wind an' gave me a mouthful an' a slap in the shop, an' that's when I got the sack.'

'Well, you'll need folk to 'elp when the time comes to nurse,' said Annie.

'I can't go through wi' this by meself,' said Ethel. 'I'm scared.'

'Well, you will, love. Don't be daft. You've no say in it now. We 'ad all this same bother when our Mary got herself pregnant, an' she 'ad you no problem. It allus works out somehow. There's lots worse that 'appens round 'ere. Now you get Jack another pint pulled. He'll show you 'ow till you get the hang of it, an' get that fire lit up again. I'm gettin' us dinner on while you get servin' in the public bar.'

Twelve

Dennis Slater opened his butcher's shop more or less when he felt like it. It was a short bike ride up St Paul's Terrace then along a couple of streets into town, but there was usually something more important to do before he set off. He might pay a call on Olive if he knew Charlie was on an early shift, or even talk to his new clutch of pigeons. Selling meat could always wait.

A few days after Ethel had left home for Rochdale, he unhooked the roller blind from the catch at the bottom of the shop door one morning and flipped the little sign in the window from '*Closed*' to '*Open*' at half past nine. He opened the door onto a line of irritated customers. They stepped in while he stepped out onto the pavement to lower the awning. His customers included the woman he despised more than any other, Mrs Sath, his next-door neighbour. *Lady muck*, he called her, and thought it was just his luck that her spotty son had gone and knocked up his daughter. He hated her. He was not alone. Most other people down the terrace did as well. Aggie Sath thought the butcher was lowlife, and she detested his bloodstained apron and the smell of raw meat he had about him. His sleek black hair and swarthy good looks irritated her too.

Mrs Pearson was at the front of the queue.

'Mornin', Mrs Pearson,' he said. 'What can I tempt you with today?' He paid no attention to Mrs Sath.

'Just six rashers of streaky, please, Dennis.'

Dennis lifted a hefty side of bacon off from a hook behind him and impaled it raw side down into the crook of the bacon slicer. Turning the wheel with one hand, slowly he slid six thick slices into a sheet of grease-proof paper laid out in the palm of his other hand. Mrs Pearson counted out some copper from her purse onto the counter between them. He wrapped the paper round the bacon, dropped it on the scales, put the little pack into her hand, and slid some of the pennies into the till.

'How's your Mary going on?' said Mrs Pearson.

'So-so, you know,' said Dennis. 'She's still badly with 'er nerves.'

'Well, look, Reverend P and me are always here to help. We're only up the road, you know that. All you have to do is knock on our door. I'll try and bob in to see her later today. I know you've got the shop to see to. And your Ethel, how is she doing? I hear she's gone off to her auntie's in Rochdale? That'll do her a world of good. She's salt of the earth is Annie.'

'That's kind, Missus P. We're gettin' by as best we can, thanks. We thought it would give our Ethel a break; she's a lot on. An' Olive's comin' over to sort out Mary at bedtimes and cook us summat.'

Mrs Pearson turned to go, leaving Dennis to serve Mrs Sath. She faced him square on. He returned her scowl. The urge to slap her was almost unbearable. All Mrs Sath had to do was be there in Dennis Slater's thoughts, for him to see the misery of her pinched, sour face, her piggy eyes overlooking her spectacles, her straggly hair bunched under her stupid hat.

She placed her shopping bag onto the counter between them. 'I've not come in 'ere to buy owt,' she said.

'Just as well,' replied Dennis. 'You're barred.'

Mrs Sath didn't so much as flinch. This was nothing new to her.

The two remaining customers turned round and left.

'I've come to tell you this to your face,' Mrs Sath continued. 'I'll not be buyin' owt in 'ere again, and nor will most other decent folk.'

'Apart from the vicar's wife and all 'er cronies, you mean?'

'Your mucky daughter led my Eddie on, and now she's payin' for it.'

'Piss off.'

'And you can tell 'er when you see 'er not to expect any 'elp from me or anybody else round 'ere. She'll get no brass out of us.'

Dennis had been expecting this. He knew from old what to expect from the sharp end of Mrs Sath's tongue. He leaned across the counter, brought his face up to hers, and whispered his attack.

'Tell your son if he ever shows 'is face again that he should've kept 'is cock in 'is pants. Ask 'im if he likes 'ospital food. 'Cos I'm gonna break 'is legs next time. Now sling your 'ook, you stupid old bitch.'

She grabbed her bag, turned on her heels, and was gone.

*

Olive was glad to find Dennis alone in his shop. The three dried pork chops languishing on a tray in his window had put the finishing touch to her plan for the evening. She'd worn her tight leopard-print jumper and left the front of her coat unbuttoned to show herself to best effect. Dennis had often told her that her pert nipples were his favourite feature. She'd also put a bit of lippy and eyeshadow on, even though she was only wandering into town, nowhere special. She was very fond of both Dennis and his wife Mary, but in such very different ways. She'd been through a lot with her old friend Mary and she worried about her illness. She knew Mary was dying, but there was nothing she could do to stop that. She worried too that Dennis might lose interest in her. He'd put some spark, some sort of loving, and sex, plenty of sex, back into her boring life. A man who noticed her.

Dennis heaved the side of bacon back onto its hook and took a deep breath.

'Old Aggie's said 'er piece, 'as she?' asked Olive. 'Got it off 'er chest?' News of an Aggie Sath row travelled fast. 'Good riddance, ey? It's not as if you need her business exactly.'

'I just told 'er to sling 'er 'ook. I didn't 'it 'er. I was really nice to 'er. I'll give 'er Eddie a serious kickin', though, if he shows 'is ugly face again. I've 'eard tell the little shit 'as gone to 'is mate in Preston.'

She took his hand in hers on the counter and leaned across it.

'Bubbles to Aggie Sath,' she told him. 'Forget 'er. You expectin' me this evening?'

'She's a fucking cow. She wants slappin'.'

'You can still 'ave me, you know? Any time you want.'

'I do know, an' I do want,' he replied. 'How about now?'

She didn't react to his suggestion, and he left his hand where it was.

'You'd 'ave to take your apron off first,' she said. 'Look, Charlie's on a late today, and won't be 'ome till tomorrow breakfast. An' your Mary is wantin' me to stay over. Be nice to see you.'

Dennis grinned and, grabbing her cheeks with both hands, plonked a kiss on the end of her nose.

'Ger'off, your big 'ands smell o' bacon, you daft ha'p'orth.' She laughed. 'Mrs Sath might come back in!'

'Let 'er.'

'How about this, then?' said Olive. 'Why don't you bring us those nice chops round to number 14 an' I'll cook 'em and bring 'em over? I'll feed Mary and get 'er bedded down.'

'An' stay on. Mary's dead to the world by nine.'

*

Olive walked across St Paul's Terrace in the early evening carrying a plate, a bowl, and a jug of gravy on a tray covered over by a steaming towel. She balanced the tray on her knee as she pushed open the door to number 13 with her foot and carried her delivery down to the kitchen. Dennis removed the towel with a mock flourish and lifted his hot plate of a pork chop, mash, and boiled cabbage onto the kitchen table.

'Gor blimey!' he said.

'I've 'ad mine already,' Olive said, and bent down to kiss his forehead. She ruffled his fringe. 'I'll take this through for Mary.'

'You smell nice, Olive,' said Mary. 'You been in the bath?'

'No,' replied Olive. 'I've got body mist under me arms. You've a nice cheerful fire there, Mary. You're better off in 'ere than out there, I can tell you. It's freezin'.'

Olive put her hand behind Mary's head and lifted it off the board then pulled up the pillow. She'd cut up the meat at home already and minced it together with some potato and gravy. She spooned it to Mary's lips, wiping the drips off her chin with the towel with each mouthful.

'You 'eard from our Ethel yet?' she asked.

'No, but I wouldn't expect to yet really. She's only been gone a few days, I think. I'm gettin' ulcers on me 'eels, Olive. They sting.'

Olive lifted the blankets up from the bottom of the bed and was hit by the pungent smell of bed sores. Her heels were wrapped with coarse grey bandages secured with safety pins.

'Do you want me to take this lot off an' 'ave a better look?'

'There's no need, love; the nurse 'as been. She comes most days. She's very good. You're a grand lass an' all, Olive, steppin' in like this while our Ethel's away. I'd be lost without you.'

'It's the least I can do, Mary. You've not eaten much, though. You've got to keep your strength up.'

'I think I'm ready for me bed, Olive.'

'Do you need your bedpan?'

'No, I've been not an hour since. The nurse sorted me. Thanks, love.'

'Alright, Mary,' said Olive. 'Give me your teeth. An' I'll close your door to keep it warm while you nod off, an' I'll be back early to get you sorted in the mornin''

She took up the tongs and put a few more lumps of coal on the fire, peered out of the window at the snow, and drew the curtains across the gap, then squeezed Mary's hand and tucked in the sheets.

'Night night, Mary,' she said. 'Sleep tight.'

'And don't let the bedbugs bite,' Mary returned.

Olive chuckled.

'Just think of our dancin' days, Mary. Sweet dreams. See you first thing.'

Olive closed the bedroom door from the hallway, pulled the handle firmly so the catch clicked shut, then leant her forehead against it. She knew only too well that what she was about to do, or rather what Dennis was going to do to her, wasn't right. It never had been. She loved her old friend Mary deeply, as only women can, and she hated herself nearly as much. But, and she had been through this in her head so many times, what Mary and Charlie didn't know couldn't hurt them. And she might leave her Charlie if she didn't have Dennis, and then she couldn't look after Mary. None of all this sex and guilt was about love and betrayal, not really. It was all about survival, and human needs, pure and simple.

She put her ear to the door and could hear the coals crackling, turned and shouted, '*Bye Dennis*,' down to the kitchen, then opened the front door and closed it again in front of her. She slipped her shoes off silently onto the floorboards then tiptoed back down to the kitchen.

Mary turned her head towards the window. She liked to look at the spaniels and watch the fire reflected in the glass cabinet doors. She strained to hear Olive's footsteps scuttle across the street to her own front door but couldn't. She wished she could remember happy days dancing in town, the evening Dennis had held her hand, walked her home, and first kissed her, but those memories had turned bitter now. She just listened to her own heartbeat instead.

Olive found Dennis smoking a cigarette in the kitchen and softly closed the door. He patted his thigh then ran his hand up underneath her skirt as she put her arm round his neck and lowered herself down onto his lap.

'I've made you a quick brew,' he said. 'You 'ave that while Mary gets off. She generally goes out like a light.'

'By, don't things change, Dennis?' she said. 'I've just told Mary to think on our dancin' days. She was a spring chicken then. Look at 'er now.'

'I 'ad me eye on you on the dance floor, you know that?'

'You've allus 'ad your eye on everybody. Dance floor or anywhere.'

He squeezed her around her waist.

'Come on,' he said. 'Sup up. She's asleep, I can 'ear 'er snorin'.'

'Like 'ell you can. Any road, this tea's stone cold.'

Her hand felt for his groin and they kissed.

'We're just wastin' time now,' Dennis said.

He smacked her rump as he crept up the stairs after her.

'Shush, you idiot,' she whispered to him on the landing and held her finger up to her mouth. 'She might not be off yet.'

'Stop gigglin' then,' he whispered back, and pushed her through the door into Ethel's old room. But she couldn't stop herself, as he threw her onto the bed and removed her pinny, skirt and bra with practised ease. He quietened her down with a pillow pushed into her face. 'An' start moanin', he told her into her ear, and rolled her onto her front.

Olive always did what Dennis told her, and this time was no exception. But it was not their lovers' laughter and muted voices, or the emptiness of her life with her Ethel gone, or her fear of dying alone that kept Mary awake that night. It was the noise through the floorboards of the rhythmic creaking of Ethel's bed, as she cried herself to sleep.

Thirteen

Albert liked to tell Ethel that running The Junction was just like trying to navigate a destroyer across the North Atlantic. You would think you were ploughing through clear blue water, and a storm would blow up. You could hit mountainous seas when you least expected it.

Ethel and Annie were both at the helm in the tap room when they hit a squall in the middle of the evening session on the busiest Saturday of the year a week before Christmas. Annie was led by the hand through to the lounge to get the knees-up underway, Jack came to the hatch and ordered a round for everyone in the room, and the barrel went off. All within the space of five minutes.

Annie had lugged the Christmas box down the ladder from the loft, and Ethel had spent the morning decorating the tree, licking and gumming paper chains for the ceilings and draping some tinsel along the picture rails. Her belly was uncomfortable now after all the stretching and bending, and her back ached more than ever. They'd stood the tree in a bucket of water in the far corner of the lounge and slid it up against the little window facing the street. Annie and Albert had then wheeled the piano across the front to wedge it upright. They'd learned this trick from previous years. If you left the tree out in the middle of the room, Annie reckoned, or even tucked it in the corner behind the door as they tried once, drunks were forever stumbling and crashing into it. And then she spent all her time twisting baubles and fairies and little parcels and Santa Clauses back onto the branches and scratting up needles with a dustpan and brush. It got to be hard work by New Year and she couldn't be doing with it.

Unlike the tap room, the lounge at The Junction was carpeted, and even had two plush scarlet drape curtains. The polished wooden bar ran the length of the room, there was a fine selection of spirits dispensed from gleaming optics, and the room was lit by a warm red crystal chandelier. Annie liked to think that the atmosphere in there was genteel and more suited to her customers with taste. It also had easy chairs and a dozen or so little round tables scattered around the room, mainly for couples who met the same friends on the same evening week in, week out. They would make each other laugh about all the petty things in their lives that gave them grief, and forget the dwindling ration coupons and the meagre pay packets for a while.

Annie set her port and lemon down onto the top of the piano and raised the lid. She kicked off her shoes under the tree, pulled out the stool, and lowered her weight onto it in as ladylike a fashion as she could. She paused for a second, as if trying to make a decision, then closed her eyes and launched into the tune she played first in her repertoire every Saturday evening. '*You Made Me Love You*'. It was Annie's favourite. The room burst into song. This was why they had left their own four walls on this snowy dark night.

Ethel could swing her bulging belly round to get to the till and the crisps much easier with Annie playing landlady in the lounge. There was standing room only in the tap room on this evening. In fact there was no room at all. Any latecomer who tried to get in from the corridor was met by a wall of bodies. Jack pushed his way to the bar.

'You should 'ave some mistletoe above this 'atch, love,' he said. ''Ow about a kiss for Christmas?'

He leant through the hatch at Ethel, breathing stale beer and pipe smoke, and pouted his lips.

'Be'ave yerself, Grandad,' she replied. 'Act your age. Pint of mild, is it?'

Ethel felt the panic rising in her throat as Jack twisted round to the room and asked every man on the bench in turn if he'd join him in a festive pint. This didn't happen very often and there were no refusals. She made no attempt to count the shouts of mild, best bitter, or stout, so reached up for a glass and began pulling the first pint of best.

'That's eight best, I reckon, to start with, love,' said Jack, 'and three milds.'

He delved into his coat pocket and slapped a pound note onto a beer mat in front of her.

'Give Annie a shout, Jack, please,' said Ethel. 'Uncle Albert's not 'ere. He's gone down the Legion playin' billiards.'

'Don't be daft, lass, you're alright,' he told her. 'She's just nicely got goin'. You just keep linin' 'em up, and I'll round up some empties. It's eight times one an' three to start with. That's ten bob for the bests.'

She set the first two down on the cloth for their heads to settle before topping them up, while Jack took hold of the empty pint glasses from outstretched arms and stacked them up on the bar. There was no time to rinse them out. But her wrist was almost too shaky to start pulling the third, when just gas and froth sputtered from the nozzle.

'Jack, I need you!' She snatched two empty pots off him and dropped them into the sink behind her. 'I can't do this. Go get Annie. The barrel's gone off. She needs to change it.'

'C'mon, love, frame yourself. You can't stop Annie in full flow. She's beltin' out the carols now. There'd be a riot. I'll 'elp you. We can sort it.'

He elbowed his way out through the tap-room door and pushed some young men back against the wall in the corridor so Ethel could squeeze out from behind the bar.

'Make way, lads. Ey up,' he shouted above the singing from the lounge. 'We need to get to t'cellar door. Best's gone off.'

He followed Ethel slowly down the weathered stone steps into the dank den of spiders, beetles, and silverfish, as she steadied herself with one hand running down the rail and held on to her belly with the other. The cellar lay just beneath the tap room and was lit by a single dim bare bulb hanging low in one corner. They could hear the muffled voices and scrapes of shoes through the boards above. Two thick planks just about a barrel-width apart ran down onto the slabs from a hatch above in the pavement, and the full wooden barrels were stacked neatly in line along a brick wall. Some empties ready to be hauled back up the ramp lay scattered on their sides around the room, and coal and empty bags were heaped up away from any spillages in a dark corner behind the stairs.

Ethel screwed the pipe off the top of the empty barrel and Jack rolled and manhandled the new one into place.

'I've 'elped Annie with this many a time before, love,' he said. 'Just screw the pipe into the top then tighten that nut up there, and Bob's your uncle. You're best learning to do it by yourself.'

He stood aside and smiled to himself as Ethel steadied the pipe and pulled round the spanner. He was sorry she would be leaving The Junction soon, and he hoped she would be back.

The third pint back up in the tap room pulled clear after half a bucket of spurts and hisses, then Jack passed the pints back round the room.

'Ethel,' he said, leaning onto the bar, 'I've totted 'em up as we've gone along, an' I reckon it comes to seventeen an' six if you take a Cherry B for yourself and a port an' lemon for Annie.'

'You're a love, Jack,' she said. 'It were all 'ands on deck, ey?'

'Pleasure were mine, darlin',' he replied. 'I buy one round a year. It's Christmas.'

'It's also me last night in 'ere, Jack. I'm on me way back 'ome to me folks.'

'We know that, love. Annie's told us yesterday, but you don't get away that easy. We've 'ad a whip-round, 'an't we, lads? You've done us right proud, lass, an' we're sorry to see you go.'

He pulled out a bulging little brown envelope from his coat pocket and pushed it into Ethel's hand. Her face glowed a pale red tinge. Plucking up courage to dart under the peak of his cap, she placed a quick kiss on his stubbly chin. Glasses round the tap room were raised and chinked, with cries of '*thanks, love*', '*look after yourself*', "*appy Christmas, Ethel*', and '*spend it on yourself*.'

'An' you look after that new bairn too,' said Jack, and squeezed her hand round the packet. 'I know you will,' he added, putting his pipe back between the few teeth he had left and turning back to his pint on the table.

She'd never known men could be so kind for nothing in return.

The call back to number 13 St Paul's Terrace had knocked Ethel off course. The letter had dropped onto the doormat at The Junction the previous morning. Ethel didn't recognise the writing on the envelope and was scared of words anyway, so Annie had opened it and read the letter aloud then given it back to her for safekeeping. The handwriting was Marjorie Pearson's, the vicar's wife. Her letter left so much more unsaid than it did say.

Dear Ethel. It's not really my place to write to you, but I can't bear to see your mum any longer in such a bad way by herself. She's left in bed all of the time and is very poorly and terribly lonely. Please come back home to help her if you can. God bless, Marjorie.

Ethel was now desperate to go home. Albert had sorted out a ticket for the next train back to York from Rochdale, and Ethel had thrown her few things from her room into her suitcase. Annie gave her a bundle of leggings, cardigans, and bonnets she'd knitted, packed her up a pork pie to see her through the journey, and took her on the bus back to the station.

'Look after your mum, Ethel,' Annie told Ethel. 'She needs you more than ever, by t'sounds of it. But you see to yourself too. An' keep out of your father's way as much as you can. You can ask Marjorie or Charlie Songhirst if there's owt you can't 'andle, I should think. And think on this, our Ethel, mark my words. It'll be right. Everything always works out. I'm allus 'ere if you ever need holdin', an' next time you come to see me an' Albert, you'll 'ave a bran'-new little baby.'

Fourteen

Ethel was sitting forward on a sofa and gazing at a bone china cup and saucer and plate on a glass-top table when her troubles really began. The fireplace behind the table was laid with sticks just waiting to be lit and the clock on the mantelpiece told the right time. There was a well-stocked bookcase built into one corner and a television set stood on four spindly legs in another. The doors to the garden looked out onto a bird table, a bank of trim lavender, and a lawn with an apple tree in the centre. It was easy for Mrs Pearson and Ethel to pretend in this room that everything in their worlds was in order and calm, and always would be. And there was never any mention of God in it. Or the baby.

Marjorie liked to walk on down to Mary Slater as often as she could, and to invite Ethel up to the vicarage when she knew her husband would be in the church or on his visits. She had known Mary and her troubles for more than thirty years. She had taken pity on Ethel when she saw her slapped down in the stores. Marjorie was a plump woman who smelled of soap and was old enough to be Ethel's grandmother. She spent her days busying herself in her home trying to make her husband's life as comfortable as possible. To be kind was all she ever wanted. She'd just brought Ethel a cup of tea and a ginger nut biscuit.

These afternoons had come to mean something to Ethel too. They were an escape from the grease of the kitchen at home, from the dread of her mother's bedroom, and from the loneliness and tears in her own room. She was almost certain she could trust Mrs Pearson not to take her baby away for adoption, even if the vicar would. But she couldn't be sure of Olive anymore, ever since the day she'd told Ethel she was lucky to fall pregnant; she should count her blessings; and she'd bring up the baby if Ethel couldn't cope. Ethel knew in her bones that if Olive took the baby away from her, it would belong more to her own father than to herself. There was nothing worse.

Her knickers and thighs turned warm and wet, and some drops of clear fluid fell onto the carpet. Ethel had leant forward from the edge of the sofa to take her biscuit off the plate and felt something give in her pelvis. Had she wet herself, just like her mum had done in the street all that time ago? It couldn't be the baby coming, surely. Dr Chis had told her that wouldn't happen till early spring. And because she didn't want it to happen anyway, she hoped it never would. Annie had told her that her labour pains would start soon after her waters burst, and it was best if Ethel could find a friend who would stay with her and help. But who? Her mother was bedbound, her father frightened her, her Eddie was no more, and she had no friend she dared trust with her baby.

Ethel stood and a warm trickle ran down her legs. Her knees buckled and she took the arm of the sofa for support. She called through to Mrs Pearson in the kitchen that she had to go; she'd remembered it was rent day; and let herself out through the front door. She was home within the half hour, peered behind the door at her sleeping mum in the front room, then climbed the stairs in some discomfort and shut the door quietly on her tiny room.

The day was fading so she left the curtain open to catch the light from the streetlamp. She stepped out of her knickers and skirt and left them on the floorboards, draped her dressing gown over her shoulders, and picked up her mirror. Her lazy eye stared back at her, more dull and ugly than ever, her belly taut and bulging and ripe, her breasts too large, drooping and full. She lay down on the bed and stared at the shadows on the ceiling. Her world was ache and panic in one. The bed was pushed up into the corner of the room. Ethel could grab and squeeze the bars at the head of the bed when her time came. She could also bite onto the pillow if she had to. The only other bits of furniture in the room were her dressing table and a chest of drawers under the window to the street outside. One picture, a young girl with an open, round face leaning in her flowing white dress against the bowl of a tree, hung on the wall. And Ethel had slid under the bed her mother's old dance shoes box packed with a couple of cot blankets, a length of string, and Annie's few knitted baby clothes.

Annie was right. Her belly tightened and the pains soon came deep and regular. She writhed silently as the pain built then eased but refused to cry out for fear of waking her mother. The endless afternoon ebbed into an even longer night. She heard the back door open as her father returned from his shop but set off again with no words for his wife or daughter. Her labour pains soon merged into constant agony, waxing and waning. Time stood still, and nothing and nobody else existed. She stretched out her arms behind her and clung to the head of the bed. She rolled off the bed and onto the floor. She screamed out in silence for her Eddie. She stood, groaned, retched, edged round the bed, and crouched. She returned and lay back on the bed, her breathing in short, shallow gasps, and bit into her blanket. She stood again, grabbed and leaned into the iron rail across the foot of the bed, and rocked. Nothing she could do, no lying, no standing, would take the pains away. She was dying, she knew it, ripping apart. Pulling the mirror off the side, Ethel held it down to see the shock of her baby's wet hair, reached for the scalp, threw her head back, pushed, heaved, and howled at full pitch a final piercing animal scream.

*

Aggie Sath's jaw sagged and she snored quietly with each breath she took. Her mouth writhed with her dream as she spoke to her Eddie. '*Bring us back a trout for our tea, Eddie,*' she told him. She stood to watch him ride away up the snicket with his fishing rod strapped to his back, then saw her son's face turn back to her and scream. She stirred, rolled over onto her side, and the blanket slipped off to the floor. She opened her eyes, and a shattering blow crashed into the wall above her head.

She flung her legs out of bed and hurtled downstairs into the dark street then into next door, armed with nothing more than her handbag. Ethel lay curled at the foot of the bed in the room bordering her own, naked, a baby lying lifeless on the floorboards. The torn thin white glistening cord dangled between its mother's thighs. Mrs Sath snatched the helpless blooded little thing up, untangled the cord from around its neck, and blew warm breath gently onto its face.

'Is my baby alright, Mrs Sath?' pleaded Ethel. 'Is she hurt?'

.There was still no sign of life.

Mrs Sath cradled the baby in her hands for a moment and stared at him, speechless. She took an old grimy handkerchief from her bag and wiped some sticky, bloodstained fluid from his head. The eyelids were closed, but then he blinked and seemed to gaze into space, his eyes roaming and unfocussed. She felt a gentle wriggle in her hands. The baby's arms twitched a little once or twice at the shoulders and he drew his knees up towards his belly. The mouth gaped and his tongue fell back as he started to cry, a pitiful, needy, pleading whimper. New life, thought Mrs Sath.

Ethel had shifted to the foot of the bed and dragged down the sheet around her. She sat on the floorboards against the wall, her head down, her arms round her knees, rocking gently to and fro. Mrs Sath pulled her nightie off over her head and wrapped it round the baby's body. It felt firm, warm and new to her, her own like a naked sagging shivering sack. She covered herself with Ethel's coat from behind the bedroom door. It was nearly daybreak, but the old familiar waking of the terrace had passed them by: the shouts from the shunting yard, the rattles of the engine wheels, the whistling of the milkman.

She knotted his cord as best she could then held him over to Ethel's breast. Her eyes were fixed on his face. It was her own Eddie's of twenty years ago. The very same slope of the eyebrows, the dimple in the cheeks, the exact angle to the chin.

'Good God!' said Mrs Sath. 'You've 'ad your baby all alone. Why didn't you shout for someone sooner?'

'I don't want anyone else,' Ethel replied from the corner.

Mrs Sath reached down to touch the baby's cheek.

'It's a boy, Ethel, and he's beautiful,' she said. ''Ave you thought of a name for 'im yet?'

'It was Lydia for a girl and now it's William for a boy, Mrs Sath,' replied Ethel. 'Same as me grandad, Bill.'

Mrs Sath had struggled to keep her tears in check, but she couldn't hold them back any longer. They welled up to her eyes from a mixture of love, memories, and shock.

'And Eddie's father too,' she said. 'My Bill, he would 'ave been as pleased as punch. Why are you on your own, Ethel?'

'I don't trust nobody,' Ethel replied. 'They just wanted to send me away to an 'ome or somewhere to 'ave 'im, and then give 'im away. I want this baby for meself more than owt else, Mrs Sath.'

'I should never 'ave slapped you, Ethel.'

Ethel had no answer to that.

She looked up from her baby. She had always been scared of Mrs Sath's nasty ways and vicious tongue, like most other people who crossed her path, but maybe not any longer. Aggie Sath was family now, like it or not.

'Well, we'd best get Dr Chis down to see you, Ethel.'

'No, I want me mum to see 'im,' she replied. 'She's downstairs. But fasten my coat up, Mrs Sath. You'll catch your death.'

'Less of the Mrs Sath,' she said, pulling the coat around herself. 'It's Granny Sath now.'

Fifteen

Granny Sath scurried down the stairs and opened the door onto a sparkling white pavement. The shock of the sharp, frosty air took her breath away. First light had risen on an unbroken sky above the gates. A perfect clear day for the birth of her grandson.

She returned from her own house with a towel to keep the baby warm, then tottered back down to the kitchen and up again to bring the tin bowl and floor cloth. She would need these to deliver the afterbirth then clear the mess from the floor. Mary in her own chair downstairs was the next to hold the baby in her lap, then Olive across the street heard the news and Dr Chisholm later that morning. He had known for months that this day was looming, but the baby had arrived a bit earlier than he wanted and Ethel had ignored all his offers of help. The doctor called at this house far too often, he thought, and he would normally open the front door without so much as a tap. But today was much more difficult. The vicar had taken it upon himself to find a couple in Leeds who wanted to adopt a baby, but they wouldn't be ready to take him for a few more weeks. Dr Chis hadn't expected to break this news to Ethel quite yet, and she would have to look after the baby by herself for a while. He knew she might struggle with that.

He knocked on the door and waited for Mary to make her way from her chair to answer it. He was weighed down as usual with his brown leather bag stuffed with bottles, tablets, potions, syringes, and tubes. He put his bag down and took off his hat and coat as he stood on the step.

'Good morning, my dear,' the doctor said in his posh Edinburgh accent. He was dressed in his customary tweed suit, pressed shirt, and tie, but Mary thought he might have lost some of his usual swagger. He peered down at his most taxing patient over the top of his spectacles.

'Them tablets have done nowt for me, Doctor,' said Mary. 'I'm just as doddery as ever.'

'Give them time, my dear,' he replied. 'They've got to work their way into your system. But I've just heard the good news, Mary. It's your Ethel and her new baby I've come to see, not you today. If I can squeeze past, I'll go on up.'

'Please come and see me soon, Doctor,' said Mary. 'I'm fadin".'

She leaned to one side and Dr Chisholm brushed past her and made his way up the stairs. He rapped twice on Ethel's door with his knuckle as he pushed it open. Ethel lay awake on the bed against the wall with William in the crook of her arm.

'Oh my goodness!' said Chis. 'What have we here? A little wee feller arrived before we expected him, ey?'

He picked up the baby from Ethel and lay him along the length of his forearm.

'A beautiful bonny bairn. Is he taking his milk, Ethel?'

'Yes, he is, Dr Chis. He's slept most of the time. But he's got a bump on 'is 'ed, Doctor.'

'He has, I can see that,' he replied. He ran his finger across the baby's forehead. 'But it's nowt to worry yourself about. Lots of babies have funny-shaped heads. It's a rough ride and a tight squeeze coming into this world.'

He took out his stethoscope from his bag, flicked its two tubes into his ears, warmed its cup in his fist, and held it onto William's chest for a few seconds. He then laid the baby flat on the mattress and lifted him up by his fingers, and tapped his knees with a little rubber hammer.

'He's a grand little chap. Bring him up to the nurse when you're back on your feet, Ethel, and we'll weigh him and check you both over. This little belly-button stump will shrivel and fall off soon, so don't you fret about that. And you might try giving him a little bath in the kitchen. He'll like that. We'll have to try and get you a cot sorted out soon as well. We can't have you two sleeping together like Darby and Joan, can we?'

He realised he'd said the wrong thing from the puzzle on Ethel's face. I'd best not mention the couple in Leeds yet, he thought. The vicar's carefully chosen words from God would be much more suitable for that kind of thing.

Chis crept down the stairs and was relieved to see in the hall that Mary had let her bedroom door swing closed. He took his hat and coat from the peg, let himself out into the street, and set off at a brisk walk up the terrace to his car. It was only a short drive to his next grateful patient.

Ethel lay back against the wall, lifted William's mouth to her nipple, and relaxed into the mutual pleasure of their own little world. She smiled down on his face, her Eddie's face, watched his eyelids opening and closing over dark liquid eyes, and stroked his hair and his forehead as he swallowed. She lifted him and kissed his cheek then set him down into the sheet on her bed. He didn't stir as she pulled on the handle on the bottom drawer of her chest, wedged it open with an old spoon pushed down the side, and emptied some dance shoes, slacks, and a scarf onto the floor. She lifted a cot blanket out from the shoebox under the bed, swaddled her baby in it, and laid him out in the drawer still sleeping with a warm woollen hat for a pillow.

Nobody else mattered in Ethel's world now, just William, her mother, and Granny Sath. She could never visit Dr Chis in his surgery, or the nurse. What would they do? Weigh him, no use in that. And then give her baby away. She spent all hours of the day and many more in the night cradling and talking to her baby, boiling nappies in a pan and washing them out in the kitchen sink, settling him down in the drawer, and snatching some sleep of her own when she could. Olive would come over the street with a bowl of mash for Mary in the evening, and Ethel would sit nursing her baby while Olive spooned food to her mother. Ethel could see Mary's life had some meaning again, some spark, some joy and hope for a future. And Olive tried to explain to Ethel that she and Charlie could give William a better life in their own home, if only she would let them. A baby might even rescue their barren marriage, she'd said, just as she'd tried to explain to Mary even before the baby was born.

The pigeons in their loft got more of Dennis's attention than his own grandson over the next few days. He had a helpless baby as well as a helpless wife in the house now. The washing line in the yard was forever draped with vests and nappies, but not his own shirt or socks. A bulky pram appeared in the hall from nowhere, and he was forever kicking it and pushing it out of his way. The whole house stank of babies and milk and sodden clothes. And the ugly old hag Mrs Sath from next door drove him out of his own home when she paid her calls.

Granny Sath tried to ease Ethel's burden by taking William out for walks and had determined to call on Mr Waggett. He'd laughed in her face on peering at the baby's forehead under the hood of the pram. 'Blow me down with a feather, so you've thumped the baby as well,' he'd said, and told her there wasn't a chance Ethel could have her old job back. Dennis Slater was down on the canvas, he reckoned; he'd topped Slater's prize racer and taken some brass out of his pocket, so why would he take his boot off his neck now?

Sixteen

With her baby but three days old, Ethel was in no doubt that the vicar had come to take William away when she heard him park his car outside in the terrace again and gently swing its door closed. This was her day of judgement. She had not done as Olive had told her and gone to see him when she found out she was pregnant, and she had not taken up William to show to his wife. She laid the baby in his drawer and came down to join Reverend Pearson and her mother and father in the kitchen. Her father was brooding. He stood with his back to the stove. Dennis always thought the vicar looked like an undertaker. He wore black and was too serious for his liking and had that musty smell of the dead. But he stubbed out his cigarette in a saucer as a mark of respect, and pulled out a chair for the vicar.

Reverend Pearson sat down away from the table and took out a brown envelope from his inside pocket and opened it. Mary took the hint and hurriedly cleared the milk bottle, a half loaf, a salt cellar, and the saucer to the other end of the table. The vicar leaned forward and spread out a letter on the board in front of him.

'Mary and Dennis and Ethel,' he said. 'God bless you and this house.'

He didn't raise his eyes from the letter. Mary could sense this was difficult for him.

'Have you time for a cup of tea, Reverend?' she asked. 'Are you here to talk about the Christening?'

'Thank you, Mrs Slater. But no, I'll not take much of your time. I can't stop. I'm here to offer you my help again.'

He turned to look Ethel in the face and tapped his fingers on the letter.

'Ethel, my dear girl, there are things we cannot avoid. God will judge the fornicators and the adulterers, but I do not. I urge you to make things right with Him. We would want to see you with the baby before God in church on Sunday and to receive William into His fold.'

Dennis scraped back a chair on the lino, snatched his packet of cigarettes from the side, and took hold of the yard-door handle.

'But I have some wonderful news for you, Ethel. We have found a young, God-fearing couple in Leeds who have not been blessed with a child and will take William into their home soon. All we need is for you to sign this paper.'

Ethel erupted.

'No!' she cried. 'Never. He belongs to me. And nobody else.'

'Sign the paper, you selfish little bitch,' shouted her father. 'Do as you're told. What about your mother and me! You've brought us nowt but shame. You disgust me. Think of us for once.'

He grabbed the end of the table and upended it together with the milk and the bread and the crockery, and slapped Ethel across the cheek.

'And you,' he turned to face the vicar, 'leave your paper an' take your God an' your stupid fuckin' words an' get out of my 'ouse.'

The vicar did just as he was told, stumbled into the hall, slammed the front door behind him, and vowed never to return. Dennis took hold of the bun at the back of his daughter's head and pushed her face down onto the letter to sign. And Mary told Ethel through her own tears that maybe it was for the best.

*

Ethel closed the curtains in the front room later that day and turned round the two spaniels on the cabinet to look straight at her mum, and then perched on the edge of the bed. She clutched the vicar's letter in her hand.

'Can you read this out to me, Mum?' she said. 'I don't know what it says.'

'No, love, I won't. There's no need.'

She knew it would make her daughter cry again.

'I could never do this, Mum. I want to keep 'im for ever an' ever.'

'Sleep on it, Ethel. If I know owt about you at all, I know you'll do what's best for others. And that includes our William.'

She put her hand over Ethel's wrist on the bed and gave it a squeeze, and the letter crumpled in her grip.

'Put it under me mattress, love, with the other scraps

you've kept from The Junction. They're from folk like us who are far kinder than the vicar.'

*

Ethel said she woke the next morning to heavy knocks on the front door. The rent man liked to vary his time to collect, but he'd never called this early before. But she didn't want to miss him again. She would say to the coroner's officer that she jumped out of her bed, collected Jack's little brown packet from The Junction hidden under her mum's mattress, and flung open the door to the street.

*

Dennis would stick to his story to the police that he wasn't at home when the postman called that morning. The postman had never needed to knock at the Slater's door before, but today he had brought a parcel, wrapped in brown paper and tied with string. Ethel had thanked him and tore open the parcel as she dashed across the street to show Olive – the court would never question that – but then a few minutes later her screaming and another thud on her bedroom wall had shattered Granny Sath's dreams next door for the second time in a week.

PART IV

Leeds, Spring 1953

Seventeen

'Your brief's here to talk to you, Slater,' said the warder. 'Follow me down.'

Ethel had learnt not to react to the hourly flicks of the observation panel in the door, but she raised herself to a sitting position on the bench when she heard the jangle of the bunch of keys in the lock. The magistrate had sent her to Armley Jail on remand, and she had been moved to a cell by herself for her own safety. She wore the regulation pyjamas and soft shoes without laces, and her wrist was heavily bandaged since the attack with boiling water in the canteen. Child killers were legitimate targets in jail.

She followed the clank of the warder's boots along the caged walkways past the jeers and whistles from behind locked doors, and clattered down the steep iron stairwells to the visitors' room on the ground floor. Mr Joyce QC sat at a small table opposite an empty chair. He was senior partner in Bilson Barristers Chambers of Leeds, and his job was to defend any clients that walked through his door, no matter how high they had climbed up in the world, or how far they had fallen. Clients were allocated to barristers in his chambers in the order they arrived, and whether he thought the accused was guilty or innocent was irrelevant. What really mattered to him was winning a fight, nothing else. He had already sat in the comfort of his own office to read through Dr Lawson's post-mortem report, PC Jackson's report for the coroner, and his client's typed copy of her confession. It had been his misfortune to be instructed to defend a hopeless case.

He tried to ignore the painful conversation on the next table of a daughter visiting her mother. He found women in prison more unnerving than men. It was a few weeks since he'd been instructed. He'd taken a file of papers out from his briefcase to refresh his mind about the case. Her baby had fatal injuries that only she could have inflicted. The only other person in the house was her bedbound mother downstairs. A witness had heard the violence. She had admitted to the police how she had battered the baby, and pleaded ignorance to the coroner. She had lied to somebody already, and probably, he thought, she is about to do the same to me.

Ethel sat herself down on the chair opposite Mr Joyce without looking at him or speaking a word. Any glimmer of hope he'd had for her case vanished. His client was miserable, dejected, and ugly, and that, he knew, wouldn't look good to a jury.

'Miss Slater,' he said. 'Look at me, please.'

She raised blank eyes to his face and continued to pick at her bandaged wrist. Another cruel man sent to hurt me, she thought.

'Try to relax, Miss Slater,' he continued. 'I'm here to listen to your story so I can speak up for you in court. You must try to tell me exactly what happened.'

Ethel looked at him still but remained silent.

'I'm here to help you if I can.'

She doubted it.

'Just the truth, Miss Slater, that's all I want to hear you say, nothing else.'

'I didn't kill my baby.'

'Before you tell me anymore, though, you must understand one thing. If I find out that you're lying to me, I can't speak up for you.'

'I didn't kill my baby, sir. That's all there is to it.'

'Do you know who did?'

'Nobody. Who'd want to hurt a baby?'

Her reply landed.

She was making sense.

'Do you remember what you told Beryl Jackson at home the day William died?'

'She brought me my teddy bear back an' she made me a cup o' tea. She didn't stare at my face either. She was kind.'

And I wonder, he thought, if you are too. He paused to take a second proper lingering look at the girl in front of him. Perhaps her eye wasn't as ugly as he had thought at first sight. She didn't have that glazed expression of a killer.

'And you told her all about the day William was born. Is that right?'

'He'd just died that morning.'

'Tell me about the birth, Miss Slater. I need to know where you were and exactly what happened the morning William was born.'

'I was at Mrs Pearson's when me waters burst, but I needed to come 'ome. I didn't want nobody there with me 'cause everybody just kept wantin' to take my baby away. I didn't know it would hurt so much an' take so long.'

'So you stayed by yourself in your bedroom at home?'

'Yes. Mum was downstairs in bed 'cause she's very poorly, but I didn't want to wake 'er up an' make things worse.'

'And there was nobody else with you in your bedroom until after he'd been born? Is that correct, Miss Slater?'

'Yes, that's right,' said Ethel. 'I wouldn't 'ave anybody with me. But Mrs Sath from next door 'elped me out. I was frightened at first he was dead, that I'd killed 'im, but she picked 'im up off 'at floor an' cuddled 'im an' he took a breath an' came round.'

'Miss Slater,' said Mr Joyce, 'this is very important. How did Mrs Sath know to come to help you?'

'I looked down an' saw the baby's head bein' born, an' I touched 'im, an' it panicked me an' I screamed. I didn't mean to. I couldn't 'elp myself, an' I smashed me 'and against the wall. I knew Mrs Sath sleeps through there.'

'And how come he was on the floor and not born onto the bed?'

''Cause I 'ad 'im standin' up.'

'And this is really important too, Miss Slater. Think very carefully if you can. Think back to that day. Did you injure William at all?'

'He was very still at first. He just lay in an 'eap, an' there was some blood on the floor round 'im, but Mrs Sath rubbed 'im an' he cried. He 'ad a bump on 'is forehead, an' I showed it to Dr Chis an' he said babies get them when they're born, an' it weren't nowt to worry about.'

Mr Joyce leaned back on his chair and flicked through the pages of PC Jackson's report. My client, he thought, has stuck to this story. And she has said something telling. That she was frightened she'd killed her baby, frightened by that fear, just by giving birth to him, nothing more sinister. These few simple words spoke volumes. He looked up to study the eyes in front of him. They had stopped crying, they were clear and dry, and Ethel's right eye had steadied and fixed on his.

He had learnt over many years locked in rooms such as this how to read faces. His training was to accept his client's words as the truth, but a blink at the wrong time, a shift in posture, a flick of the gaze to one side, the slightest twitch of the head could give the game away. This client, he knew, was telling him just as it was. She was one of life's innocents, gullible, naïve, and slow, yes, but nothing worse than that. He doubted she was capable of deceit, let alone murder. He gave her a half-smile. He even felt sympathy for her, and he had, he thought, gained her trust.

'And the father of your baby?' he asked.

'Eddie Sath?'

'If that's his name. Did he help you with William?'

'He lives next door—'

'With his mother, Mrs Sath?'

'…but he's run away. He wants nowt to do wi' me. Or the baby.'

'Did he force himself on you?'

'No, not really. Not at all. I loved 'im.'

'So you wanted this baby?'

'Not at first. I was just scared, but then I wanted 'im all

to meself. I wanted 'im more than anythin' else I've ever 'ad.'

'How about Mrs Sath then? Did she help you?'

'She took 'im out in 'is pram, did Mrs Sath. She showed 'im off as her Eddie's, one of her own.'

Mr Joyce was more than satisfied with Ethel's account of herself so far, and took a moment to thumb through the list of reports and exhibits the prosecution would use. He could see where most of them were heading: the post-mortem reports, the photographs of the baby, the report on the microscope slides, what the neighbours in the terrace and her family had to say, all the photographs of her bedroom. The most damning bit of evidence was her confession to the police: a piece of paper that, standing alone, could convict her of murder. But there were a couple of other things Ethel would have to explain as well.

He bent to take a flat brown envelope out of his briefcase and slid a small pile of photographs onto the table in front of Ethel.

'Tell me about that, please, Miss Slater,' he said, and put his finger on the bright, focussed image of a box, set against a shadowy dim background of dusty floorboards, dangling metal springs, and a sagging mattress.

'That's 'is baby box. I kept 'is things in there.'

Mr Joyce then pulled out a photograph of a teddy bear, marked exhibit B in the top corner, and laid it on top of the picture of the box. Sporting his smart, speckled waistcoat, his soft, upturned, thin line of a mouth and shining black buttons of eyes grinned up at the camera.

Ethel leaned forward and touched each of the teddy's eyes in turn.

'What about him?' said Mr Joyce.

She picked up the photograph from the table and held it into herself.

'Auntie Annie sent me teddy in a parcel. That's what the postie 'ad brung.'

'So you were woken up by the knocking on the door and went down to answer it, and brought the parcel back upstairs. Is that correct, Miss Slater? Tell me exactly what happened.'

'I went over the road to show Olive, an' when I went back up I saw William was laid on the bed. I thought he should 'ave been asleep in the drawer. He didn't move when I went to pick 'im up, an' he 'ad some blood under 'is nose. He was gone an' I just knew he was dead. An' I didn't know what to do, an' I panicked, an' I screamed an' thumped on the wall for Mrs Sath again.'

'How long were you with the neighbour?'

'Not long. I 'ad to get back.'

'Your father has told Police Constable Jackson he was out fishing at the brick ponds all night. Is that correct, Ethel?'

'He's never gone fishin'. Like Eddie does. Dad was at 'ome sleepin' on 'is own mattress.'

And woken up by the postman, and with just enough time, thought Mr Joyce, to snatch the baby out of its drawer and batter it.

Ethel was innocent of any crime, Mr Joyce was certain of that. And he knew now that it had never even crossed her mind that the key suspect, her own father, was not on trial. She was.

'Did you do anything else?'

'I don't think so. I can't remember. My baby was gone.'

Mr Joyce placed two more photographs in front of Ethel, both of a couple of grey floorboards nailed side by side and running from between the legs at the end of a bed to the front of a drawer pushed back into place. A dark patch a few inches across lay on the boards in one of the images, and in the other it had been covered by a circular rug.

'Is that the drawer William slept in?' he asked.

'Yes. The policeman must 'ave pushed it back in.'

'And the stain on the floor?'

'That's where he was born. Mrs Sath gave me that rug to cover it over.'

'And this wall, Miss Slater?'

His last photograph showed the bedroom wall, framed by the chest of drawers to the right and the end of the bed to the left. A gaping zigzag crack in the plaster snaked up from floor to ceiling, and an arrowhead stuck to the side of it pointed at a dark smear.

'The bomb,' Ethel replied.

'The bomb?'

'It dropped during the night two doors up the street. The air raid. In the war. It killed Ruby an' Mrs Broadbent an' Eddie saw their ghosts. The blast shook all the 'ouses down the bottom of the terrace. There's cracks everywhere.'

'And the smear of blood?'

'Me fingers probably, when I thumped for Mrs Sath. I'd touched 'is 'air.'

Mr Joyce had swallowed countless stories in his career, told to him by criminals he disliked and distrusted, that did not have the ring of truth about them. But this one did.

'Miss Slater,' he asked, 'do you remember signing this piece of paper?'

Ethel lunged at Mr Joyce for the paper, but winced, grabbed her bandaged wrist, and slumped back onto her chair.

'Yes, he's a bastard,' she shouted. 'He lied to me.'

And I don't think Inspector Harrison got the truth out of you either, thought Mr Joyce.

'These are the words you said to the police inspector. I'll read them out to you.'

I gave birth to William alone. I was exhausted and deserted by the father so I hit his head on the bedroom wall. I never wanted this baby. On the morning I killed him, he had been crying all night and I hadn't slept. I came upstairs from answering the door in the morning, something snapped inside my head, and I pushed the pillow into his face then threw him at the wall.

I confess that shortly after giving birth alone to my son William on 8th February, I threw him against my bedroom wall. He was unwanted and I felt I had been abandoned. On 12th February I threw him against the wall for a second time. I'm sorry, I didn't mean to kill my baby. I have read over this statement and it is all the truth.

Mr Joyce looked up from his reading.

Ethel had slumped back slack-jawed on the other side of the table.

Her eyes fixed and staring ahead.

He had no need to ask the question.

'That didn't happen,' she whispered. 'I swear to God.'

'Did you read it, or did the inspector read it out to you?'

'No.'

'And what was the lie?'

'He said Mum 'ad fallen downstairs. He said she might 'ave broke 'er bones, so I 'ad to get 'ome. I ran back an' Mum was fast asleep in bed.'

Mr Joyce could see from the times written on the statement that Inspector Harrison had started to interview his client on the same day her baby had died and undergone a post-mortem, completing it with her signature in the small hours of the following morning. The turmoil he could picture for himself.

Neither the truth nor the lies needed any more explanation. She was innocent. She had fallen headlong into a simple trap and signed a false confession.

Ethel had started to weep again.

'Will I ever get my teddy bear back, please?' she whispered from behind her hands.

'Yes, you will,' said Mr Joyce. 'If it's the last thing I do. I'll fight for you every step of the way.'

Eighteen

Mr Joyce's office in Bilson Barristers Chambers was plush and spacious and lined from carpet to coving with shelves of dusty legal tomes and portraits of the business's founding fathers. He sat at his inlaid rosewood desk facing out into the body of the room. He was working on a lengthy and lucrative contested will, when the clerk tapped on the door and ushered in Dr Jean Samuels. He screwed the cap back onto his pen and closed the file, came round from behind the desk, and extended his arm to the doctor to take a seat at a conference table.

He had been given to understand that Dr Samuels was an expert in her field. A medical practitioner and specialised pathologist, she had been recommended to him by a colleague. She did not suffer fools gladly, he had been warned. She was feisty, would stand up to a battering in a witness box. Mr Joyce had set out all the available evidence against Miss Slater on the table pending the doctor's arrival.

'I'm obliged to you, Dr Samuels,' he said. 'You've come a long way south. I must be honest, I'm not too sure you'll be able to help my client very much. I hope I'm not wasting your time. I fear she's a lost cause.'

'O ye of little faith,' she replied. 'Let's see what we find.'

They had never met in person before, but they'd had brief conversations on the telephone on a couple of occasions. Jean Samuels worked out of Glasgow and was called to cases around the country. She had made something of a name for herself by investigating the deaths of children. This was a very strange occupation in anybody's book, but it was a job that somebody had to do, Mr Joyce supposed, a bit like an abattoir worker. By all accounts she was good at it. And although Jean Samuels knew the world might think her calling was odd, that bothered her not one jot.

Mr Joyce had posted a package up to her in Glasgow with Dr Lawson's post-mortem report together with a little box of microscope slides and the coroner's report. They laid all the bits of evidence out on the table between them.

'I've met with Miss Slater on remand in Armley Jail,' began Mr Joyce, 'and got the tale from the horse's mouth. That's the one thing going in her favour. She's stuck to her story…'

'Which is?'

'…that she's innocent. Simple as that. Not me.'

'Pick her story apart bit by bit. She gave birth standing up?'

'So she says,' Mr Joyce said. 'She delivered her baby standing at the foot of the bed and leaning forward onto the frame.'

'And then called for help?'

'Yes. Thumped on the wall to attract a neighbour.'

'And then four days later she came back upstairs from answering a knock at the door to find her baby dead in her own bed. That's correct, isn't it?'

'Bang on the nail, Dr Samuels. Exactly what she's said. She's given me a simple flat denial that she's killed her baby. And she's stuck to the same line with the coroner's officer and myself. That's where I run into a major problem, and that's why I've asked you to travel all the way down from Scotland. She said she came back upstairs after visiting a neighbour to find her baby had fatal head injuries. Her father claims he was out fishing all night and has not been charged with any crime, so that leaves just herself and her bedbound mother in the house.'

'You don't believe her?'

'You know the answer to that question as well as I do, Dr Samuels. It's not my job to believe her. I'm paid to defend her in the best way I can.'

'And how will you do that?'

'Exhaustion, in a word. Loss of control.'

'And what will the prosecution say the motive was?'

'Revenge. Premeditated violence.'

'Has she said to you that she wanted this baby?'

'Yes, but not in so many words,' said Mr Joyce. 'She's not got a lot going in her favour really. She's drawn a few short straws. She's easily led. She's only a kid herself, I reckon, and she's got herself pregnant by the tyke next door. She lives with her parents. Her father is a small-time crook, and she tries to look after her mother as best she can. I understand her mother is disabled. I suppose Ethel Slater is too, in her own way.'

'Mr Joyce,' Dr Samuels said, 'let me stop you there. I've looked at all of this baby's injuries. I'm convinced you have good reason to believe every word that Ethel Slater says. She's telling us the truth. The whole truth and nothing but the truth. That's your defence.'

Mr Joyce closed his mouth, sat motionless, and stared at Dr Samuels.

'You mustn't fail her. *We* mustn't fail her.'

She spoke softly – words that would resonate with him for the rest of his days.

He liked this woman, admired her style. She spoke only when she had something worth saying. She had followed his train of legal thinking, he could see that; she had led him along, then cut him dead. He looked at her carefully, for the first time since she'd walked through the door. She was delicate, sharp features, attractive for her age, probably late forties, wearing pearl earrings and matching necklace. Not at all what he would have expected for someone working in her brutal world. Her elegance made him feel a little shabby and under-dressed.

'This baby has serious injuries. Even I can see that,' he continued. 'And she says she woke up in bed and went downstairs to answer the door and didn't notice anything wrong. A jury won't swallow that, Dr Samuels.'

'Show me these injuries.'

Mr Joyce took a set of prints out of a brown envelope and set them out side by side on the table. He didn't baulk at blood-soaked post-mortem photographs any longer. Dr Samuels read through the descriptions in Dr Lawson's report as he laid them out one by one.

'Start with this,' he said. 'A bruise in his scalp…'

'The shape of a hen's egg, it reads here. Speckled browns and red?'

'Correct,' said Mr Joyce. 'Where she's thrown him against the bedroom wall.'

'Twice?'

'Yes, two colours. At birth, then four days old.'

'And he's happened to hit the wall twice on exactly the same part of the forehead just by chance, you suppose?'

Mr Joyce paused to reflect on what she'd just said, scratched his temple, and read Dr Lawson's findings again.

'That's not impossible,' he said. 'There are two impacts there, Dr Samuels.'

'No, there aren't, I don't think. There's one, where his head landed on a hard surface, the floorboards, when he was born. We'll come back to that in a minute. Carry on with the rest of these injuries, please.'

'The fatal injury,' he said. 'Let's get to the point. The cause of death.'

He picked up the grainy colour photograph taken from above the top of the baby's head. The scalp had been drawn back and the skull bones splayed open and apart to the sides to reveal a thick clot of dark blood over the surface of the brain. A finger and thumb in a bloody glove held a pair of scissors into the picture, its tip resting on a crack in the bone.

'A skull fracture and a brain haemorrhage, Dr Samuels,' said Mr Joyce. 'And inflicted at the time of death by severe force from a blunt instrument, consistent with impact against a wall, says Dr Lawson's report. The jury will be shown this image, and it will shock them. It's pretty difficult to argue against his conclusion, isn't it?'

'Not really, no, as long as you ask me the right questions,' said Dr Samuels. 'Because that crack isn't a skull fracture. It's a fissure. It's normal. We'll come back to that in a minute too. Can we take a look at the photograph of these injuries taken before Dr Lawson picked up a scalpel and began his post-mortem?'

'I haven't seen that one,' said Mr Joyce.

He sifted through the set of photographs on the table, peered inside the envelope again, thumbed through the pages in his file, then returned to his desk to rummage through some papers.

'I'm sorry, Dr Samuels,' he said. 'It doesn't ring a bell, to tell you the truth. Did I post it up to you in Glasgow?'

'No, Mr Joyce, you didn't. It doesn't exist. He didn't take a photograph, because there was nothing to see.'

'No injuries?'

'William looked the same as he did when they both went to bed. Either she's glanced at him as she dashed out of bed to answer the door, or assumed he was still fast asleep in his drawer. That's why Ethel didn't see any terrible injuries in the morning, because there were none to be seen.'

'She says she saw some blood under his nose when she came back upstairs.'

'I'm sure that's right. It's come up from his lungs, Mr Joyce. And been washed off before Dr Lawson ever got to the mortuary.'

'And the brain haemorrhage?'

'The same reason he's bled into his lungs,' explained Dr Samuels. 'His mother has accidentally rolled over during the night and smothered him. It doesn't take much with a new baby. She's no more thrown him against a wall than you could throw me. She's guilty of sleeping with him in the same bed. She's guilty of nothing worse than exhaustion, as you so rightly said before.'

She held the barrister's gaze and smiled at him, and he broke into a relieved smile too.

'Are you confident about all this? Are you sure enough to give evidence in a witness box and stand your ground against Mr Cox? He'll attack you. It sounds to me like you've seen this happen before?'

'Yes, I have,' replied Dr Samuels. 'Many times. Though it doesn't usually get as far as a murder trial.'

'What's different about this one?'

'Two reasons probably. One, she's a fallen woman from a rough family who grew up in a backstreet built on wasteland next to the railway sidings, so who cares? And two, I don't think the truth has even crossed Dr Lawson's mind.'

'Tell me, in that case, about a skull fracture and two bruises then, Dr Samuels.'

'Show me this crack first,' she replied.

Mr Joyce flicked through the little pile of photographs and pulled the picture of the baby's head to the top. The doctor pushed her spectacles back into her hair over her forehead and brought the picture close up to her eyes. She ran the tip of her fingernail up and down a line in the skull bone an inch or so in length.

'Well, let me tell you why it's not a fracture, first. Fractures are jagged; this is straight. Fractures are wide; this is thin. Fractures cross bones; this runs up just to the edge of one. And fractures bleed; this is as clean as a whistle. This isn't a fracture, Mr Joyce; it's a join where two plates of bone have grown up against each other but not fused.'

'Are you sure? Why has Dr Lawson diagnosed a fracture then?'

'Maybe because he's never seen one of these before, because he's never chosen to look before. This one just happens to lie beneath a bruise.'

Mr Joyce leant back in his chair to watch her brain at work. To admire the skill of this beautiful woman pondering on the insides of a baby's head, a spectacle that would revolt any other right-minded person.

'Dr Samuels,' he said, 'if you don't mind my saying so, I can see how well you do your job, but I don't know why. I can't imagine anything more painful than losing a child.'

'There are things even worse than that, I think,' she replied.

She looked past Mr Joyce to a family photograph she'd spotted on the corner of his desk. She seemed flustered, embarrassed, taken off guard by his personal question.

'Like not knowing why, or being blamed for it, to name but two. It matters. That's why I do it.'

He nodded his head slowly and pursed his lips.

'The bruise, Dr Samuels. Tell me about that.'

'That's your most difficult argument, convincing a jury there's only one.'

'Convince me first.'

Dr Samuels picked out the photograph of the bruise in the scalp and ran her finger round it, then slid the box of microscope slides across the table.

'These slides are crucial,' she explained. 'Dr Lawson made slides from different parts of this bruise. Just like a bruise changes colour on the skin as it gets older, it does down the microscope too. From red to brown. There are some areas of new blood in this bruise and some areas of old blood. They're two different colours. Dr Lawson says there's an old bruise and a new one, so there must have been two impacts. And I think it means that some of the new blood hasn't changed yet into the old colour, so there's only one injury. I think it's maturing, slowly. It's the lump on his forehead that Dr Chisholm said was nothing to worry about, just healing over a few days. Does that make sense?'

'Probably,' said Mr Joyce. 'But it's not so easy, just your word against his, and juries like things simple. If I can get them to listen, they'll want to know who is right and who is wrong. Which is it, Dr Samuels?'

'Whichever one they want. It comes down to who they want to believe. There's no certainty about the age of this bruising, and I'm the first to admit that. Dr Lawson is certain about everything, and he's wrong about a lot of things. That's his weakness. It's your job to show the jury that, isn't it?'

'It's my job to get witnesses to say things that help my client. The bruise isn't my biggest problem, though. This signature is.'

He returned to his desk to find Ethel's confession and paused to glance at his family photograph: a framed portrait taken of himself, his arm resting on the shoulder of his young wife, and three children, their youngest daughter Emily dressed in her christening gown and sat on her mother's knee. He wished he could show them off to Dr Samuels but daren't.

He took the page back to the conference table and pointed to the two words '*Ethel Slater*' typed at the bottom.

'She's admitted she's thrown her baby at a wall, twice.'

'I know, and she's signed it,' said Dr Samuels, 'but did she say it, and has she read it?'

'How do you think this baby died, Doctor?'

'By accident. Ethel Slater is an innocent. A victim. Of careless men who think lives like hers don't count for anything.'

'Are you convinced Ethel Slater didn't kill her baby with a blunt instrument, Dr Samuels?'

'I am. But she's been hit with one. Dr Lawson. What do you think?'

'I don't. I'm just paid to ask questions to which I know the answers,' said Mr Joyce. 'But I will ask you again when you're standing in the witness box.'

*

Mr Joyce slept fitfully that night, his dreams disturbed by the spectre of a beaming foreman of a jury rising to his feet.

Nineteen

Ethel was the last person to make her appearance in the courtroom on the first morning of her trial for murder. For weeks she had languished in Armley Jail in dread of this day. She climbed the stairwell from the cells in the basement and surfaced into the dock, an open square box where countless other shattered people had been judged before her. She stood on the last step, gasped at the sea of faces out of focus beyond the rail, and turned to retreat. The warder in her wake took the backs of her shoulders and pushed her forward to the front.

The dock was raised on a plinth in the centre of an ornate oak-panelled room. Polished wood jutted out from every angle. Ethel stood at eye level with the judge seated some yards in front of her. She watched as the jury on their two long benches in another box down to her left gaped at the barristers and their legal teams adjusting their robes and wigs down to her right. Bundles of papers had been stacked on a table between them, together with her shoebox and teddy bear, and a skull. Ethel's neighbours from back at the terrace could enjoy this drama unfold over the next couple of days from the public gallery in the balcony behind her.

All voices were hushed as Ethel arrived in the dock, but all eyes were drawn to the skull. Mr Cox for the prosecution rose from his bench, flicked the tails of his robe out from behind him, took his spectacles in his hand, and launched into his opening speech.

'The case for the Crown, ladies and gentlemen of the jury,' he said, 'is this.

'The defendant you see before you in the dock is Miss Ethel Slater, an eighteen-year-old woman. Spitefulness and rejection drove her to snuff out her defenceless newborn baby before his life had even really begun. She made two attempts to kill him. She failed at the first when she was interrupted by a neighbour, but succeeded when he was just four days old.

'Miss Slater lives with her parents in a terraced house in York that is rented from the Railway Company. Her father is a butcher and her mother struggles with illness. The family is penniless and Ethel Slater is unmarried. She befriended the boy next door, a young man with prospects, by the name of Edward Sathersthwaite, with the aim of seducing him, and she fell pregnant. This ploy to trap a husband failed. Edward deserted her and she was left to carry an unwanted baby. You will see that Ethel Slater is a loose, feckless woman who lacks ambition or foresight. She was unable to hold down a job serving in a corner shop and was then incapable of supporting herself, let alone a child. She made no plans to care for a newborn baby, she turned down all offers of help, and she made no preparations for the birth.

'The defendant chose to deliver her baby alone in a bedroom in her parents' house, even though she knew that her mother in the room below, a vicar's kindly wife nearby, and a helpful caring neighbour were on hand to help. She attempted to destroy him by throwing him at the wall as soon as he was born. The impact attracted the attention of Edward's mother in the adjacent bedroom in the house next door, and Miss Slater's first attempt at taking his life was thwarted. Mrs Sathersthwaite revived the baby. Four days later Miss Slater received the gift of a teddy bear from the father of their child. Bitterness and revenge drove the defendant to suffocate her baby with a pillow and hurl him at the wall again. On this occasion her efforts were successful, as she has confessed to the police.'

The judge and the jury had lifted their eyes up onto the figure frozen in the dock. Ethel stared down at her hands gripping the rail.

'My lord,' Mr Cox continued, 'I should like to call my first witness to the stand, Dr Lawson.'

The man seated on his left rose to his feet and made his way between the table and the jury box then climbed the three low steps to the witness box. Dr Lawson, an upright and confident man dressed for the occasion with bow tie and buttonhole, took the Bible in his right hand and swore to God that he would tell the truth, the whole truth, and nothing but the truth.

'Dr Lawson,' said Mr Cox, 'are you experienced in the examination of victims of violent crime?'

'Sadly yes, sir,' he replied. 'I have carried out thousands of post-mortem examinations on the bodies of fatally injured people in my career.'

'Indeed, and over the course of many decades, as I understand it. Did you carry out such a post-mortem on the body of a four-day-old baby by the name of William Slater on the 12th of February of this year, and then make microscope slides of an area of bruising and write a detailed report?'

'Yes, sir, I did.'

'And how had this baby died?'

'Sir, he had died of violent injuries.'

'Please describe for the jury the most significant injury you found.'

Dr Lawson turned slightly to look at the judge.

'The most serious injury, Your Honour, which would have required extreme force and resulted in death within a minute or so, was a fracture of the skull.'

Mr Cox raised his hand to pause his witness.

'Please hold your reply there for a moment, Doctor,' he said.

He bent forward over the table to pass a photograph to the clerk of the court and took up the weight of the skull in his hands.

'Members of the jury,' he said, 'I ask you to brace yourselves and look carefully at the photograph. Be prepared. It may well shock you, but I make no apology for that. You have been asked to turn your minds to a truly shocking matter.'

The clerk held the photograph up to Justice Weaver sat at his bench at the head of the court. He glimpsed at it over the top of his spectacles, nodded his approval, and waved it back, and the clerk handed it to the nearest juror. There the jury looked down upon the unmistakable top of a baby's head: the scalp pulled back and away, a glistening big bruise lying under the skin, the bones cleaved open and apart, the thick dark blood pooled over the surface of the brain, and a gloved finger and thumb holding the tip of a probe to a crack in the skull.

'Before I ask you to take a closer look at the detail, ladies and gentlemen,' he continued, 'I ask you to focus on the fracture, please, just here.'

He held the skull in the palm of his left hand and turned its top to face the jury, then with a flourish of a pen held between finger and thumb of his right hand, brought its nib to land on a line he had drawn on the bone.

Mr Cox could not have hoped for a better opening salvo. The photograph had served its purpose. Few of the jury could bear to look at the image for more than a second, but they could all now see in their mind's eye this devastating attack unfolding on a helpless baby. Jurors looked to the dock for any reaction in the face at the rail but saw not a flicker. Two wandering eyes fixed on nothing.

'Dr Lawson,' Mr Cox resumed, 'we can all see the fractured bone, the bruised skin, and the bleeding over the brain in that disturbing image. Are all of these injuries the result of one fatal blow?'

Dr Lawson always enjoyed his privileged position in a witness box, where he could parade his opinions and expertise to a captive audience, whether they wanted to listen to him or not. And courts paid well. He had appeared before this judge and barrister on numerous occasions. He counted them among his friends. He remained standing erect and raised his shoulders to their full height. He spoke slowly and clearly to the judge and jury.

'No, sir, they are not. The skull fracture and the brain haemorrhage were both caused by a single heavy blow, but there were two separate blows to the scalp several days apart.'

'Please tell the jury how you are able to reach that conclusion?'

'I made microscope slides of the two distinct areas of the bruising in the skin, Your Honour. I can see with the aid of a microscope a fresh red bruise inflicted at the time of death and a separate older brown bruise inflicted, I would suggest, around the time of birth.'

He tilted his head back slightly to give the members of the jury a view of his best profile.

Mr Cox brought a second photograph to the top of the pile on the table, and asked the clerk to show it round to the jurors and then hand it to his witness.

'Doctor,' he said, 'you see here Miss Slater's bedroom wall the day after William died. You have told the jury that the most serious injury was the result of extreme force. Would you care to describe the photograph to the jury, please, and explain to them what you mean by that?'

'Correct, sir, extreme violence,' said the doctor. 'There is a crack in the plaster on the wall overlaid at one point at shoulder height by light blood staining. In my opinion the fresh scalp bruising, the fracture, the brain haemorrhage, and death were caused by a heavy impact with the wall.'

'Are you suggesting, Dr Lawson, this baby has been thrown against that wall?'

'I am.'

'A fatal impact?'

'Absolutely.'

'And the earlier bruise to the scalp?'

'By the same means, sir, doubtless around the time of birth.'

'Doctor, I don't want to detain you for any longer than is necessary,' Mr Cox continued. 'I know you have other important duties to attend to. But tell me if you would, please, did you find any other injury in this baby?'

'Yes, sir, I did. Bleeding into the lungs, a sign of suffocation.'

'And finally if I may ask your opinion on two further photographs of the room in which this baby died? One shows a pillow on Miss Slater's bed, and the other the floorboards at the foot of the bed.'

'The pillow, Your Honour,' replied the doctor, 'shows staining with blood coughed up from the lungs as it was pressed into his face. And a large pool of dried blood on the floor marks the position in which this baby landed after his impact with the wall and was left to die from his injuries.'

The clerk took the photographs from the witness and passed them to the jury, but most of them had seen and heard more than enough. They would never be able to forget the image of injuries to a baby's head. Or get out of their minds the violence that had erupted in this angry life in a sordid room and the sufferings of this innocent baby at Ethel's hands. It was hard to see how on earth she could be innocent.

'That completes my examination, m'lord,' Mr Cox said, and sat down.

The judge seemed to wake with a start, bent his arm down along his leg, eased the left shoe off his foot, and nodded his approval to Mr Cox.

'Thank you, Dr Lawson,' he said, 'you have been most helpful. Please remain standing where you are. My learned friend Mr Joyce may have some further questions for you.'

*

Mr Joyce rose to his feet. He always enjoyed Mr Cox's performances and Dr Lawson's bluster. This arrogant doctor has made plenty of assumptions I can expose, he thought. He's stumbled into so many blind alleys where I can trap him.

The trick now, Mr Joyce knew, was to unravel all this evidence for a simple jury; to puncture this pompous man and expose him for what he was. He'd taken a risk allowing Mr Cox to show them the bloody photograph of the baby's head. He could have jumped to his feet and objected. He knew it could so easily turn them against his client, but he was hopeful his gamble had paid off. He'd seen the revulsion on the faces of most of the jurors, and one or two of them hadn't got the courage to give the picture a second glance. But one woman had held his attention. She'd kept hold of it, pored over it as Dr Lawson described the injuries, pointed out the crack in the skull to the man on her right. This elderly smart woman, Mr Joyce felt, is an ally, my crowbar into this jury.

'Dr Lawson,' Mr Joyce said, pushing the photographs back onto the table, 'may I ask you, have you had occasion to deliver many babies during the course of your long career?'

'Indeed I have, sir, yes,' he replied. 'I trained in the art of obstetrics under Sir William Gilliatt, the Royal Obstetrician, at King's College Hospital in London.'

'Marvellous.'

Mr Joyce retrieved the image of the splayed head from the top of the pile and asked the clerk to pass it to the witness.

'And has your expertise been called upon to examine many cases of death during childbirth or newborn babies?'

'Sadly, yes, sir. Obstetric disasters are not uncommon in my experience.'

'Every day, Dr Lawson? Once a week? Once a month?'

'My last case was just before Christmas,' replied the doctor.

'Really? Then I would suggest not common at all in your practice. But I take it you are very knowledgeable about fractures of the skull in older people?'

'Yes, I see them all too frequently. Assaults, mainly, and accidents on the railways.'

'Then please describe for us, in as much detail as you can, the fracture in baby William's skull, the injury that you say was caused by a heavy impact and extreme violence.'

Dr Lawson took the photograph from the ledge in front of him and angled it towards Mr Joyce.

'There it is, you see it here, at the end of the pointer. Straight as a die and runs to the middle of the bones of the forehead.'

'And please tell us, in your opinion, why this fracture hasn't splintered into the soft tissue underneath it, and more to the point, why it didn't bleed? Why is there no bleeding on the bone around this fracture, Dr Lawson?'

'There's extensive bleeding over the brain, sir.'

'We can all see that, can't we? That's separate, though, deeper down. But why not on the bone itself? It's as clean as a whistle, isn't it?'

The doctor ran his finger down the line and stared at the image as if that might bring it back to life.

Justice Weaver's pen came to a standstill over his notebook, and he looked over to the witness box. This hesitation was completely out of character.

'Dr Lawson?'

'I don't know the answer to that question, Your Honour.'

Rarely had the judge heard such a feeble response from his good friend Dr Lawson.

'Have I heard you correctly?' said the judge. 'You don't know why a fractured bone didn't splinter and bleed?'

'No.'

'Well,' said Mr Joyce, 'I'm sure that if a man of your distinction doesn't know the answer to this very important and simple question, then I put it to you that there probably isn't an answer. Perhaps you can help the jury with another point. Take this skull in your hands if you would, and apply the pressure it would have felt during its slow travel down Miss Slater's birth canal into the outside world.'

The hollow skull rang to Mr Joyce's idle knock with his knuckle, and he handed it over to the witness box. The doctor took it in both hands and made to squeeze it from side to side.

'Tell us, please, why doesn't a thin skull fracture when it's forced through the narrow space of a mother's pelvis?'

'The bones of a baby's skull aren't fused like this. It's not a solid box,' explained the doctor. 'They ride over and under each other when they're squeezed. It's like a concertina.'

'Thank you, Dr Lawson, nicely put. They slip and slide, as I understand it. They can bend. Would you agree that a baby's skull bones rarely fracture during a normal birth, but when they do, they bleed?'

'I would.'

'I suggest to you, sir, that you haven't stopped in your busy, headlong life to consider any other explanation for this crack. You wear blinkers. Is it possible that the reason this fracture didn't bleed is that it isn't a fracture at all? Could it just be a fissure where two bones meet?'

'This is a fracture, sir. It's just beneath the bruise in the scalp.'

'Dr Lawson,' interrupted the judge from his bench. He leant forward and down again to massage his big toe. 'Do I understand you correctly? It's a fracture because you say it is? Is that the long and the short of it?'

'The fracture, Your Honour, sits just beneath an injury—'

'...And there, members of the jury,' interrupted Mr Joyce, 'we have a coincidence, the bruise in the skin over the crack in the skull, but a coincidence the doctor cannot accept.'

'And at that point,' said the judge, 'we shall adjourn for lunch. It's nearly half past twelve. Reconvene at two o'clock, please.'

The judge eased his shoe back over his foot, raised himself out of the chair, and tried not to limp to his door. He needed this gout gone by the close of play tomorrow. A glass or two of sherry with lunch should take the edge off it. The jurors waited for him to exit then filed out of their box in a line; the two barristers fell into an easy conversation; and Ethel's warder followed his prisoner down the stairwell back to her cell below. She'd caught a glimpse of her baby as the doctor had tipped the picture to Mr Joyce but felt numb and it had meant nothing.

*

The clerk rapped on the door at the front of the court promptly at two o'clock and opened it for Justice Weaver to make his entrance in his flowing robes. Dr Lawson had already taken his position in the witness box. He straightened his tie, dropped one hand into his trouser pocket, and stood with the other just resting on the rail.

He took this chance to look up and study the killer in the dock.

He saw just grime and cross eyes.

'Mr Joyce,' the judge resumed on taking his seat and picking up his pen, 'where were we?'

'I propose to question Dr Lawson about the bruising to the scalp, Your Honour.'

'Then please do, by all means. Hurry along.'

'Dr Lawson,' Mr Joyce began, 'be so good as to describe the bruise to us, then tell the court how you know there are two separate injuries here, inflicted several days apart.'

The barrister's ally in the jury caught the clerk's eye and he passed the photograph back to her again. The bruise had fascinated her. She'd never seen one cut open before and so vivid, a jigsaw pattern of beautiful shades of colour.

'Yes, certainly, it's a couple of inches across, quite flat and thin, oval, just beneath the surface of the forehead, and shades of red and brown. I made microscope slides of different areas of it. These slides show some fresh red blood, and the brown areas are old blood that has been sitting in the tissue for a longer period of time.'

'I want you to be very clear about this, please, Dr Lawson. A young woman's life may hinge on your answer. You're telling us some of the bruise is recent red injury, and some of it is old and brown. Have I understood you correctly?'

'You have.'

'And what would we have seen in this bruise if William had survived his more recent injury? What would have happened to the fresh red blood?'

'It would have started to turn brown after a day or so, and then stayed in the skin for a long time.'

'Like the old injury?'

'Yes.'

The witness hesitated.

This line of questioning was heading in the wrong direction.

'But this is what really matters, isn't it, Dr Lawson? How quickly does all the fresh blood turn brown? After how many days has all of the red blood disappeared? Every last trace?'

'It goes within a few days, I'd say.'

'A few days, Dr Lawson? Two days? Three?'

'Science doesn't know all the answers, sir.'

'And nor do you. But please answer my question. Use the benefit of all your vast experience.'

'Two or three days, in my opinion.'

'Thank you. So, all of this bruise could be three days old, some still red, some turned brown. Do you agree?'

Dr Lawson took his hand out of his pocket and put them both on the rail in front of him.

'Answer the question,' said the judge.

'Possibly.'

'Let me push you even further, Doctor. How about four days? Is it conceivable that all of this bruise is four days old?'

'I doubt it.'

'But not inconceivable?'

'No.'

'Let the jury be crystal-clear about this. You are telling the court that it's possible that all of this bruise was inflicted by one injury, on the day he was born. You doubt it, but science can't exclude it.'

Eyes had shifted from Ethel in the dock to the witness in the box.

'You've relied on ignorance and assumptions, haven't you?' Mr Joyce continued. 'When really there should be so many genuine doubts in your mind. Dr Lawson, you are negligent and incompetent.'

The doctor rocked back on his heels without attempting an answer. His shoulders slumped and he took a shaky sip from a glass of water. He looked to the bench up on his left. The judge was bent over his notes. He looked to Mr Cox in his seat in front, hoping he would be rising to his feet to object to this outrage. But he wasn't.

'Dr Lawson,' said Mr Joyce, 'you took all these photographs after the post-mortem was completed, the skull, the bruise, the bleeding over the brain, all the organs laid out in a tidy row. Can we assume that you had photographs taken of every shred of evidence?'

'Yes, sir, I always examine every organ in minute detail. I leave no stone unturned.'

He eased his grip on the rail.

He was more comfortable now.

'But there are no pictures of the baby taken before you took up your knife, are there? Why's that, Doctor?'

'Because there were no external injuries, sir.'

'Well, this comes as an enormous surprise to us, surely. You've told the jury this baby was thrown at a wall, then left to die of his injuries from a heavy blow in a pool of blood on the floorboards. We can't bear to imagine it, but we can see it in slow motion. We can almost hear the violence. And yet there wasn't a mark, not so much as a scratch, on the surface of his little body. Do you want us to take you seriously, Dr Lawson?'

The doctor didn't answer this question but exchanged a look with the judge.

'Then where is the injury that bled onto the floor?'

Dr Lawson opened his mouth, then closed it.

'Members of the jury, the witness has lapsed into silence. Let me ask him two final very straightforward questions. One, could a crushing injury to the baby's head have caused a brain haemorrhage?'

'It could, I suppose. But we don't have a crushing force, sir.'

'I put it to you that we do. Two, could you accept that

baby William might have accidentally been overlaid and suffocated under his exhausted mother sleeping in her bed? Would that explain the bleeding in the lungs and over the brain, Dr Lawson?'

'Yes, but not the fracture or the bruise.'

'Thank you, Doctor. I'll take your answer to my last question as yes.'

Mr Joyce turned his fire on the jury, raising a finger to the smart elderly woman in the second row back.

'Let me explain the doctor's last answer to you very clearly, ladies and gentlemen,' he said. 'This experienced doctor would accept that baby William died by accident, overlayed by his mother in bed, were it not for the crack in the skull and the bruise in the scalp. And yet he admits in truth that he has serious doubts about those two findings as well.'

He turned his finger back to the doctor in the box.

'And you, sir,' he said, 'your theory doesn't quite fit any of the facts. It doesn't hold water. Just like a baby's skull.'

Twenty

Ray Cooper had told the other jury members that he was a highly successful businessman and that he would speak up for them as their foreman. They could leave it all up to him. He had listened very carefully to Mr Cox's opening speech and then watched Ethel's reactions in the dock as the doctor had gone through all the horrific injuries she had inflicted. She hadn't flinched. What he didn't tell the rest of the jury was how much he would enjoy delivering their verdict.

He watched Inspector Harrison take the stand and knew before the policeman opened his mouth that he could be relied upon to tell the truth. The inspector had that air of seasoned authority about him that Ray Cooper envied and respected: that self-assurance, the familiar ease, that would cut out any nonsense they didn't need to hear. But Linda Moxley in the second row just thought the man looked shifty, more like a villain than a policeman.

The clerk told the inspector to take the Bible in his

right hand, repeat the oath after him, and tell the court his name, rank, and position.

'I'm Ian Harrison, Detective Inspector with York City Police,' he said as he looked behind him to take his coat off and lay it over the chair. He then turned back to face the court, pushed up the knot of his tie, and looked up at the little head poking above the rail in the dock.

He'd forgotten her, it was so long ago, but now he remembered the eyes. Frogface. He recalled that she had killed her child, a newborn baby, if his memory served him right, and that she was guilty of murder. He'd put the fear of God into her probably to get the confession, but the details escaped him. All he could really think back to was standing in the snow on the Leeds canal towpath for the best part of the day. He was sure it would all come back to him when he saw what he'd written down.

He gave Ethel a half smile.

Ethel looked down from the dock in horror. She realised as soon as he began to take his coat off that this was the man who had lied to her on the day her baby had died. He had kept her scared and alone in a cold dark room in the police station all day; she'd felt naked just in her nightie, coat, scarf and slippers; and she'd ached. She'd ached in her breasts, she'd ached in her bones, and she'd ached for her baby. He'd sat down at a table with a lamp between them after she'd spent hours waiting, he'd blown billows of smoke across her face, and he'd stared at her eyes. Her baby had died and there was nothing left to live for, and all he could do was write down stupid, empty words.

And then he had told her that her mother had fallen

down the stairs at home and broken her bones. He'd let her run back through town in the snow in the middle of the night, but her mother wasn't at the foot of the stairs. There was just the old pram and the nappies hung out to dry in the hallway. Mum was asleep in her bed downstairs, her fire had been stoked up for the night, and Olive was tucked up in Ethel's own bed upstairs next to William's empty drawer. Ethel had broken down in a turmoil of despair and relief when she found her mother unhurt and her home in darkness and full of her baby's ghosts. She couldn't understand then or now why anybody would want to be so cruel and tell such a lie.

Mr Cox stood and passed four pieces of paper to the clerk of the court, one each for the judge, the witness, Mr Joyce, and the jury.

'Your Honour,' he addressed the bench, 'you have Miss Slater's statement to the police.'

The judge glanced down the page then flipped it over to look for writing on the back; Mr Cooper clung on to it and smiled at the witness; Mr Harrison was grateful to read it and remembered the girl's fear for her crippled mother; and Mr Joyce laid it on the table in front of him without a second look.

'Inspector Harrison,' Mr Cox said, 'do you routinely interview suspects of serious crime?'

He smiled then chuckled.

'Yes, you could say that. I've been doing it for years.'

'And do you recall taking a statement from Miss Ethel Slater?'

'Yes,' replied the inspector. 'I remember it like it was yesterday.'

'Then let me refer the jury and yourself to this signed confession.'

Mr Joyce jumped to his feet.

'Objection, My Lord,' he addressed the judge. 'This confession is not signed.'

Justice Weaver picked up his page again and looked at the names '*Ethel Slater*' and '*Ian Harrison*' typed at the bottom.

'What?' he said. He straightened his leg under the bench and winced in pain. 'Come again?'

'The names are typed, Your Honour, not written in their own hand.'

The judge pursed his lips and blew out his breath quietly.

'It is an exact copy, Your Honour,' Mr Cox said. 'The words are just the same as the original.'

'Then I fail to see your point, Mr Joyce,' said the judge. 'Hurry up, Mr Cox. Just get on with it, please.'

'Thank you, Your Honour.' Mr Cox turned to the witness box. 'Inspector, I'll read to the jury the final words of Miss Slater's confession. Please confirm them as the truth then if you can.'

'*I confess that shortly after giving birth alone to my son William on 8th February, I threw him against my bedroom wall. He was unwanted and I felt I had been abandoned. On 12th February I threw him against the wall for a second time. I'm sorry, I didn't mean to kill my baby. I have read over this statement and it is all the truth.*'

Ethel stared at the judge. Surely he would speak up for her. She remembered the policeman's promise. He said he knew the judge. The judge would be kind to her if she signed that piece of paper. He would tell the inspector now that he could see that she was worried about her mother and she couldn't have meant anything he'd written down.

'Inspector Harrison,' asked the judge, 'do you confirm this statement to be true?'

'I do.'

'No! No!' shouted Ethel from the dock. 'He's lyin', he's lyin' again.'

Her warder wrestled her back from the rail.

The jury turned to the dock and then to the gallery behind. A lanky youth with slicked-back hair and thick sideburns had leapt to his feet.

'That's our Ethel,' Eddie shouted down at the room. 'An' my baby too.'

Ray Cooper saw the man with a future but who'd been snared by the slut next door; Linda Moxley saw a feisty youth who was still in love with the mother of his child.

'That can't be right,' he bellowed at the inspector. 'You're a lyin' bastard, it's not right. Ethel couldn't 'urt nobody. No way she's done all that.'

Charlie Songhirst grabbed the tail of Eddie's jacket and hauled him back into his chair.

'Remove that man from my court,' the judge shouted up at the gallery.

A warder pushed along the row past Mr Waggett and Charlie, grabbed Eddie by the sleeve of his jacket, and bundled him out of the door at the rear of the court.

Mr Cox cut through the bustle and noise. 'Inspector Harrison, did Miss Slater say these words, and is there anything you would wish to change?'

He had been asked these two questions many times by a lawyer, and the answers were always the same. He loosened his tie and relaxed now the shouting was over.

'Yes, she did, and no, there isn't.'

This was just what Mr Cooper needed to hear. She had killed her own child, and who could doubt it? She had said so herself.

'Tell me in her own words what Ethel Slater said about the birth of her baby, please.'

'*I gave birth alone on my bed at home. Eddie had left me and I didn't want my mother downstairs to know. The labour pains were terrible. I tried to kill the baby by throwing it at the bedroom wall, but the noise disturbed Mrs Sath next door and she came round.*'

Mr Cox picked up the shoebox from the table, took off its lid carefully, laid out the teddy bear neatly inside it, tied on the lid with a piece of string, and held it up for the jury.

'And please, Inspector, read out for us what Miss Slater had to say about this shoebox.'

'*I hid the shoebox under the bed because I was going to hide the body in it.*'

'No,' Ethel shouted. 'That's not true. That's a little box like Monica 'ad made for 'er new baby in the 'ome. He's lyin'.'

The warder slapped his hand round Ethel's mouth from behind and dragged her back from the rail.

'For God's sake, shut that woman up,' Justice Weaver bawled at the dock. 'I'll not have anybody shouting in my court.'

Mr Cox coughed politely as the judge slumped back in his chair.

'May I continue, Your Honour?'

'Yes, Mr Cox, please, if you must. We've all read it anyway.'

'Mr Harrison,' continued Mr Cox, 'let me take you back to the confession. Spell out for us please what Miss Slater said to you about the baby's death.'

'I never wanted this baby. On the morning I killed him, he had been crying all night and I hadn't slept. I came upstairs from answering the door in the morning, something snapped inside my head, and I pushed the pillow into his face then threw him at the wall.'

'Very good,' said Mr Cox. 'And if I may quote to the jury myself, Miss Slater told you that she was carrying an unwanted bastard child, that she had been deserted by the father of the child and her own parents, and that nobody else was involved in the planning or the execution of the killing. Is that correct?'

'It is, absolutely.'

'Finally, Inspector, are you able to confirm that the accused signed this confession of her own free will?'

'She did, yes, sir. And the relief was written all over her face.'

Mr Joyce rose from his seat again and thanked Mr Cox, then took up his copy of the confession, held it up to the jury, and slowly ripped it into shreds and let the leaves drop down onto the table in front of him.

*

Eddie Sath bounded up the marble steps of the court building two at a time with a double whisky from the

Town Hall Tavern coursing through his veins. He had needed it, but he also needed to hear the rest of what this bent copper had to say.

He turned the knob on the door to the rear of the public gallery as slowly and as quietly as he could, took out a cigarette from his packet and held it out to the warder, got a knowing wink in reply, and slid into an empty chair on the back row.

He knew the likes of Mr Cox and Mr Harrison from his army days. The officer class, bastards, he loathed them. They were playing a game with our Ethel. She was their cannon fodder. She was simple, no doubt, but she was gentle, and she was kind. She was no killer of babies. He might even have married her but for her wonky eye.

'Your Honour,' said Mr Joyce, 'I have here Miss Slater's real confession signed with her own hand. Tell me, Inspector, have you got signatures from any other mothers suspected of murdering their babies?'

He leant on his fingertips spread out on the bench in front of him and tilted his head to the witness.

'I interview suspects of all serious crimes, not just murders. It's my job.'

'Answer my question, please.'

'Most murder victims are adults.'

'I'm sure you're a very busy man. Did you think this mother had killed her baby before you set eyes on her?'

'No, sir, but I knew the baby had serious injuries, or she wouldn't have been arrested.'

'And you knew that nobody else could have caused them?'

'I was open-minded.'

Linda Moxley mouthed the word *What?* at the policeman, then tapped on Ray Cooper's shoulder and held her hand out for the confession.

'Did you ask how her baby might have got his injuries?'

'She just wanted to tell me.'

'This interview lasted for more than six hours, but we've just the one page of writing. Can you explain that?'

'I just ask the questions and write down the answers. It's very easy, really.'

'Words like disturbed and abandoned and execution? Long words. Words that a girl with no learning would never use. These are your words, not hers, surely, aren't they?'

'I just helped her along the way, that's all.' He shrugged.

Linda passed the confession to the woman on her left. 'It's all nonsense,' she whispered into her ear.

'Did you offer to let your suspect speak to a friend, or even a solicitor?' Mr Joyce continued.

'Course I did. I wanted her to telephone her neighbour, or we could even go and collect her in a police car. But she said no, she just wanted to get the job over and done with.'

'Had the duty sergeant told you that her mother needed her daughter at home?'

'No. She told me that her dad would look after her mum.'

'Really? Did you lie to Miss Slater? Tell her she could get home to her mother as soon as she confessed to a murder?'

'Objection, Your Honour,' interrupted Mr Cox. 'These are all leading questions.'

'Yes, Mr Joyce, they are. The witness is under oath,' said the judge, 'but you're making him out to be a liar. Don't answer that last question, Inspector.'

The judge knew barristers would get nowhere doubting the word of a policeman. They could wriggle out of any corner.

'Mr Harrison, look at Miss Slater's signature, please.'

The inspector glanced at the bottom of the page, a gaggle of jumbled letters in two words tumbling away from the line.

The judge clicked his fingers to the clerk, who passed the confession over to him.

'This is not the writing of a girl who is used to words,' Mr Joyce continued. 'Let me tell the jury what really happened in that room. You arrive at the police station to make everybody's life easier, including your own. A baby has just died a few hours before. With injuries. You know the woman in custody has killed him. She's terrified. Exhausted and alone. The duty sergeant has brought in the suspect from home and told you her mother can't stay alive without her daughter's help. Miss Slater agrees to what you write down, any words you like to say, your long words, just so she could get home, Inspector Harrison. And she's left the police station clueless of what she's signed.'

'Too fuckin' right!' a voice called out from the back. 'She can't fuckin' read either.'

The judge erupted.

'Jesus Christ, I've said get that man out!'

Mr Joyce dropped down onto his seat without waiting for an answer as Mr Cox leapt up.

Eddie Sath had come good and done his job for him.

'Sit down, Mr Cox,' Justice Weaver snapped. 'I know, I know, you object. I agree with you. But I've had enough for one day.'

He bent under his seat to slip his shoe back on again.

'We'll kick off again in the morning.'

Twenty-One

'In yer go, me darlin',' her warder said, and threw a blanket over Ethel's head.

He'd led her down the stairs from the dock into the basement then straight out from the court building into the back street to avoid the reporters. He placed the flat of his hand over the top of the blanket, pushed her shoulders down, and bundled her into the back of the van. He climbed in after her, sat on the bench opposite, and thumped twice on the metal plate behind the driver. It was not his place to talk to prisoners and they travelled in silence back to the jail.

Her cellmate old Winnie had taken the bottom bunk. Ethel had been moved into this cell to share with Winnie, and so she had no option but to take the mattress on top and lie inches from the lightbulb. The cell had been home for Ethel since a couple of days after her baby had died. There was a small, barred window looking out at blank sky, whitewashed brick walls, and cold stone slabs for the floor. Two wooden shelves and a chair stood in the corner with some tin plates and pots, the slop bucket, and some folded clothes and a towel. She knew it better than her own bedroom in St Paul's Terrace, every scratch on the chair, every crack in the slabs, every patch of peeling paint on the ceiling.

She climbed the few rungs on the ladder. The springs under the mattress groaned as they took her weight. Winnie had squatted over the bucket just before Ethel arrived, and the air stank of warm urine.

Winnie had propped herself up on her elbows when she heard the key scrape in the lock.

'Blimey, they've let you come back,' she said. 'For one night, anyway. I'd started a book we'd not see you again.'

'I don't know what's 'appenin',' Ethel replied.

She felt too stunned to talk yet. She couldn't say if she'd got through the day or not. The doctor had told the judge he was sure she'd killed William, and then the policeman had told him that she had wanted to talk about throwing her baby at a wall. That was all wrong, surely, she thought. But William's little life had ended so long ago it was just a fog, and she didn't really know for certain what had happened anymore. Who would take any notice of her anyway? But she did remember the inspector's face as he lit his cigarette and warned her that the judge would hang her if he caught her telling him lies. And then Mr Joyce seemed to be arguing with everybody. Perhaps the judge didn't like that and had made up his mind already.

Ethel was one of the few people that Winnie had any time for in jail. She saw Ethel for what she was: she was simple, posed no threat. She had told Ethel her story, or at least the bits of it that mattered, as they huddled on their bunks when they couldn't sleep, the light from the corridor flooding their cell. She had murdered her husband. She had no regrets. Good riddance. He had it coming. She had told the whole story to the police, gladly and with no questions asked. She spoke little more of her past life; there was nothing she could do about that; and she didn't have a future. She had told Ethel it was no secret her husband had sex with other women, showed lurid photographs of them round the public bars, spent his wage on beer the same day he got it, and beat his wife if he was in drink and life wasn't going his way. She had finally squared up to him, snapped when he hit her once too often, grabbed a bread knife in the kitchen, and plunged it into his chest. She had been sentenced to hang by the neck until she was dead.

The jailers got sense that Winnie hadn't quite accepted her sentence yet. If and when she did, she could find some peace for her last few days, some solace. She would soften and relax and might spend her time playing clock patience in her cell. Until then, she would fight against her guards whenever she could. There was no real defence for her crime. Pending a stay of execution in the coming days, she would soon set her eyes on the hangman for a second or two before he covered her head with a hood and she paid the price for her crime.

Winnie's marriage to a cruel husband put Ethel in mind of her own mother. They were both of an age, but unlike Mary's crippled limbs and empty shell, Winnie had a stout body and a strong face that had been lived in, thick-skinned and lined. And Ethel could sense in her a resolve, a toughness, that can sometimes come from a life of knocks and setbacks.

'Eddie was there.' Ethel spoke to the lightbulb above her face.

'What?' answered Winnie after a few moments. She was aiming to get some sleep and in no mood for talking.

'Eddie's come back, Winnie. He was sat be'ind me and he shouted out that I 'ant done 'owt wrong. Mrs Sath 'ad told me he'd left 'ome an' gone for good.'

'You're well shut of 'im, Ethel, from what you've told me. He's a bad lot.'

'No, he's not really,' Ethel said to herself.

She reached under her pillow then dangled a creased and faded photograph over the edge of her bunk into the void below.

'That's Eddie,' she said.

Winnie took the photograph and held it out to catch the light from the window above the door.

'Big trunk,' she said.

The picture was of an elephant standing on a lawn of dandelions, held by a circus clown complete with bulbous red nose and spiky yellow hair. It stood twice the height of two children wild with excitement grappling to stay astride its neck and hang on to its massive grey ears. Its trunk played across a grinning soldier in uniform with his arm round the shoulder of a beaming woman in a floral frock.

'An' Mum and Dad,' said Ethel, 'when the circus came to town.'

'Blimey,' said Winnie, 'I've never been anywhere near a fuckin' elephant. Lucky you. 'Appy days, eh?'

Happy days, you can say that again, thought Ethel. The elephant came to her street before everything started to go wrong. Happy kids, when everybody in the terrace knew that Eddie Sath would marry Ethel Slater; it was only a matter of time. Dad, after he'd come back home after fighting his war and still loved his family, and Eddie with his arms tight round her waist before he went to fight his. And Mum, before she started to fall over with her illness, and before Dad had started to slap her down.

'Eddie would 'ave married me, Winnie, if all this 'adn't 'ave 'appened. An' Reverend Pearson was reckonin' to baptise William too.'

'Ethel,' said Winnie, 'listen to me. Don't dwell on these things. It does you no good. Never get your 'opes up with any man if you get yourself out of 'ere, love. I know. Then he can't let you down. Eddie would 'ave 'urt you sooner or later, one way or another.'

'He's soft, deep down, is Eddie.'

'An' you're daft.'

'My dad 'its Mum, Winnie. It's made 'er poorly.'

'Or t'other way round? Perhaps he thumps her 'cos she is poorly, more like. Men 'its their wives, Ethel; it's the way o' the world; it's what they do. But folk as 'urts babies are another thing, and you're not one o' them. But maybe your father is from what you've said. It's as plain as the nose on your face. Now think on, an' try get some sleep.'

*

Ethel knew they were Winnie's last words for the night and slumped back onto her pillow. She couldn't think any more about today, and even less about what might happen tomorrow. She just wanted the old days back, when everybody was sure about everything and nothing ever changed. And her Eddie flooded her mind. She could see why she loved him. He'd told the judge what was right. He was strong, and he knew what he thought and would say it, and she couldn't.

The screech of the bomb and the blast at Mrs Broadbent's house jolted her out of her drift into sleep, then she saw dead Ruby emerge from the ruins in the fireman's grasp. But soon she floated away as the peeling paint formed angry faces on the ceiling, and slipped into a dream of Eddie's face above hers in dappled sunlight through a canopy of leaves.

Twenty-Two

Ray Cooper stood to his feet as instructed by the clerk of the court, watched the judge rise and shuffle to his own private exit behind his bench, and looked at his wristwatch. His day away from the scathing comments of his boss Mr O'Sullivan had been more than welcome. He believed strongly in the British rule of law and it was a privilege to be a part of it. And to be seen to be a part of it. With all expenses too.

He had a snap decision to make. Either he turned left outside the court and returned to his desk in Planning in the Town Hall next door, or turned right and took a leisurely walk through town to the Blue Moon Gentlemen's Club for an early start to his evening. O'Sullivan might guess that a court would finish its business for the day by four, but he could say he had a few tricky points to talk over with the other jury members if he was ever asked. Ray clipped down the courthouse steps and turned right.

Ray's years of waiting on the prospective members list for the Blue Moon had paid off handsomely. He enjoyed the discreet banter with influential businessmen at the bar and its wide range of whiskies, the library laid out with deep red leather armchairs, busts on plinths, and the daily papers, and the exclusive use of the green baize of the billiards and card tables in the games room. But the real attraction was the hushed lounge-cum-dining room, where he could sign in and be entertained and flattered by non-members eager for his attention. The club was the haven in which he could escape from the drab outside world and his wife and daughter for a few hours, and even take a room for the night if the opportunity arose. He could mix with the right sort of people and create a good impression. And he could do business deals in here away from prying eyes and ears.

'The usual, Mr Cooper?' the bar steward asked. 'We've escaped from the office ahead of close of business today, have we, sir?'

'No, not yet, it's a bit too early for the hard stuff,' he replied. 'Even for me. A gin and tonic, if you would. Leave it off my account and put it on a tab just for this evening, though. I'll take it in the dining room.'

Ray took exception to overfamiliarity with members of staff, and drew the line at carrying a drink across the lounge himself. He selected the evening menu from the bar and found a table for two in the corner of the dining room. He pushed out the creases from the cloth and lined up the cutlery and wine glasses perfectly, and awaited his cocktail.

'I told a tradesman I might visit the club this evening,' Ray told the steward. 'If you could let me know if he arrives, I'll sign him in. A Mr Tom Dakin. I'm obliged, thank you.'

'I'll recognise Tom, don't you worry, Mr Cooper. He does plenty of work round town, but I've not seen him inside these premises before. Hardly his sort of place, sir? I'll sign him in for you.'

Ray Cooper put his elbows on the table, closed his eyes, and dropped his face into the palms of his hands. He hoped Tom Dakin would go home and have a wash and change out of his overalls and boots before they met, like he'd told him. They were going to talk serious business and big money, not build a brick wall.

'Just show him in,' Ray said.

Mr Dakin duly arrived at the front door of the Blue Moon and asked if a Mr Cooper had arrived and if he'd mentioned that he was expecting a guest. Wearing polished shoes, a suit and tie, a waistcoat and shirt buttoned tight round his belly, he looked, and felt, out of place.

'Evening, Tom,' said Ray. 'Do join me. What'll you have?'

Tom stood back for the steward to pull his chair out from the table and ran a finger around the inside of his collar.

'Very generous, Mr Cooper, thank you,' said Tom. His mouth felt dry. 'Just a pint of best for now. How's things, and the wife?'

'Never better. And the wife's fine, since you enquire, last time I asked her.'

Tom smiled a wan smile.

'And your daughter?'

Ray chose not to hear that question.

Joyce and her problems were none of his business.

He picked up the menu instead and looked down the main courses.

'Is Planning all hands on deck, Mr Cooper, now the Hunslet scheme is off the ground?' asked Tom. 'Are decisions being made?'

Tom Dakin was far too blunt for Ray Cooper.

'We'll come to that, Tom. No, I've been in the Assizes. Doing me bit for Queen and country, you know how it is. Murder trial.'

'So I've heard,' said Tom. 'And I'd heard they'd wanted you on the jury. Suppose you're not allowed to talk about it, I expect?'

'Tom,' whispered Ray, leaning into him across the table, 'keep your voice down. What's said inside the Moon, stays inside the Moon. Understood?'

Tom nodded then bowed his head slightly and downed half his pint of ale in one swallow. He was lost for words now. Ray glanced from side to side. One or two gentlemen had taken a table each for an early dinner, but nobody he recognised.

'A dumpy cross-eyed scrubber from one of those cramped old terraces built by the railway over in York.'

'They want knocking down.'

'Yes, I'm told the Germans have started the job. Anyway, she gets herself pregnant by the yob next door. He clears off to Preston—'

'Who could blame him?'

'...so she drops it in her bedroom and throws it at the wall.'

'Jesus!'

'A few days later, finishes it off the same way. Flings it at the wall, job done. A right sticky mess.'

'No!' said Tom. 'What's there to talk about?'

'Nowt,' said Ray. 'She's admitted the whole thing. Wrote out a confession.'

'Christ! Will she hang?'

'She will when I've had my say, Tom. This country is going to the dogs. An eye for an eye. The punishment should fit the crime. If you break the law, it must come down on you like a ton of bricks.'

'I couldn't agree with you more, Mr Cooper,' said Tom.

Tom Dakin hadn't been invited to the Blue Moon to discuss crime and punishment, however, and he visibly relaxed when the steward sidled up to their table to take orders for dinner. Mr Dakin declined, telling Ray his pie and mash would be on the table at home at six. Happily, thought Mr Cooper, as he preferred not to be seen dining with a local builder and his tab for the evening would be that bit smaller.

Ray lowered his voice.

'Tom,' he said, 'let me speak to you in the strictest confidence. We've put out a request for tenders to demolish the row of slum houses in Hope Street in Hunslet. Would you be interested in that contract?'

'I would, Mr Cooper. I'm always available.'

'The lowest bid so far is £800 to take them down and clear the site. To start work in March next year. If you come in with a lower bid, that's going to look dodgy, and O'Sullivan will smell a rat. But how about you come in with a slightly higher bid, maybe £820, but say you could start the job by February? I can get that through for you, I reckon. And if there's a bit of slip with the timing, a month or so if you're stuck, they'll swallow that, or probably forget they ever agreed Feb. How does that suit you?'

'Very generous of you, Mr Cooper. That would do me very nicely. And how about a day at York races for your kindness?'

'Look, Tom,' whispered Ray, 'there's probably a lot more work with this slum clearance if things go to plan. And I've got influence, so we can do plenty more business. The missus is wanting an inside toilet. It would save us struggling to get Joyce into her wheelchair for the one outside. Could you see your way to that?'

'I'll see what I can do.'

'No, I think we need the deal a bit more secure than that, Tom. Yes, or no?'

'It's a yes then. Thank you, Mr Cooper.'

They both stood up and shook hands across the table on the deal. Tom picked his pint up, finished the dregs, and put his glass back down on the tablecloth.

'I'll make tracks,' said Tom. 'Good luck with your trial.'

'Thanks,' said Ray. 'Remember, what's said in the Moon goes no further, and get the paperwork to me by Friday.'

'Agreed and understood, Mr Cooper.'

And he left Ray to line up his knife and fork again, put a placemat on the linen over the circle from Tom's pint pot, and eat his fish of the day just with his own thoughts for company.

Twenty-Three

Olive heard the telltale squeak of the hinge on Dennis's back bedroom door, followed by the creak of the floorboard in the couple of steps from his bedroom to hers and the slow turn of her door handle. She rolled over from her back to face into the wall and closed her eyes. The early mail train had thundered past the gates about an hour ago. She tried not to think that she had to pull on some smart clothes and get herself all the way to Leeds. She couldn't even get out of bed.

Sleep was a luxury of the past. She hadn't slept for two nights now, not since the day before the trial began. She'd heard all the news from Charlie, then brought Mary across a bowl of soup in the early evening and got her settled down to sleep. Olive stayed over in Ethel's bed most nights now so she could turn Mary during the night, help her use the bedpan if she needed it, and rub the cramps in her legs.

Olive knew in her heart that Mary wasn't going to live for much longer now. She just hoped she could cling on to comfort her Ethel again. She was forever telling Mary that she had visited Ethel in jail as often as they would let her, and that her daughter was bearing up. Last night Mary had been desperate to hear about the first day in court. Did our Ethel look frightened? Was she crying? Would Olive take her to court in the morning, please, so she could be in the same room as her daughter? She'd pleaded with Olive, surely all the serious, clever judges would see that Ethel could never hurt a baby, wouldn't they? Olive had done her level best to calm Mary's fears. She had told her as much about the trial as Charlie dared tell her: that there was nothing for her to worry about, that Mr Joyce was on her side, and that Eddie had spoken up for her. But not that her husband had listened to every word from the public gallery and feared the worst.

Olive and Dennis had known each other for as long as she could remember. They had played together when they were snotty little kids in the terrace, just as Ethel and Eddie had done. Dennis had told Olive that he'd married Mary only because he had to; she was in the family way with Ethel; and Olive then told Dennis that she'd married Charlie only because he was comfortable. Their greedy sex together had started after they'd shared these confidences. She thought that Mary's illness had killed what little there had been of their marriage, and any feelings Olive had for Charlie had ebbed away slowly when she never fell pregnant. Love of sex was the only thing she thought she had in common with Dennis. It had seemed to be free before baby William died, but now it came with too big a price tag to pay.

Dennis had already left the house for the evening by the time Olive arrived from over the road. He had rolled back in some time after midnight. She'd heard the kettle whistling and smelt his cigarette smoke down in the kitchen. She'd felt the icy draught from the yard when he went out to check on his pigeons last thing. He'd crashed up the stairs to his own bed soon after, slammed his bedroom door shut, and was snoring within minutes. Olive knew this routine well, and what was to come when he had sobered up in the morning.

Olive had no hope. Yesterday had been a day of unbearable tension, but today threatened to bring new terrors all of its own. The day about to dawn was Olive's private torment in the witness box. A policeman had delivered the summons into her hand some weeks ago. What would they make me say about Ethel, she thought, and what's even worse, about myself? They might ask her what secrets Ethel had told her. Had Ethel told the police she'd seen her own father humping Olive like a whore up against the wall in the snicket? Please God, that wouldn't come out for all the world to hear. How could she look at pitiful Ethel in the dock, a prisoner in a cage? How could she face her ever again? How could she face today at all?

The mattress sagged as Dennis turned down the blanket and settled along her back. She froze. She felt his hand brush across her belly from behind, then his palm move up to rub gently over her nipple. She was aware of his erection nestling between her buttocks.

'Dennis, no,' she said to the wall.

He parted the hair on the nape of her neck with his nose and planted a kiss, then squeezed her breast and pulled her into him.

'Don't.' She looked at the craze of cracks in the plaster.

His reply was to reach through the gap between her thighs and lift the strength of his hairy forearm up firmly against her vulva, then pin her against the wall.

'No, Dennis,' she said, and wriggled free to lie on her back.

'C'mon,' whispered Dennis. 'Mary won't be awake; it's not seven yet. Come on top. We can be as quiet as mice.'

She turned her face to his and got the smell of stale beer from last night and his first cigarette of the day.

'I mean it. I said no, Dennis. Not anymore.'

He eased back onto his edge of the bed and looked at her eyes.

'Fuck me,' he said. 'You've changed your tune. What's up wi' yer?'

'Your grandson died in this bed, Dennis.'

'Or on the floor at the end of it,' he replied.

Olive moved back away so that no skin of hers was touching his, leant into the corner of the wall, and pulled the blanket up over her breasts and shoulders.

'What did you just say?' she said.

Dennis hoisted himself up against the headboard, lit his second cigarette from the packet, and took a long, deep draw.

Olive watched him inspect the flame burn down the match for a few seconds then blow it out.

'Do you reckon she killed 'er baby then?' she asked.

'What do you think?' returned Dennis.

'Course she didn't.'

'I meant, do you know what I think?'

Olive gave him a quizzical look.

'No, I don't, now you ask me,' she said. 'Tell me.'

'I know she didn't, for a fact.'

'How?'

She took a close look at his face, the thick black tousled hair spoilt by a night's stubble. He scared her now. There were so many things about Dennis that she didn't know, or like.

'Our Ethel could never thump anybody, she's not got it in 'er. That's how I know,' he replied. 'Never.'

'You could 'ave told her you knew that, you cruel bastard.'

'Well, I 'ave,' said Dennis. 'I've visited 'er in jail an' told 'er.'

'My oh my,' Olive whispered at him. 'Your gob stinks, but maybe you're not all bastard after all, eh?'

He dropped his cigarette onto the floorboards, rolled towards her in the corner, and took hold of her chin.

'I wanted to adopt that baby for me an' Charlie,' she told him.

'So I'd 'eard. Well, nobody's got it now, have they? So there's nowt stood in our way.'

He took hold of the blanket at her neck.

'No, I meant no, Dennis,' she said. 'It's too difficult now.'

She had to kill this affair, stone dead, and she'd worked out how she could do it with a simple lie.

'Charlie's rumbled us,' she said. 'He's found a packet of your johnnies in my handbag. I reckon he must 'ave wondered for a long time; everybody else 'as.'

And you've left them in there, you stupid cow, thought Dennis. Charlie might be dumb, but he could handle himself; one more jealous husband's fist to duck.

He slid off the bed, drew the curtains, and, standing naked at the window, looked up and down the terrace. First light was breaking. The trains were pulling into the station every few minutes now, the shunting had started for the day in the sheds, and clouds of steam were starting to puff over the gates into the street. Olive found some knickers and a bra in Ethel's chest of drawers and peered into the mirror. She rolled a finger over cheekbones under dark careworn eyes, but she knew she still had the face and thick glossy hair that could turn men's heads. She picked her best shapely dress for the day from a bag, then came downstairs to find Dennis in shirt and pants out at his loft in the yard.

'I'll try get some porridge down Mary an' get 'er dressed,' she called out of the door, 'then I'll say mornin' to Charlie and get on the train back to Leeds. I said I'd take Mary too.'

Dennis ignored her.

He'd forgotten it was her day in court.

Keeping pigeons fed and happy was a lot easier than working out women.

Twenty-Four

Justice Weaver lived for the cut and thrust of a battle of wits. He liked to think of his beloved courtroom as a chessboard, and of the barristers and their juniors and solicitors as his rooks, bishops, and knights. The witness box down to his right was the square on the board for all the dispensable pawns to be lined up one after another. He enjoyed watching the match play out over the few days of a trial, when his chessmen lulled pawns into a safe, cosy position with a raft of soft, easy questions, only for an opponent to knock them off the board with a quick, devastating swipe.

He rarely gave these pawns much attention, but the first witness this morning was an exception. She caught his eye as she tripped down the aisle at the start of play and mounted the few small steps into the box. She wore the gaudy, cheap clothes of her type, but she walked with the poise of a woman of his own class. Olive Songhirst, ruminated Justice Weaver, had the hourglass figure, the thick, lustrous, auburn hair, the chiselled face and the piercing blue eyes that were sadly lacking in Mrs Weaver.

Olive stood erect in the witness box and swore to Almighty God that she would tell the whole truth, with no such intention. The truth out in the open would cause far more damage than all the lies she had told, and lived, already. She would speak up for Ethel given the chance, certainly, but she must keep her long affair with Dennis hidden and save her marriage at all costs. Kind, dull Charlie would never recover if it hit him that the love of his life had been taken by Dennis Slater in any bed they could find and even in the snicket, and whenever he was out of the way. And she did love her husband in a queer sort of way. Hearing the gossip coming true that had smouldered behind her back in the terrace for years would finish off her oldest friend Mary. And the judge might find it easier to pass a heavier sentence on a woman if he could see that her father and her only real friend were such cowardly lowlife.

'Tell me, Mrs Songhirst,' asked Mr Cox, 'would you say you were on friendly terms with the Slater family? Good neighbours?'

'Yes,' she replied. 'Everybody looks out for each other down the terrace.'

'I understand you've been friends for a good many years. Please tell the court how you came to know the accused and her parents.'

'We go way back,' Olive continued. 'Me an' Dennis were kids down the terrace, an' Mary and me were on the Kit-Kat line at Rowntrees. We'd go dancin' the three of us an' meet up at the Regent in the middle of York before the war. Charlie and Dennis knew each other from the darts team at the Legion, an' Charlie started comin' to the Regent as well. Charlie an' me struck up together an' got wed, then he served his time in the sheds an' got a job at the carriage works. We got one o' them houses let out by the railway at the bottom end of the terrace. Anyway, Dennis's folks in the house opposite died soon after. And Mary moved in with Dennis after their Ethel came along.'

Olive's features relaxed. What had she been so worried about?

'So it's fair to say that you've lived opposite Dennis and Mary Slater and their daughter for all the years of Ethel's life. But I understand from another good neighbour that this has changed a bit over the last few months, since Ethel is no longer living at home in fact. Do you sleep in Ethel's bed now in the room next to her father?'

Nosy cow.

Olive Songhirst hated the old gossip's tiny mind that went with her tidy house. Now that her Eddie had sown his seed and left home, the old bitch next door had nothing to do but sit in her chair in the window, ease her curtain aside, and watch the comings and goings of Olive and Dennis. Nothing, but nothing, escaped Mrs Sath.

'I do stay over sometimes to see to Mary, that's true,' said Olive. 'She's bedridden now. She needs feedin' and turnin'.'

'And her husband's needs?'

The question floored Olive.

The guilty memory of noisy sex with Ethel's father in Ethel's bed and in her paralysed mother's earshot flashed through her mind.

'Do you see to him too, Mrs Songhirst?'

'He can fend for himself,' replied Olive.

She could feel her husband's stare from the public gallery and fixed her eyes ahead on Mr Cox.

He just let her answer hang in the air. Perhaps a moment's hesitation in the witness' reply, perhaps the hush that fell in the public gallery, had given their little game away. The jury and the judge, Mr Cox knew, would come to their own conclusions. He need say no more.

Mr Joyce hauled himself to his feet. 'Your Honour,' he said, 'I can't see how these neighbourly domestic arrangements are of any relevance to the case.'

'Maybe, maybe not,' Justice Weaver replied. Envy of Dennis Slater and the vision of a warm, naked Olive Songhirst had flooded his brain. 'Anyway, change the subject, please, Mr Cox.'

'Let me take you to Dennis and Mary's daughter,' Mr Cox continued. 'Would Miss Slater confide in you, would you say? Tell you her worries? Did she talk to you about her baby?'

'Yes, she did. She'd allus come to me when summat was up. She'd bob across through the day quite often if 'er mum was badly.'

'But to talk about her poorly mother, not so much about her new baby on the way?'

'She did tell me when she found out she was expectin', I remember that.'

'And did she ask your advice about where she should have the baby, how to look after a new baby, where she could live with a baby, how she could get money out of the father? Did she talk to you about her baby at all?'

'She was scared more than anythin' else, I think,' said Olive. 'She just worried about her mum. Her mum is the only person in her life.'

'But you did talk together about the baby, didn't you? Did she ask you to write a letter to her aunt about the baby?'

'No.'

Olive shook her head.

Mr Cox turned to the jury.

'Ladies and gentlemen, a pack of lies,' he said. 'We know that Ethel Slater and this witness plotted and schemed. Slater didn't plan for this baby because she knew it wouldn't have a life of its own. That's all she really wanted, an end of it. And that's the reason she asked this neighbour to write to an aunt in Rochdale. So she could get away from violent men and wagging tongues. And get rid of the baby where nobody even knew she was pregnant. You wrote to Annie Lofthouse in Rochdale to arrange a backstreet abortion. Isn't that the truth, Mrs Songhirst?'

'Never! I never did that.'

'Never,' screamed Ethel from the dock, jumping forward at the rail.

'Sit down, be quiet, or I'll have you taken down,' the judge shouted up to the dock.

'Is this your writing, Mrs Songhirst?' continued Mr Cox, and had the clerk pass a letter up to the witness box.'

'Yes, I did write it.'

'Read out the words for us, please.'

'Dear Annie, ar Ethels in the family way and Dennis as teken agenst it. Can she stay at the junction pleese

*to sort evrything out? You always know whats for
the best with babies.'*

'And can you confirm that you posted this letter to
Annie Lofthouse, landlady of The Junction public house
in Rochdale, and that Ethel Slater took herself off to live
there and escape?'

Olive's reply that these were Mary's words written in
Olive's hand was drowned and lost in the emotions in the
room. The words backstreet abortion had struck both fear
and disgust in most hearts and minds. Fear, at the spectre
of dark practices with knitting needles, pumps, and soapy
water; and disgust, that Ethel and her friend could have
sunk so low as to seek out the services of an abortionist.

Olive's worst fears had been realised. Horror on her
husband's face in the gallery, confirmed in his suspicions
that his wife had done far more for Ethel and her father
than any good neighbour should; surprise in the judge's
expression, that such an attractive woman could possibly
be involved in such a crime; and smug satisfaction on the
face of Ray Cooper. Why else would a slut who found
herself pregnant take herself to a place like Rochdale, if
it wasn't to get rid of the baby? It all made perfect sense.

'Mrs Songhirst,' said Mr Cox, 'a final easy question for
you. Would you say you were Miss Slater's closest friend,
perhaps?'

'I think so,' she whispered. 'I'd do anything to help her
if I could.'

'Yes, quite so,' he said. 'We can all see that.'

*

'Mrs Songhirst,' Mr Joyce said as he rose to his feet, 'tell us this, do you feel a mother's love for babies?'

'I wouldn't know,' Olive said.

'Is Ethel Slater the daughter you never had?'

'She is, sir. We were never blessed with children of our own.'

She hesitated, then stole a glance at the judge.

'Some things are meant not to be, Your Honour.'

'Well, there's our reason Miss Slater couldn't ask you how to have one,' Mr Joyce continued. 'But did she talk to you about a mother-and-baby home called Albany House?'

'She told me all about it. The vicar drove 'er there. They wanted 'er to stay an' 'ave the baby and then give 'im away for adoption.'

'Do you know why that never happened?'

'Because the place scared 'er out of 'er wits. An' she'd never let anybody take her baby away. She wanted 'im all to herself, nobody else.'

'And were you aware that Ethel refused to sign an adoption paper for a couple in Leeds?'

'No, she din't tell me that.'

'I have the adoption paper here, Your Honour. An agreement made by the vicar Gerald Pearson with a Mr and Mrs Richard Petty in Leeds who wanted to adopt a baby. The space for Miss Slater's name is left blank.'

'Mrs Songhirst,' Mr Joyce said. 'What would you say to the suggestion that Ethel Slater turned down both these offers of adoption because she knew the baby wouldn't live? Because she intended to kill her baby at birth.'

'No, that's not true, it's wrong,' said Olive, 'because Ethel wanted to keep that baby for 'er own. She'd never 'ave let 'im go.'

'Would you have adopted that baby?'

'If only…'

'If only, Mrs Songhirst?'

'If only our Ethel hadn't needed 'im so badly for 'erself.'

*

Justice Weaver held a helping hand out across the bench to guide Olive back down to the well of the court but withdrew it the second he realised his error. He watched this pawn glide back up the aisle without so much as a sideways glance to the gallery and out through the exit, the sway of her buttocks, the curve of her ankles, the shining hair falling away down her neck.

Mr Cox might have holed your marriage below the waterline, he said to himself, but he wasn't sure that Mr Joyce had repaired enough damage to save his client's life.

Twenty-Five

Justice Weaver felt mildly amused and couldn't help but smile. He had an uninterrupted view of the shape of his next witness down to his right.

'Please be seated and feel free to remove your hat if you wish,' he told Mrs Sathersthwaite.

Aggie Sath's shoes, ankles, coat and waist remained hidden from the rest of the court by the front oak panel of the witness box, but her head and shoulders stood bristling and proud. Her fixed, thin smile disguised the fact that she was terrified.

She chose not to look up at the judge, remove her hat, or sit down. Her customary dark blue felt bonnet with grey knitted rose was fastened securely to her bun and she knew it would have required some time and effort to dismantle. Extracting hatpins was a task performed last thing every night and she would have felt naked during daylight hours without her hat. And had she taken the chair behind her, her view over the top of her spectacles would have been restricted to the public gallery up in front of her.

The clerk instructed her to swear an oath on the Bible and tell the court her full name, date of birth and address.

'Agnes Emmeline Sathersthwaite, 25th December 1903, 15 St Paul's Terrace. Down near the railway station in York,' she replied.

Ethel in the dock felt relief that the neighbour she'd once feared so much would surely now speak up for her. Her father in the public gallery behind her could barely suppress a chuckle when he heard Mrs Sath's full name. He'd never found anything even remotely amusing about her before; and he guessed that the old cow must have spent her life looking out for Olive arriving with his dinner on a plate, then craning her neck to hear the rocking and the squeaking of Ethel's bed through the wall an hour or so later. He did feel disappointed, though, not to see the old woman remove her hat for once. Mr Waggett in the front row just hoped he would witness Mrs Sath in the same great form as her right hook that had floored Ethel in his shop a few months ago.

Mr Cox aimed to put his witness at her ease and disarm her.

'Mrs Sathersthwaite,' he said, 'have you lived at number 15 St Paul's Terrace for a long time?'

'For ever.'

'That is a long time.'

'Yes, sir,' she said. 'I was born on Christmas Day in that 'ouse in the back bedroom overlookin' the yard—'

'The second coming?'

She ignored a belly laugh from the public gallery.

'…The 'ouse 'as been in't family since it were built, donkey's years, a century ago, when the railway came. Grandad were a train driver; he came down from Durham way; then Dad worked in the railway offices.'

'And I understand that you are widowed and have a son, but he has recently moved away?'

'My 'usband, Bill,' continued Mrs Sath, 'worked 'is way right up to the top. He was manager of the sack department at the station by t'time he finished. He got early retirement on account of 'is shrapnel wound, and he'd not been left long when he was taken sudden like on 'is allotment. He was a good man. He deserved more time an' we 'ad no warnin".'

'And your son, Edward? Why has he left you to live alone?'

'He said he 'ad to get away from folk next door for a while. He went over to Preston to stay with an old pal from 'is army days till he could come back 'ome when the bother had blown over.'

She pushed her spectacles back up to the bridge of her nose so she could get a clear view of her son's face in the public gallery. Eddie gazed back at her in disbelief and shook his head gently from side to side. What the daft old bugger has just said, he thought, is news to me. She hadn't got a clue. And he had a good idea what Mr Cox's next question would be.

'And what might that bother have been, Mrs Sathersthwaite, and how and when did you think it might, as you put it, blow over?'

She had no ready answer to this question. She looked up to Eddie in the gallery for help. He held his breath.

Once he had managed to escape from the clutches of his mother, he had no intention ever of coming back to live at home again. He had outgrown her fussing, her cleaning of the windows, her scrubbing of the step, her beating of the carpets; and seen through her carping and bitterness and spite and backbiting. If there was one thing he had learned from his time in National Service, it was that the world was bigger than St Paul's Terrace. There was nothing to keep him at home anymore, and Ethel's mistake had been the final push.

'Mrs Sathersthwaite,' the judge said, 'you must answer the question.'

'Ethel next door was 'avin' my Eddie's baby,' she replied.

'So the bother was a baby on the way that nobody wanted. Is that correct?'

'Folk allus thought that Eddie would marry Ethel, but Bill an' me knew that my Eddie could do a lot better for 'imself than settlin' for 'er.'

'Sin and shame made you punch Ethel Slater in her shop and argue with her father in his butcher's shop. You got her the sack, didn't you?'

'Look 'ere, it's like this,' Mrs Sath said. 'She'd led my Eddie astray. She got nowt worse than what she 'ad comin' to her. But I must say, I do regret it now.'

'And so when the bother had blown over, you supposed your son would come back home with his tail between his legs as if nothing had happened. What did you think would get rid of the problem? An adoption, perhaps, or even an abortion?'

'Go away; I thought nowt o' t'sort. To tell you God's honest truth, I just thought she'd 'ave it then bring it up at 'er mum's next door, same as when Dennis got Mary pregnant. An' then try badgerin' my Eddie for maintenance.'

'Mrs Sathersthwaite,' Mr Cox said, 'I see from the house plans that you sleep on the other side of the party wall from Ethel Slater's bedroom. Do you sometimes hear commotion through the wall from next door, voices, shouts, banging, knocking?'

Any lingering fear Mrs Sath had for the court evaporated with this question. She liked nothing more than an open invitation to talk about herself, and here was a glorious opportunity to put a knife into those neighbours who didn't live up to her standards. She had genuine sympathy for her old invalid friend Mary, the more so because she had to live with a revolting man who had abused her since the day they had married. But she'd been given permission to unleash years of pent-up anger. She tucked a ringlet of hair back under the brim of her hat, settled on Dennis Slater's face in the public gallery, and launched her revenge.

'Yes, I do, now you ask.' She raised her voice. 'I've 'ad years of that man shoutin' the odds from next door. He shouts at Mary, knocks 'er about when he's in drink, and then clears off an' leaves the poor woman to fend for 'erself. She's bedbound, for pity's sake. An' he's played around wi' mucky women for as long as I've known 'im. An' the rowin' got worse after the poor baby was born. Shoutin' at Ethel and slammin' doors. An' now the baby's gone and he 'as the run of the 'ouse to 'imself, he brings in that trollop from over the road. You should see the state of 'er 'ouse. She brings 'is tea and stays over, and Lord knows what they get up to in Ethel's bed. His poor wife listenin' downstairs.'

Dennis's head rocked backwards, as if dealt a blow.

'You bitch!' he bawled at the witness box.

He leapt to his feet and stormed along the row of bodies in the gallery.

'You think I'm daft, don't you?!' Mrs Sath hurled her abuse after him as he made for the door. 'An' nobody knows your little games?! Well, they do now!'

Mr Waggett leaned forward to the rail, clasping his hands. This was the just the fight he had hoped to see. Aggie Sath at her finest.

'Mrs Sathersthwaite,' said the judge, 'that is all very interesting.' He flicked back a page in his notebook and drew a circle round the words '*Olive Songhirst*'. 'But you must restrict yourself to answering the questions.'

Mrs Sath thought she had done exactly that and was stunned into silence.

'Let me take you back to the 8th of February this year, if I may, the day Miss Slater gave birth,' Mr Cox resumed. 'Did you hear noises from her room through your bedroom wall in the early hours of the morning?'

'I'll never forget it. I 'eard t'poor lass thump on the wall. It woke me up with a start. It were still pitch black. To tell you the truth, at first off I thought Mary must 'ave died.'

'Tell me exactly what you heard, Mrs Sathersthwaite.'

'I've just told you, lad. I 'eard Ethel thump on the wall.'

'You heard a thump? One thump, or several?'

'Might 'ave been several. I were fast asleep. One woke me up.'

'One crash?'

'I 'eard 'er thump the wall, for God's sake. 'Ave you got cloth ears or what?'

Mr Cox looked to the bench for guidance. The judge's head was bent forwards as he scribbled his words in his notebook, but Mr Cox could see that he was smiling to himself.

Eddie looked over the ledge into the well of the court at the two women in his life. At Aggie Sath, a lonely old woman who was despised and avoided by almost everybody that knew her. Eddie was ashamed of his mother and scared of her when she was in this frame of mind. He knew that she would plough through anybody that stood in her way, and her vicious loose tongue in the next few minutes could strip Ethel of any hope she might have had. And he had a clear view of the back of Ethel's head as she slumped forward over the rail in the dock, her lank brown hair falling over sagging shoulders. Today was the first time since their childhood games in the bombed house he'd felt the need to protect her from the world. She was lost and harmless.

'I can hear you perfectly well,' Mr Cox resumed. 'How did you know it was Ethel who thumped the wall?'

Mrs Sath blew out through pursed lips. 'Because it's her bedroom, and she slept by herself.'

'But there were two people in that room, weren't there, Mrs Sathersthwaite? There was Ethel, and a baby.'

'Sorry?'

'Can you be certain it was Ethel's fist that woke you up, and not the baby's head thrown at the wall? Can you be sure?'

She shifted on her feet, looked back at Mr Cox, and frowned.

'I suppose not, no,' she said.

'What did you do?'

'I flew downstairs, grabbed my handbag off the side, and let meself in next door. It were dark still, an' frosty; I slipped on me step an' nearly went, I remember that. Their electric was off. I looked in on Mary off the hallway. Her fire was glowin' and she was awake lyin' flat out in bed. She were prayin', I think. Dennis's door were open so I knew he weren't in. Ethel 'adn't closed 'er curtains and the lamp outside was enough for 'er room. She were slumped in the corner with 'er back against the wall propped up against 'er bed. She looked as white as a sheet.'

'Why?'

'Gawd 'elp us,' Mrs Sath said, 'she'd just 'ad her baby, 'adn't she? And my Eddie's. He were bonny, the spit of my Eddie, same nose, same chin.'

'And where was he, the baby I mean?'

'He were on the floorboards. It looked like a dog's dinner, splattered, like summat out of 'er dad's shop. I must be honest, I thought he were dead to start off; he didn't move a muscle.'

'Was he injured?'

'How would I know? Don't be daft. He were covered in blood an' slime.'

'What did you do?'

'What do you expect? His cord 'ad snapped an' one end were tangled round 'is neck an' oozin' blood. I unwrapped it an' tied that off sharpish, then picked 'im up an' wrapped 'im in my nightie. Then gave 'im to Ethel.'

Ray Cooper shuddered and shut his eyes. Her words had cut deep. A tangled cord had wrecked his own life.

'So you were stark naked then?'

'I took Ethel's coat off from the back of the door. It were freezin' in there. He seemed to warm up a bit, anyroad, an' I rubbed 'im in me nightie, an' he wriggled an' opened his eyes an' cried. It 'it me then like a train, it was my Eddie born all over again.'

Few in the public gallery knew that Aggie Sath could ever shed a tear, but they all witnessed it now. Her voice cracked as she tried to speak. She paused to take a clean handkerchief from her handbag, pushed her spectacles back up again, and blew her nose, then folded her handkerchief carefully and tucked it under the end of her sleeve.

'I'm sorry,' she whispered, 'he was beautiful.'

Mr Cox needed to show Mrs Sath's bad temper to the jury, though, not soft, sentimental tears.

'Let me take you forward a few days to the end of that short life, Mrs Sathersthwaite. Noises from next door woke you again on the 12th of February, didn't they?'

'Yes, I was fast asleep again. Then Ethel started screamin'. She must 'ave woke the whole street up, howlin' and bawlin'. I'd never 'eard owt like it, and I don't mind sayin' I don't ever want to 'ear owt like it again. She sounded like a wild animal. I'd no idea what it was this time. All I could think of was 'er father must 'ave killed Mary.'

'Did you hear the thump on the wall again?'

'Yes, I did. The wall shook.'

'But Dennis hadn't hit anybody again, had he? What did you find?'

'Ethel was sat on 'er bed in 'er nightie holdin' William, like cradlin' 'im an' rocking backwards and forwards and sobbin' and wailin'. Poor little mite was drip white, an' he 'ad a bit o' blood on 'is face. I took William off Ethel an' 'eld 'im, but he'd gone. I just ran up the street to Reverend Pearson's to get 'im to fetch an ambulance.'

Mrs Sath broke down once more and buried the spectacles at the end of her nose in her handkerchief again.

'Mrs Sathersthwaite, two short questions for you,' Mr Cox said. 'Was there anything else that you didn't expect to see in Ethel's bedroom?'

'Yes, there was, there was the teddy bear and wrappin' paper thrown on the floor by the bed.'

'Now remember you're sworn to tell the truth. I'll ask you this for a second time. Can you be sure it was a fist and not a head that hit the wall? Twice?'

Mrs Sath shook her head and wept.

*

Eddie could see from the shock on the jurors' faces just how much damage his mother's tongue had done to Ethel's chances.

Mr Joyce rose to his feet.

'Mrs Sathersthwaite,' he said, 'Mr Cox has made you cry in court. Did you weep alone with Ethel Slater too?'

'We wept with joy after he was born, and we wept with grief after he died.'

'Did you help out with William on the days in between?'

'I took 'im out in 'is little pram whenever I could. Every day. I showed 'im off, I suppose. He was my Eddie's.'

'Did Miss Slater mind? Did she push you away?'

'No, she doted on 'im. She was all in, exhausted, but I think she'd got the only thing she ever really wanted. And 'er baby was a little bit of me too.'

Twenty-Six

The judge retired to his office behind the courtroom, unlocked the wall cabinet and took out his crystal decanter, poured himself just a small sherry as it was still quite early in the day, sat behind his desk, and kicked both his shoes off. He opened his notebook and licked the pulp of his fat thumb, then began to peel back through his notes on the trial with a vague sense of loss. Today was the last day for the prosecution, and it was probably the penultimate day of his long but not particularly distinguished career. Mrs Weaver had begun to pack their suitcases before he left for work. They were bound for Southampton in a couple of days' time to pick up their cruise.

He always enjoyed the prosecution more than the defence. His old friend Dr Lawson had put on a creditable last show for him, even though he was possibly slightly out of his depth. Mr Cox had been his usual theatrical self, and the skull had been a nice touch. All today had on offer was the last prosecution witness, the landlady of a grubby backstreet pub in Rochdale and no doubt a wizened gin-soaked old hag, and then the defence would open their case. The accused looked to be a miserable, cross-eyed specimen, thought the judge, who wouldn't put up much of a fight. Then they had some upstart doctor drafted in from miles away. He hoped he could wrap all that up by end of play today, then in the morning he could rattle through the closing speeches and summing up before he sent the jury out to decide. He couldn't see them taking more than an hour. Justice Weaver rarely guessed a verdict wrong. With luck he would have wrapped everything up by noon tomorrow. He had only ever sentenced one female to hang, a coarse, thickset woman who had stabbed her husband to death, and whose name he had forgotten. Mr Joyce could possibly launch an appeal in due course, but that was no concern of his. He would be dining at the captain's table on the *Queen Mary* by then.

The highlight of the case had undoubtedly been Olive Songhirst. The judge had drawn a box around her name on the page with his pen. Why, oh why, reflected the judge, had Mrs Weaver never had a body like hers, even when she was in her prime? He closed his notebook with a pleasing thud, took his robes from the peg and made for the courtroom door. He expected little of his last full day in power. Rochdale had never been on his list of holiday destinations.

The court rose as one as the judge made his entrance. He nodded the slightest of bows to the court before lowering himself onto his seat, pleased that at least Mr Cox's last witness was a woman. Yet again reality far exceeded his expectations. She looked, he thought on first impression, as if she was about to pull a pint of best in the witness box. She had the common lined face and thick vulgar lipstick he would want in a landlady, plus some bulk barely concealed by tight clothing and a cleavage to match. Justice Weaver wrote down the name of Annie Lofthouse at the top of the last page in his notebook, and drew his customary box round it.

'Mrs Lofthouse,' said Mr Cox, 'I understand that you are the landlady of The Junction Inn in Rochdale, and you live there with your husband and children. Is that correct?'

'Yes, that's right, love,' she replied. 'And I could really do wi' bein' back there for openin' time if you could see your way to it.'

'Well, we can only do our best,' Mr Cox said.

This woman is a straight-talker, thought the judge. He nodded his approval to Mr Cox.

'How many children live in the pub with you, Mrs Lofthouse?'

'Ee, you've started with a crackin' good question, love. I lose track meself sometimes. I've got Sadie, Colin, and Ada for the present. An' there's our Raymond just turned fifteen now, an' he comes an' goes as he pleases. I've sometimes a job on to know if he's stayin' with us or with his gran. Sadie's me youngest. She'll be eight in a few weeks' time.'

'And you've other children as well, haven't you? Have they left home now?'

'Yes, they have, thank the Lord. Not that I don't love 'em, don't get me wrong. An' they've not moved far. It's just jugglin' beds for 'em all can be a problem. The pub's only got four bedrooms at a push so we 'ave to double up.

There's Ann an' our Molly, and Molly's a young 'un of her own now. We 'ave 'im to stay over an' all if Molly's stuck for a sitter. She's on her own, you see.'

'Have you lost any children, Mrs Lofthouse?'

'Blimey, I 'ave, love,' she replied. 'How on earth did you know that? There was little Flo. She died of scarlet fever the same week the war ended. An' she were born the same week it started.'

'And I believe you've a sister a couple of years older than yourself. Is that correct?'

'By, you 'ave done your 'omework, 'aven't you, lad? Yes, Mary, our Ethel's mum. We 'ad a brother too, Reg, a good few years younger than the both of us. He was a bomber pilot. We lost 'im in a raid over Berlin in 1944.'

There was nothing Annie liked more than talking about family. She could tell that Mr Cox was a nice man, who had taken an interest in her children. She'd taken to him. This was going well. She raised her hand in a friendly wave to Ethel facing her in the dock and gave her a smile.

'Mr Cox, please,' interrupted the judge, 'this is all very homely, but where is it all taking us? Please get to the point as soon as you can.'

'Very well, m'lord,' Mr Cox said. 'Mrs Lofthouse, tell the jury if you would. With The Junction full of children and short on beds, how did you find room for Ethel Slater over Christmas last year?'

'There was bother back at home in York. She's family.'

'What kind of bother?'

'I'd probably best not say.'

'I'll make things easy for you, Mrs Lofthouse. The police seized several letters from Miss Slater's handbag after her baby died. I have here one that was addressed to yourself at The Junction Inn in Rochdale and posted from St Paul's Terrace. Be so good as to read it out to the court, please.'

Annie believed things were always better said face to face than written down. She remembered meeting Ethel off the train at the station last Christmas, but she'd not seen the letter since. She took the folded scrap of paper from the clerk and put it down on the ledge in front of her while she rummaged around in her handbag for her spectacles.

'*Dear Annie*,' she read to the court in a slow, stumbling voice, '*ar Ethels in the family way and Dennis as teken agenst it. Can she stay at the junction pleese to sort evrything out? You always know whats for the best with babies.*'

'Do you recognise this letter?'

'Yes, I do remember it now.'

'Who wrote it, do you know?'

'Mary. Or at least she probably 'ad Olive write it down for her, I reckon. Our Mary's badly.'

'Your sister, you think, Ethel's mother? And did you try to sort everything out, Mrs Lofthouse?'

Annie hadn't read anything much into Mary's letter, and she didn't understand the question. Of course she'd taken Ethel in and looked after her and the baby in her womb. That's what families are for; everybody knew that. She had to get her out of Dennis's way. He'd started to hit his wife when Ethel was a noisy new baby in their cluttered little house, and there was nobody at home now to stop him doing the same to his daughter, or even to a baby.

'Of course I did,' she replied. 'I'm her auntie, for God's sake. Of course I looked after 'er.'

'But that's not what this letter had asked you to do, is it? You'd been asked to sort out the baby, not look after Ethel Slater.'

What? Same difference, thought Annie.

'You have not been entirely truthful with us, have you, Mrs Lofthouse?'

'Claptrap! I'd never lie to you, lad,' she said. 'I've told you the God's honest truth.'

'Well, I'm not so sure about that. I understand from your sister Mary's statement that you spent some time in hospital in 1947. You've told us that you lost just the one child little Flo through scarlet fever. But what took you into hospital after the war? Had you just lost another baby then?'

Annie hesitated and fumbled with the letter on the ledge.

'I 'ad a miscarriage, that's true. It's not summat I like to brood on, though.'

'But tough women like you don't go to hospital with a miscarriage. They just knuckle down and get on with things. I suggest to you that you had a termination, an abortion, an abortion that went wrong, septic. You had a pub full of children; the last thing you needed was another mouth to feed. Is that the truth of it, Mrs Lofthouse? Sorting the baby out, that's what this letter meant, isn't it? Get it aborted. What better place to send a pregnant girl than to the backstreets of Rochdale to an old hand like you?'

'Nay, lad,' Annie said. 'I've never 'eard owt so daft in me life. It's insultin'. I love my babies more than life itself.'

A knowing smile crept over Ray Cooper's face. He sat back on his jury bench and looked up to the ceiling. He could see that Annie's last few words were hollow. He'd seen the scowl on this seedy old landlady's face as she dropped her gaze onto the letter and fiddled with her handbag when the questions had changed from cosy family life to backstreet abortion. Olive Songhirst had admitted to the court, or as good as, that she'd written the letter to ask for an abortion, and Ethel's auntie had just told them that she could arrange one. What more did they need to hear? Surely, he said to himself, any more witnesses are a waste of everybody's time.

'Mrs Lofthouse, were all your babies born at home, at The Junction in Rochdale?' Mr Cox continued.

'Yes, they were, lad. I 'ad a nurse there, a midwife, for the first one or two, but then Vera from the corner shop 'elped out with the others. Sadie were born wi' no-one else there, in front of the fire. I didn't even wake Albert, she came so quick.'

'Vera is a friend you trust?'

'Wi' me life, love. She's 'ad plenty of 'er own, mind you. She knows what she's doin'. She's a grand lass. She 'elps out behind the bar anytime I'm stuck. She can turn 'er 'and to anythin'.'

'Were you anxious with the first one? Things can go wrong, can't they?'

'I were a bit worried, love, I must admit. Any young mother is, but things generally work out.'

Annie understood Mr Cox's little game now and didn't like what she could see. These questions were taking aim at Ethel really, not herself. She was being led into a trap, down a blind alley, and there was nothing she could do about it.

'And you took in Miss Slater, a young mother-to-be, and under your wing in The Junction. A mother hen. Was she nervous, do you think?'

'Ethel were more worried about 'er mum copin' on 'er own back in the terrace than givin' birth, I reckon. She's selfless, is our Ethel. That's why she's in the mess she is. I tried to tell 'er that Mary was safe in Olive's 'ands. She weren't so much nervous, to be honest wi' yer, as scared out of 'er wits. She must 'ave known all hell were goin' to break loose back at 'ome with a bairn. She buried 'er 'ead in the sand. Wouldn't talk about it. But at The Junction she just served in the tap room an' mucked in. She's a good worker. The regulars liked 'er.'

'Well, maybe Miss Slater had good reason to be worried by what might be happening back at home. Olive Songhirst was sleeping in her bed, we've been told. Did you give Ethel the benefit of all your years' experience with childbirth?'

'I did that.'

'Did you offer to help Miss Slater give birth to her baby at the pub?'

'Well, no, not as such. I've enough on there as it is really.'

'Let's think about that carefully, Mrs Lofthouse. You tell the jury you have enough on there with your own children and a shortage of beds. I can see that. Yet still you could empty a room and give it to Miss Slater all to herself, but you can't let her stay on then help with the birth. Like Vera helped you. How do you explain that?'

'I've all on with our Albert. He's not a well man. He's badly with 'is chest. An' Ethel wanted to get back 'ome.'

'Your husband's chest is of no concern to me. You tell Ethel Slater she can't have the baby at The Junction, but you've told the jury you love babies more than life itself. This doesn't all quite make sense, does it?'

Annie felt she was tied up in knots. She knew just what she meant, and she had done her best to explain, but he wouldn't take it in and now she was lost for words.

'Did Miss Slater talk to you about the baby's name?'

Lydia came to her mind, but then it was her favourite name and it might have been her own suggestion. She looked at Mr Cox, then at Ethel, then shook her head.

'I suggest the jury can take it from your own silence, Mrs Lofthouse, that Miss Slater's silence didn't make much sense to you either. Do you know what plans she made to look after the new baby once she was back home?'

'She wouldn't talk about it. She were terrified.'

'Or was she hoping to have it adopted? Do you know?'

'The vicar 'ad tried that an' he'd scared 'er to death.'

'None of what you say tells me that Miss Slater was frightened at all. On the contrary, she was as calm and collected as you like. Cold and scheming. She didn't talk to you about this baby's future because you both knew it didn't have one. She knew that if this baby didn't die at the hands of a backstreet abortionist in Rochdale, it would die by her own hand in St Paul's Terrace in York. She'd been jilted, she couldn't stay at home, and you had more than enough babies yourself. Ethel Slater had hatched a plot with Olive Songhirst and then you were drawn into it too. That's the terrible truth of the matter, isn't it, Mrs Lofthouse?'

'Objection, m'lord.' Mr Joyce had risen to his feet, his hands tucked into the lapels of his gown. 'Mr Cox is putting words into this witness' mouth.'

Justice Weaver looked up from his notebook. He'd added deck shoes to his list of luggage for the cruise.

'Is he? Sorry,' the judge said. 'Mrs Lofthouse, don't answer that last question. And members of the jury, ignore those last comments. It's my job to summarise the evidence, not yours, Mr Cox. Now hurry along, Mr Cox, hurry up.'

'I've no further questions, Your Honour.'

'Grand. Mr Joyce, do you have any questions? The floor is yours.'

'One or two.' Mr Joyce remained on his feet. 'Mrs Lofthouse, what took you into hospital for a time in 1947?'

'Pain in me belly, your lordship. I was servin' in the tap room an' it came on sudden like I'd been 'it by a train an' I collapsed. Then some bleedin' down below. Albert sent for an ambulance an' I 'ad to ' ave an operation an' I was laid up for a fortnight. They said I 'ad a baby growin' in one of me tubes an' it burst. So they took the 'ole lot away. I didn't even know I was expectin'. Came as a complete shock, I can tell you. I thought I was done wi' babies with our Sadie.'

'Could you see that Ethel Slater was expecting when she arrived at The Junction?'

'You can say that again! She was a few months on the way. You could see that through 'er coat. Me an' Albert met 'er at the railway station. I was a bit shocked, to be 'onest, quite how far she was gone. I knew she was in trouble but I just thought she must 'ave found out an' told our Mary and 'er Dennis, an' the balloon 'ad gone up.'

'Did Miss Slater talk to you about her pregnancy and the baby?'

'No, she didn't really, to be honest with you, sir. Not much at all. I knitted things and we'd sit an' chat a bit about what she wanted to do, but that were about it. That's our Ethel for you, though. As I said to the other gentleman, she were just very frightened, I think, of what she'd done, an' what would happen with 'er mum, and what 'er dad would do. She's timid, I think the word is. She's allus been frightened of 'er own shadow, is young Ethel.'

'Did you knit this teddy bear for her?'

Mr Joyce reached over in front of Mr Cox and took the little bear off the lid of its box.

'Yes, I did, love, an' I posted it on for 'er.'

'Let me put this suggestion to you. Did Ethel Slater come to you at The Junction hoping you'd help her get rid of the baby, one way or another, Mrs Lofthouse? Perhaps you know of a woman in Rochdale who helps out young girls in trouble?'

'Of course not. I told 'im next to you. I've never 'eard owt so bloody ridiculous.'

She pointed her finger at Mr Cox.

'So why did she come to you?'

'Same reason most folk walk through the front door of The Junction. To get away from 'ome for a while, see a friendly face an' put their worries be'ind 'em.'

'Is that the only reason you took her in?'

'A bit more.'

'Go on.'

'Kindness, warmth and a bit o' tender lovin'. Our Ethel doesn't ask for much. She's plain an' simple.'

Twenty-Seven

'Call Ethel Slater.'

Silence fell on the room as Ethel's head jerked up from the rail in the dock. She looked down into the court. The judge watched her eyes roaming from side to side. Her dowdy figure then turned about and descended into the well of the court, shuffled along between the jury and the table top of skull, teddy bear, and papers, and climbed up into the witness box. She had left one cage for another in the space of a few small steps. She stood at a rail again, cornered, trapped, alone.

Breaths were held in eager anticipation of hearing this little voice talk for the first time. She looked tiny in comparison with the earlier witnesses, wearing a shapeless, dull dress and her lank hair tied back in a bun. In the row of benches in front of her stood Mr Joyce, her barrister, waiting for her as she took the stand. Seated on his left were Mr Cox and some juniors and solicitors, flanked by their files of statements and reports, tied into bundles by bright red tapes. To Ethel's right was the jury in their box of seats, and to her left Justice Weaver sat aloft in his scarlet robe under the Royal Coat of Arms.

There were no seats left for the taking in the public gallery. This was a brutal fight not to be missed. A contest eagerly awaited for weeks by all her nosy neighbours, friends, and enemies down St Paul's Terrace and beyond. Did she do it? A spiteful lover. Surely not. But then how could it be a tragic accident? That made no sense either. Would Ethel hold up to a relentless battering from Mr Cox? Would she even break down and confess? Or try to shift the blame onto somebody else? Or would she move hearts and turn minds and prove her innocence? All Aggie Sath knew now was that her Eddie's childhood playmate in the bombed house didn't have it in her to harm any living soul. But Mr Waggett in the row behind her had seen the hatred between these neighbours spill over in his own corner shop, and nothing would have excited him more than to watch the judge don his black cap and sentence Ethel to hang.

Anyone in the gallery who knew anything about Ethel thought they knew the answers, but only one person in court knew for certain. The next few hours were Ethel's one and only chance to convince the jury that she was an innocent victim of justice going wrong. And one man in that jury, the self-appointed foreman Ray Cooper, had her down as a killer even before she'd uttered a word.

She stood in the box, took the oath, gripped the metal bar in front of her, and tried to fix on her barrister.

'Miss Slater,' said Mr Joyce, 'let me take you back to the times before your baby was born. Where did you live then?'

'With Mum and Dad near the railway sidings in York,' she mumbled. 'I've always lived there. Down St Paul's Terrace.'

'Speak up, Miss Slater,' said the judge. 'We can barely hear you.'

She daren't look up at the judge but dropped her hand down from her mouth.

'And what did you do there before you fell pregnant?'

'I tried to look after Mum, and I used to serve in Mr Waggett's grocery stores in town to bring some money in till I got the sack.'

This reply was the first comment worthy of the judge's attention. He looked down at Ethel in the witness box then wrote '*sacked from work*' under her name in his notebook. He would need some reminders to describe Miss Slater's character in his summing up of the case after the closing speeches in the morning.

'Am I right in saying, Miss Slater,' interrupted Mr Joyce, 'that Mr Waggett gave you the sack, as you say, because you couldn't work on account of looking after your new baby? And that, if we can put it this way, was your one and only offence?'

Ethel nodded, and the judge pondered a moment before putting some brackets round his comment followed by a question mark.

'And why did you need to look after your mother?' asked Mr Joyce.

''Cos she's crippled. Dr Chis says it's called multiple serrosis. She's 'ad it for years, an' it jus' gets worse an' worse. She goes down'ill, an' she can 'ardly dress 'erself now.'

This was just the right answer, thought Mr Joyce. Back on track. The judge took up his pen and wrote '*cares for invalid mother at home*' in his notebook.

'But you have a good neighbour who cooks for your

mother and father and helps with other things round the house, do you not?' he continued.

Olive could sense Dennis's body tense up in the row behind her, without even turning her head. She knew him so well, and that Ethel wouldn't hide the truth.

Mr Cox sprang to his feet. 'Objection, m'lord. This line of questioning has nothing to do with all this.'

Olive caught her breath, her shoulders dropped, and she reached for her husband's hand.

'I'm not so sure about that,' the judge said, 'but do try and get to the point if you can, Mr Joyce.'

'Very well, Your Honour,' said Mr Joyce. 'Tell me, Miss Slater, about your relationship with the boy next door, Edward Sathersthwaite. Were you betrothed?'

Ethel shifted her weight from one foot to the other. Her mouth opened but she was speechless. Her eyes flitted round the room and landed on Eddie in the gallery.

'Answer the question,' the judge told her.

'I don't know what he means.'

'Were you sweethearts? Did you plan to marry?' said Mr Joyce.

'Yes, we did. I think so. We played together when we were children down the street, but then he went to do 'is National Service.'

'Miss Slater, let me help you,' said the judge. 'What your barrister wants to know is this, I think. Did you have a sexual relationship with Mr Sathersthwaite, and is he the father of your child?'

Ethel looked down at her feet.

'Yes,' she whispered.

'Speak up, girl.' The judge took up his pen.

'Yes, William was 'is baby too,' Ethel whispered again.

'I heard the witness say yes, Your Honour,' said Mr Joyce. 'And Miss Slater, were you faithful to him, and do you think you loved him?'

'Yes, an' I still do.'

She took a handkerchief from her sleeve to wipe her eyes.

Right on target, thought Mr Joyce.

He paused to give Ethel's tears full effect.

'Now tell the court, did you leave home for a while to visit a relative in Rochdale to help you during your pregnancy?'

'Yes,' said Ethel. 'Auntie Annie runs The Junction pub there. I could work be'ind the bar an' send me mum some rent money maybe, an' nobody in the pub would stare at me or say owt nasty. An' Annie's had lots of babies an' she'd know just what to do.'

'Quite so,' said Mr Joyce. 'I think you made plans to keep your new baby. Reverend Pearson found a childless couple in Leeds who would adopt him. But they arranged this without asking you, and you turned down their thoughtless offer in the hope that Mr Sathersthwaite, the father, might return home. Is that correct?'

Mr Cox sprang up from his bench and raised his hands up to the jury in mock surprise.

'I really must object, m'lord. This is ludicrous. My learned friend is putting words into the witness' mouth.'

'Don't answer that question, Miss Slater,' said the judge, 'if indeed it was a question. We know quite enough about your client by now. Get to the baby's injuries, Mr Joyce, as quick as you can. They're the reason we're all here.'

'Very well, Your Honour. Let me take you, Miss Slater, to the morning when William was born. We shall show the jury quite clearly that his injuries were caused by an accident and nobody's fault, least of all yours.'

Justice Weaver took up his pen again but paused to look at his wristwatch.

Oh my God, Ethel thought, of course it was my fault...

'Second thoughts,' the judge interrupted. 'Before we hear all this, I need a spot of lunch. The clock says it's gone twelve, so we reconvene at two thirty.'

*

The judge screwed the lid back onto his pen and rose from his seat; Ethel remained standing in the box, unsure whether she was allowed to speak or move; Olive Songhirst muttered, '*Thank God*,' under her breath and let Charlie's hand drop; the jury filed out from their rows of seats; and Eddie Sath made a dash for the door as he delved into his pocket for his packet of cigarettes.

Justice Weaver had realised that he was already a few minutes late for his own retirement lunch. But that was no bad thing; he always liked to stamp his authority by keeping an audience waiting. He downed a generous tot of sherry from the cabinet in his office, threw his robe over the back of the chair, and found the notes for his speech in the top drawer, and scurried out of the building to the town hall next door. Mercifully this attack of the gout was well on the wane by now and he barely had a limp. He must remember to take his robe and his wig with him tomorrow, though, for his final farewell pose for the *Yorkshire Evening Post* cameraman. He could see himself on the front page now, centre stage on the first-floor balcony, with his loyal staff smiling for the camera and snaking their way down the staircase below him.

Mrs Sath caught up with Eddie as he was about to descend the stairs, a fag perched between his lips.

She grabbed hold of the back of his shoulder.

'Just stay the afternoon, will you, please, Edward?' she said.

He turned round to face her.

'No, Ma,' he replied. 'I need a drink. I've 'eard enough.'

'You should 'ear 'er out. It's 'cos of you she's 'ere at all.'

'No, it's not. She should 'ave got 'im adopted like they said.'

'You're 'eartless an' 'ard,' Mrs Sath said to her son. 'I never thought I'd 'ear meself say it. But it's true. You're a disgrace to your father's memory.'

'He's dead, Ma, I'm sorry, an' so's 'er baby. They're both well out of it. An' it's nowt to do wi' me anymore.'

'Don't you dare speak about your dad like that, Eddie. For God's sake! Your father was a good man an' he faced up to things an' went to fight in a war. He'd be ashamed of you. And so am I. You would 'ave wed Ethel if you'd stayed on at 'ome, an' now you turn your back on 'er. What's 'appened to you? You left 'ome kind and you've come back cruel.'

'Well, Pa's not 'ere now. Korea changed me, too right it did. I 'ad summat before that, a job for life on the railway and set up, and now I've nowt back 'ome. I'm off for a few pints, and then I'm on the train back to Preston. I know our Ethel wunt 'urt a fly, Ma, but it should never 'ave got this far.'

Mrs Sath dropped her hand off his shoulder and saw the slope of the baby's eyes in his.

'He was your baby too, Eddie,' she said.

'He was, Mum. An' don't I know it.'

Mrs Sath watched her only child turn away and hurtle down the stairs without a backwards glance. She knew in a flash that she might never see her Eddie again. With her Bill and her little baby William gone too, the terrible reality hit home. She was left with nobody.

*

Mr Joyce rose from his bench again after lunch. He fixed Ethel in his sight and tried a weak smile.

'Did you have your baby at home, Miss Slater?' he resumed.

'Yes,' she whispered. 'In me bedroom.'

'And was anybody there to help you?'

'No. It was all me own fault. An' I 'urt 'im.'

Mr Joyce and the members of the jury stared at her body trembling in the witness box.

Of course it was all her own fault. Who could doubt it? She'd had over two hours to think of nothing else. She shouldn't have ridden on the back of Eddie's bike to the brick pond, or giggled or buried her face in the back of his neck, or laid out on the grass and looked up through the leaves to the sky and let him have his way with her; she should have done everything the vicar had told her, and gone to Albany House with Sister Ash and Monica;

she should have stayed with Mrs Pearson after her waters broke, and gone straight to Olive's house when the labour pains started, and shouted for Mrs Sath sooner. She had only herself to blame.

Mr Cox clasped his hands behind his head and leaned back in his seat. His friend Mr Joyce was doing his job for him.

'I dropped 'im. I let 'im fall.'

Ethel knew she couldn't stand up for much longer.

How can I rescue this? thought Mr Joyce.

'You were alone, you say? There were plenty of people you could have called on, surely?'

'There was Mrs Sath after he were born.'

'The woman next door,' said Mr Joyce. 'Forget Mrs Sathersthwaite for a minute.'

Mrs Sath in the gallery adjusted the tilt of her hat slightly, and Mr Joyce shuffled some papers on his table and pushed his wig to one side to scratch his temple.

'Why not a midwife, or Dr Chisholm, or Mrs Songhirst from over the road, or your mother from downstairs, or even your father?'

''Cos I didn't trust no-one,' she said. 'They'd 'ave tried to take 'im away. My mum and Olive can't 'elp wi' stuff like that and my father's never there, and I'm scared of 'im anyway.'

'Did you call for Mrs Sathersthwaite as he was being born?'

'I 'it the wall an' she came round from next door. I 'oped she was through there.'

'Just pause there, please, Miss Slater, if you would. The jury must hear you very clearly about this. Why did you hit your bedroom wall?'

'I was scared. I were beside meself. I'd 'ad enough.'

'With a slap?'

'More of a thump, I suppose.'

'One thump with your fist? Or more than one?'

'A few, I think. I can't remember.'

'After the baby was born?'

'As 'e was comin'. I was in such pain.'

Ethel's eyes, both the good one and the lazy one, filled with tears, and her view of the world lost any focus. She steadied herself on the bar in front of her.

'We must be crystal-clear about this, Miss Slater. I can see how difficult it is for you. You thumped your bedroom wall because you were frightened and in labour and before William was born?'

'Yes.'

'Did you lie down to give birth?'

'No, I stood up.'

'Why?'

'The pain was less.'

'Did you catch him? Did Mrs Sathersthwaite catch him?'

'She weren't there. I could feel 'is 'ead comin'. No.'

'So he must have fallen onto the floor of the bedroom?'

'Yes.'

'Head-first?'

'I think so.'

'Does your bedroom floor have a soft carpet?'

Ethel's hands shot to cover her eyes. Her eyes swam and her balance went, and her knees buckled, and she slumped forward onto the ledge of the witness box, toppling a glass of water onto the floor below as she fell. The clerk leapt to his feet, dashed round into the witness box, and lifted her back onto the chair. A stunned silence hit the room, save for some empty words from the clerk for Ethel and the roll of the glass down the steps.

The judge stared from his bench. He had enjoyed many a witness collapse in his time, but most under fierce cross-examination and none so unexpected as this. Mr Joyce sat back in his seat to wait and to study the jury. Ethel hadn't cracked under the weight of guilt, but the agony of an accidental injury she had done to her baby. He'd broken her with the truth in full view of the jury, and he could do the same again.

She reached forward for the ledge and took the glass back into her hands. She could stay seated if she wished, the judge told her, but she hauled herself back to her feet.

'Miss Slater,' said Mr Joyce, 'the early morning of Thursday the 12th of February. You woke with a start, I think. Why was that?'

'The postie were knockin' on the front door.'

'What did you do?'

'I got up an' went downstairs to answer it.'

'You got up, you say, Miss Slater. The knock woke you up. Were you alone in bed?'

'No, I think William was in wi' me. In bed next to me. I'd fed 'im and winded 'im before I turned the light off, and I must 'ave fallen asleep with 'im still there. I don't think 'e woke again during the night.'

'Did you look at him before you went downstairs?'

'No,' said Ethel. 'I'd sort of din't think he'd be in bed wi' me. I were so groggy an' just jumped out of bed. He'd generally go back in 'is drawer. I just forgot. I must 'ave just thought he was still in there.'

Mr Joyce pushed a finger under the edge of his wig again and eased it to one side while he collected his thoughts and planned his approach. He flicked over his notes with the other hand and looked down what Ethel had told him in jail, rubbed his chin slowly, then left his finger over his mouth. Ethel's answers to his last few questions must stick in the jurors' minds. He knew very well that Mr Cox could demolish Ethel so easily. If he could shake her now with the truth, best even break her down, the worst would be over and she might well stand up to a battering from Cox.

'Miss Slater,' he said. 'I must ask you now to tell the jury what happened to you after the postman called. Why did he knock at the door?'

''Cos he 'ad a parcel for me.'

'A parcel?'

'Yes, Aunt Annie 'ad sent me that.'

Ethel took her eyes off Mr Joyce and tried to focus on the small cloth teddy bear sitting on the table facing Mr Cox.

'A teddy bear for baby William? Had Aunt Annie put a letter in with it?'

'No.'

'Then how did you know who'd sent it?'

'The postmark on the packet.'

'Which was?'

'Rochdale. I saw it straight off. An' I just knew it was 'er anyway. It's what she does.'

'And what did you do with the bear?'

'I took 'im straight over the street to show Olive.'

'How long were you away from your bedroom?'

'Don't know. Not long.'

'Was there anyone left in the house with your baby?'

'My mum, downstairs, an' me father in the back bedroom.'

'How do you know your father was at home?'

''Cos I'd 'eard 'im come back in the small hours, an' 'is bedroom door was shut.'

'What did you do after you'd shown the teddy bear to Olive?'

'I took 'im back upstairs for my baby.'

Ethel leant into the rail.

If I get these questions right, with luck she might even collapse again, thought Mr Joyce.

'And what did you find upstairs in your bedroom?'

Ethel had stopped hearing her barrister now.

All she could see was the shape of her teddy bear.

The judge spoke at her to catch her attention. 'Miss Slater,' he said, 'you must answer the question. What did you find in your bedroom?'

'My baby.' She turned to his voice. 'In bed. Where I'd been lyin'. Cold an' white with some blood round his nose. He'd gone.'

She grabbed hold of the rail.

The judge watched her struggle to breathe.

'Miss Slater, I have to ask you this, I'm sorry,' said Mr Joyce. 'Did you ever throw William at your bedroom wall?'

She seemed not to have heard the question but stared at the judge. 'How?' she replied, still looking at him. She paused to try to think. 'Why? He was all I ever wanted.'

Mr Joyce could not have asked for more. His client had told the judge she was innocent with the lightest of touches.

'No further questions, m'lord,' he said, and sat down.

*

Mr Cox rose to his full height, flicked the tails of his gown out from behind him, and tucked his thumbs into his lapels. He smiled to the men and women of the jury to attract their attention.

'Stay where you are,' he said at the witness box.

Ethel sensed that this blurred figure was about to attack.

He reached his arms under the bench, brought out the shoebox, and placed it on the table next to the teddy bear. Ethel knew that box; it was hers. He lay the bear on the top, a perfect fit, then lifted off the lid, picked out a length of string from inside, and settled the bear snugly onto a blanket. Securing the box shut again with a knot in the string, he raised it head-high to the jury with a flourish. Mr Joyce watched his client reel backwards.

Justice Weaver took up his pen again and drew a square with a cross on the top in his notebook.

'Ladies and gentlemen,' Mr Cox turned to the jury, 'something rather odd has happened. And we can't have failed to notice it. Miss Slater confessed to a murder when events were crystal-clear in her mind, but now she tells us a different story. I wonder why. She's had time to think, perhaps? Let's remind ourselves of the facts.

'Miss Slater,' he said, turning to the witness box, 'I can

see from your face that you have seen this box before. Am I right?'

'Yes, it's mine,' she replied. 'It was for William's things.'

'And are you able to tell us where the police found your shoebox?'

'Under the bed.'

'Yes, indeed. And I think the string and the blanket were inside it, weren't they?'

'Yes.'

'Well, I'll ask you no more questions about that for now, but we'll come back to it.' He faced the jury. 'But for the moment, I should like to ask Miss Slater some questions about her feelings for Edward Sathersthwaite, the father of their illegitimate baby.'

Ethel looked to Mr Joyce, but he was powerless to help.

'We heard you tell the court that you love Edward. Is that correct?'

She nodded.

'Well, I wonder about that.' He paused, waiting for the judge to finish writing some words in his notebook. 'Did he love you, do you know? Has he asked you to marry him, for example?'

'No.'

'No, he never has, has he? I think we can safely assume that he wants nothing to do with you, and I would suggest he never did. He deserted you, you've admitted that. Let me turn your attention to… how did Your Honour describe it, yes, your sexual relationship with this man? Your sexual relationship with Edward was one act of intercourse, you say. It wasn't really what you would call a relationship at all. You drove together down a country lane to a secluded spot and you seduced Edward Sathersthwaite, didn't you? You wanted a way out of the drudgery of looking after your dying mother, didn't you? Were you a virgin then, Miss Slater, or had you been, let us say, more generous with your affections?'

'Objection, Your Honour!' Mr Joyce jumped to his feet. 'This is outrageous! We have a string of slurs and allegations with no basis.'

The judge kept his eyes down as he scribbled in his notebook but raised a hand to stop Mr Cox in his tracks. What had been said, though, couldn't now be unsaid. The damage had been done. The seed had been planted in the jury's minds that Ethel was perhaps a loose woman with no morals, scheming, not quite so innocent as Mr Joyce would have them believe.

Ethel's mother in the gallery shrieked then grappled with the rims of her chair wheels, and Olive took the handles, wheeled the chair round, and pushed her up the aisle and out of the back of the court; Mrs Sathersthwaite was glad her rotten son was out of her sight on a train bound for Preston; and the jurors leaned forwards in their seats and exchanged glances. All their eyes were on Mr Cox, as he placed his outstretched fingers on the teddy bear's coffin and shifted it gently from one hand to the other. And Ethel had no words she could say.

'Mr Cox,' said the judge, 'just slow down, ask the witness one question at a time, will you, and then wait for the answers?'

'Miss Slater,' said Mr Cox. He spoke to her while facing the jury. 'Am I correct in saying that you fell pregnant to Edward Sathersthwaite at your first and only attempt at sexual intercourse with him?'

'It was,' said Ethel.

'And that your relationship came crashing down when you told him you were expecting?'

'Yes, but—'

'You were unlucky, you could say?'

'No, it's nowt like that. You've got this all wrong.'

'I suggest to you that there is no other way of describing it. But let's leave that to one side too. Let's have a look at how you hid your pregnancy.'

'I—'

Mr Cox didn't want answers.

'Why are you scared of your father?'

'I'm not really.'

The judge licked the tip of his finger and flicked back a page of his notebook, and Mr Cox ran his finger back up his own notes.

'Members of the jury,' said Mr Cox, 'we have a clear contradiction here, it seems. In other words, yet another lie. She said quite clearly from the witness box in reply to Mr Joyce not an hour since, "My mum and Olive can't help with stuff like that and my father's never there, and I'm scared of him anyway."

'Tell us, Miss Slater, is your household in the habit of using violence to sort out its problems?'

'No more than any other, I shun't think.'

He repeated her words slowly and carefully…

'No more than any other.'

…then paused, turned to the jury, and raised his eyes to the ceiling.

'You must live your life in fear, you poor thing. Did you escape from your parents' house for Rochdale to avoid a violent house, only to come back when your aunt threw you out?'

'Not at all. I wanted to stay with Auntie Annie. An' I 'ated everyone in the terrace could see I was 'avin' a baby. An' Eddie had gone an' Mrs Sath was always next door. I was just scared at 'ome.'

'You didn't want anybody to know you were expecting a baby, at home or anywhere else. You weren't scared, were you; you were ashamed? Of what you'd done. Of letting the world see what a loose woman Ethel Slater is. This was an unwanted baby right from day one. You just wanted all this mess to go away, didn't you? You wouldn't see any midwife, or even Dr Chisholm, who seems to have spent half his life at your house with your poor mother.'

Mr Joyce wearily hauled himself to his feet again. 'Your Honour, we just have Mr Cox's own speech here again, and my client is given no space to answer to anything.'

'Overruled,' said Justice Weaver. 'Mr Cox is trying to build a clear picture of your client. But, Mr Cox, please state your case more slowly, if you could. I'm having great difficulty in keeping up with my notes. And let's get to the birth and the rest of it a bit quicker, please. It would be nice to finish with this witness and the last one before we rise till the morning.'

'Very well,' replied Mr Cox, and Mr Joyce resigned himself to his seat again.

This is going to plan, thought Mr Cox. He had the jury's full attention, and the judge's ear by the sounds of things. And he still had some heavy blows to land.

'Tell the jury, if you would, why you'd hidden an

empty shoebox in your room containing some string and a blanket?'

'It's 'is baby box for 'is clothes an' things.'

'Let's think about this. You'd actually made a plan to have this baby in your bedroom. And all by yourself. Had it occurred to you, Miss Slater, that your baby might be stillborn, and you would need a box for his coffin, perhaps?'

'I was terrified he'd die.'

'Really? And yet you accepted no help from anybody? Do you expect us to swallow all this nonsense? You have told the jury that William was all you ever wanted. I put it to you that he was something you never wanted. I put it to you that this shoebox was meant to be William's coffin whether he was stillborn or you murdered him at birth. And you would have succeeded at your first attempt, had Mrs Sathersthwaite not foiled your plan.'

'No!'

She looked at the shoebox but could only see her baby.

'It's Mum's old dancin' shoes box. Monica 'ad a baby box too.'

'What?' said Mr Cox. 'Who on earth is Monica?'

Her words poured out through a mix of stuttering sobs and tears.

'That box 'as got nowt to do with owt. Mrs Sath saved me and my baby. It wasn't like any of what you say at all. I didn't want anyone to see I were pregnant 'cos they would have taken my baby away. An' taken me away from lookin' after my mum. He was everything I needed. I just wanted a life for us, but you won't see it.'

She's breaking, thought Mr Cox, but she's tipping the wrong way.

One last assault.

'You didn't have your baby standing up. You had him lying on your bed, didn't you, like every other mother? You admitted that to the police. What's changed your story, Miss Slater?'

'He fell onto the floor.'

'And the thump that woke Mrs Sathersthwaite wasn't your fist. It was William's head. You threw him at the bedroom wall, didn't you?'

'No.'

'But you've admitted it?'

'I didn't.'

'What did you do in the house after the ambulance took your dead baby away, Miss Slater?'

'What? I don't know what went on. I can't remember.'

'I think you can. You lit a fire in your mother's bedroom downstairs. Why did you do that?'

'Probably the cold.'

Mr Cox raised the teddy bear to show the jury again.

'No, to burn the wrapping paper, I suggest. You used this teddy bear's parcel to light the fire, didn't you? Because Edward your old lover had posted it to you. The postmark was Preston, not Rochdale, wasn't it?'

'Annie made that bear for my baby.'

'Wrong. It was a final taunt you couldn't stomach. You flipped. So you rushed upstairs in a blind fury and smothered your baby with a pillow and threw him at the wall again. Revenge is what you're all about. Just like now, Miss Slater, it's truth, hard reality, you can't take.'

Ethel looked to Mr Joyce and took strength from his belief in her at last, and saw through Mr Cox in his silly wig, the judge in his pompous robe, the jury in their wooden pen, and the faces leering down at her from the public gallery. Pictures surfaced and flashed across her mind, of simple days long gone, and of what had once been, and of what had been taken away. Fleeting snapshots of the elephants and the clown and the juggler in the street; shinning up the forsythia bush behind Eddie in the bombsite rubble; Mum and Dad lying in the same bed on Christmas morning in The Junction. All come back in a medley of haunting memories.

'No,' she said after a while, her eyes settled on no-one, 'it's all lies.'

'No further questions, Your Honour,' said Mr Cox, and flicked out the tails of his gown again and sat down.

Twenty-Eight

Justice Weaver eased himself back in his chair and looked up at the clock after Ethel had returned to the dock. It was nearly three o'clock on the last full day he would ever be in charge of events in his life. There was not an empty seat in the public gallery, and just one free chair down below next to Mr Joyce. The only witness called for the defence had not shown up.

A man in his position did not take kindly to unscheduled delays. He had pressing matters to sort out at home ahead of his cruise in a couple of days' time and he wanted to be away from court as soon as he possibly could. He summoned the clerk with a wag of his finger, who apologised for the delay and begged to inform his lordship that he understood Mr Joyce's witness was presently on the early morning train down from Glasgow and was therefore at the mercy of the elements. A cab was waiting at the railway station to bring her up to the court.

Dr Samuels appeared at the entrance into court

shortly after three. She carried with her a smart leather suitcase, paused inside the door to bow her head slightly to the judge on his bench, caught Mr Joyce's eye, and made her way down the aisle to take the seat beside him. Justice Weaver's annoyance dissolved in an instant. Just as Olive Songhirst had the figure and face he had admired, this witness, dressed in a tailored suit with pencil skirt and short jacket, had the poise and style he respected.

'Good afternoon, Your Honour,' Dr Samuels said to him on taking the stand. 'I apologise for my late arrival.'

'That's quite alright,' he replied. 'No need to apologise. We are grateful to you for travelling such a long way to assist the court today.' He could have added that it had been well worth the wait, but he didn't.

'Tell me,' asked Mr Joyce, 'do criminal courts such as this call upon your expertise often?'

'Sadly, yes, I'm afraid they do. There are daily tragedies similar to this across the country, sir,' she replied. 'I work out of Glasgow, but I am one of the few pathologists with experience of the suspicious deaths of newborn babies.'

The judge stared at her and let his pen lie untouched on his notebook.

'So the tragic death of William Slater is not unique in your experience?'

'No, sir, it is not. His case has many features that I see all too often.'

Mr Joyce paused to settle his wig square on his scalp then took a long deep breath. At last he could relax with a solid, reliable witness he could steer whichever way he chose. He was a man in charge of his brief. This witness had none of the froth and bluster of Dr Lawson. She had that quiet authority and assurance a jury ought to believe. He reached over for the skull resting on the bench in front of Mr Cox, and had the clerk pass it to the doctor.

'Dr Samuels,' he said, 'you can see that my learned friend Mr Cox has drawn a pencil line on the top of this skull. Would you accept that this line might represent a fracture?'

She glanced casually at the thick black line and passed it back to the clerk.

'Yes, I would,' she replied.

'Please describe for the jury if you could the features that would make this a fracture.'

'Certainly. Well, this is an adult skull, of course, and not a newborn's. They behave in very different ways when they're damaged. But his pencil line is quite long, over an inch or so probably; it doesn't run straight, and it crosses over from one bone into another. All points to a fracture, I would say.'

'And this crack in William's skull?' asked Mr Joyce.

The clerk passed over the post-mortem photograph, a head the size of a grapefruit splayed open with a pointer lying on the crack in the bone.

'Quite different. It's nothing like his pencil line. This is not a fracture.'

'Then please, Dr Samuels,' continued Mr Joyce, 'in your own words, tell us why it isn't a fracture. Take your time.'

She pushed her spectacles back into her hairline and ran a painted fingernail along the crack.

'There are so many differences, it's difficult to know where to start,' she said. 'For one thing, fractured bone splinters into sharp fragments that injure the soft tissue around so it bleeds. There's not one drop of blood along this crack. For another, fractures don't follow nice, straight lines like this crack. They are jagged. They curve and bend. But the most crucial thing is that a fracture will pass from one plate of skull bone across the joint into the next plate. But this crack just runs up to a joint and then stops. Stops dead in its tracks. A fracture is a living thing for a second or two after a skull hits a wall, Your Honour. It travels, it rips, it tears, it bleeds. And this tidy little crack hasn't done any of those things. It just sits there. It's done nothing…'

She stopped speaking when she felt the silence around her. She had forgotten herself, lost in her life's work and her train of thought. She paused to look up to the judge, tilted the photograph in his direction, and ran a circle around the crack slowly with the tip of her finger.

'A fracture travelling through a skull goes on a short, rapid, violent journey, if I may put it that way, Your Honour,' she said. 'This skull crack has gone nowhere.'

He raised his eyebrows, nodded his head slightly, and asked the obvious next question.

'Carry on, Dr Samuels. You've told us what you think it isn't. Now can you be so good as to tell us what you think it is?'

'It's a normal structure, sir,' she replied. 'It's a fissure. Some babies have a fissure like this when they're born. Quite often, I find. You may even have had one yourself, Your Honour.'

'Well there's a thought,' he said, and burst into a loud, short laugh. 'I must have been a baby once, I suppose.'

'A baby's skull bones grow in the mother's womb like sheets of ice spreading over a garden pond,' Dr Samuels continued. 'Tiny crystals of bone come together to make floating islands that press up against each other, and where these islands meet they sometimes leave a join, that we call a fissure. They just don't quite fuse together. It's as simple as that. There's nothing suspicious about William's skull at all.'

'Then how, in your view, Dr Samuels, could a pathologist mistake this innocent little crack for a fracture?' Mr Joyce asked.

'Quite easily,' she replied, 'if he's never come across a fissure before, or more likely never noticed one before or given the matter a moment's thought.'

Dr Samuels tried to flatten out the creases from the grainy image on the ledge in front of her and looked to Mr Joyce for his next line of questioning.

'Pass the photograph back to the jury, please,' Mr Joyce continued. 'There may not be bleeding around the crack, but there's a great deal of blood inside this baby's head.'

Linda Moxley pored over the picture once again. She could see quite clearly the thick pool of blood over the surface of the brain where the plates of bone had been splayed apart and held by Dr Lawson's fingers.

'What about the dark blood on top of the brain, Dr Samuels?' Mr Joyce said. 'Surely you would accept that could have been caused by a blow to the head?'

'Well, yes, in theory, but not necessarily,' replied the doctor. 'I would suggest the more likely reason is that the baby's head was crushed under his sleeping mother.'

Ethel's breathing stopped.

She had no clear memory that she had slept at all in her few endless nursing days. Only the worry during the daylight hours of keeping her baby and her mother and herself alive, and her own exhausted, fitful turmoil during hours of darkness.

But she had found him dead on her bed, hadn't she?

'Mrs Sathersthwaite has told the court there was some blood on the baby's face when she found him dead, Dr Samuels,' Mr Joyce said. 'Could that bleeding have been caused by impact against a wall?'

'I really don't see how,' she said. 'There were no lacerations to be found on this baby's skin at post-mortem, on his face or anywhere else for that matter. The same cause as the bleeding over the brain, I would think. This blood has come up from his lungs. Suffocation. There can be little doubt about it, sir.' She turned to the judge. 'This innocent baby, Your Honour, died asleep underneath his mother. All the evidence points in that direction.'

'Just pause there a second, Dr Samuels,' the judge said, and carefully wrote down these last two sentences in full in his notebook.

'The bruise in his scalp, Doctor. We can't escape from that, can we?' Mr Joyce continued. 'One injury, or two?'

'One bruise,' she replied, 'just taking its time to heal.'

Linda Moxley took another opportunity to study the image of the head. It had lost its power to shock. She had seen plenty of harmless bruises on her own skin, but not one on a baby or one upon which a woman's life depended. The scalp had been peeled back from the skull such that its shiny, smooth, deep surface faced up to the camera. Some wisps of black wet hair poked out around the cut edge. The bruise was a rough oval shape of lakes and strands of reds and browns merging together.

'Then, please,' Mr Joyce said to the witness, 'show us the bruise and tell us its story.'

'Well, a bruise is quite a complicated little thing, really,' she said. 'And like everything else that lives, it changes as it grows older then disappears without leaving a trace, just like you and me. Dr Lawson helpfully made some microscope slides from areas of this bruise, and we can see these changes taking place. The blood in the bruise is red when it's fresh or young, and after a day or so parts of it turn brown and start to heal. But this change doesn't all happen in the same part of the bruise or at the same time. So most of it is red and a little of it is brown about a day after the injury, but several days later most of it has turned brown and not much remains red. Eventually all of the bruise changes colour before it fades. You can think of it as a pear ripening if you like. It all turns soft eventually, but it doesn't all ripen at the same time.'

'Doctor,' Mr Joyce asked, 'this is the really important question, isn't it? For how many days does some of a bruise remain red? How long does it take for all the red areas to disappear?'

'We don't really know, to be honest,' she replied. 'But at least several days.'

'So what you are telling us, and correct me if I'm wrong, is that this bruise may be one injury healing at different speeds?'

'I am, yes. In my opinion, William's scalp was injured only once, probably when he was born.'

'When he fell onto hard floorboards?'

'Yes.'

'Can you be certain his scalp wasn't injured twice, once when he was born and once when he died four days later?'

'No, I can't. All I can be sure of is that it's not certain he was injured twice.'

'Let me put this a different way. You're saying there is room for reasonable doubt that his scalp was bruised when he died?'

'There is, certainly.'

Mr Joyce eased a finger under his wig to scratch his temple again then rubbed his chin. This was a lot for him to take in, let alone a jury.

'Finally, Dr Samuels, what do you say about the photograph of the blood on the floorboards at the end of the bed? William's blood?'

'No, there's far too much there for a small baby's body. Mother's blood, I would suggest, when she gave birth onto the floor.'

'And the blood splatter on the wall?'

'The same. Not from the baby. He had no external injury.'

'And the crack in the plaster on the wall? What caused that, do you think? Impact?'

'No, there's no good evidence he was thrown. This is a crumbling old house a few yards from a bomb blast and a railway line and a shunting yard, as I understand it. There are probably cracks on every wall you care to look at.'

'And last of all, Dr Samuels, give the court your view on how William Slater came by his death, please.'

She turned to the judge and waited a second or two as he finished a note.

'Overlaying is the cause of death in my opinion, Your Honour. He was bruised accidentally at birth, then overlaid by an adult in bed a few days later.'

Shock buckled Ethel's knees in the dock. What the doctor had said all rang true. She'd watched the bruise fading, knowing that Chis had said it was nothing to worry about. How wrong he had been.

*

'Dr Samuels,' Mr Cox launched into his own questions, 'you are an oddity with a very strange calling. You just look after dead babies, do you not?'

'No, sir.'

The wrong answer.

Mr Cox looked up at the witness.

'Sorry?'

'No, I don't. I look after grieving mothers.'

'That's a smart answer. I like it. You've clearly said it before. But you've told us you have long experience of suspicious deaths of newborn babies. Does that include babies injured by a fall at birth?'

'Mothers usually give birth lying down.'

'Well, blow me down with a feather! Even I know that! Please answer my question.'

'I can't remember dealing with such a case before, no.'

'And babies dying in mother's beds, do they often have bleeding over the brain?'

'No, not usually.'

'That's how I understand it too. Perhaps your ideas are not so certain after all. Would you agree with that?'

'I'm certain about very few things.'

'Mm. Maybe you're better with theories than facts.'

Mr Cox took up the photograph of the baby's scalp again and peered at the bruise. He paused to study the detail for several seconds before passing it back to the witness.

'Good doctor,' he said, 'I'm sure you will agree with me on this point, though. We two look at this with very different eyes?'

'And brains,' she replied.

'I like that too,' Mr Cox continued. 'Then tell us, what does your cool, scientific brain see in this bruise?'

'A patchwork of reds and browns, shades of light and dark.'

'No, Doctor, that's not good enough by a long shot. That's what my legal brain sees. Your brain can pick out patterns and it knows what they mean; it's much more precise than the brain of a lawyer. Describe it for us, please.'

She took the photograph off the ledge in front of her and spoke to it.

'There are vague geographic shapes of different shades of red and brown colour merging into each other.'

'Good. We're getting there. Is it the same all over?'

'No, it varies.'

'Carry on.'

'Well, I'd say most of it was the pattern I've described, with a larger area of reddish bruise towards one edge.'

'And the remainder of the edge? How would you describe that?'

'Mainly browns, and then merging into more reds in the centre.'

'So, Dr Samuels, for a lawyer's simple brain, would I be right in saying there's a pattern of mainly reds in the centre, and shades of light and darker browns with a separate larger area of red around one edge?'

'You would.'

The judge held a finger up to catch the clerk's attention and motioned for him to pass the photograph up to his bench. He angled it around to figure out which side was at the top of the baby's head, placed it down square on his notebook, then sketched its shape as accurately as he could on the adjacent page. He drew round edges he thought were more brown than red, decided to shade red areas with blue ink, and then leant back to admire his skill.

'How does a bruise heal, Dr Samuels?'

'Slowly, over time.'

'No, not when. How?'

'New healthy tissue grows in to repair the damage.'

'Where from?'

'The edges of the injury, generally.'

'The edges, thank you. So we'd expect the edges to turn brown first, would we, then move towards the centre?'

'Well, in general, yes, broadly speaking. Though it heals from the deep edge underneath too. It's not as straightforward as you make out.'

'So a single injury would explain the brown rim nicely. But the big red area at the edge is a bit of a fly in the ointment then as far as you're concerned. Dents your theory of just the one injury, doesn't it?'

'As I've said, it's patchy.'

'Or, more likely, there's been a second later injury at the side of the first?'

The witness remained silent.

'Dr Samuels? More likely two injuries than one?'

'I can't say that.'

'Can't, or won't?'

'We can't be sure.'

'You're quite sure about the fissure, though. And how do you explain that the bruising lies just above the fracture or the fissure and just above the brain haemorrhage? Impact against a wall possibly?'

'That's coincidence.'

'Oh dear! We don't like coincidences in this room. Or uncertainty. We just go round in circles with your notions, Dr Samuels. Your theories are Scotch mist, it seems to me. They just vanish into thin air when we get up close.

'But finally, before we put you back on the train to Glasgow, tell us this. Can you be certain this poor wee baby hasn't been thrown at a wall? Twice?'

She hesitated, then looked over to Mr Joyce.

'No. As I've said already, I'm certain of very little.'

'Thank you,' Mr Cox said, lowering himself back onto his chair. 'M'lord, I rest my case.'

Twenty-Nine

Linda Moxley's priority after unlocking the front door, unlacing her shoes and lining them up on the rack in the hallway, and hanging up her coat on the hook, was to open the back door and call for Tommy. She just hoped he'd not been fighting with Barker's bruiser from up the street again. He appeared as usual from inside the shed, his spidery daytime refuge from driving rain or scorching sun.

She lifted him up and set him down carefully onto the kitchen table, slid his bowl of biscuits under his nose, and stared at the ulcer on his forehead while he chewed. It had been at the back of her mind all day. It worried her. He hadn't opened it up again by scratching it, thank goodness, but she could tell that he'd been grooming it by the streaks of blood on his paw. She'd have to bathe it with cotton wool soaked with tepid saltwater before she went to bed.

She had arrived home a little later than usual today. Even though she had nothing to get out of the cupboards for her class in the morning, she'd still called into school on her walk home from the court. It had been eerie to hear the silence in the building, strange to see it so empty of teachers and children, just Mr Cropper the caretaker pottering around with his broom. Anyway, she didn't like to let a day go by without checking up on things.

She had taken her usual seat at the front of the orderly rows of empty chairs in her classroom, squared up the stack of exercise books on the table, tidied the box of blackboard chalks, and lapsed into private thoughts she knew were forbidden. How could she not push the facts to the back of her mind for a while, not wonder about the lives paraded into the witness box, not pity Ethel Slater? She could see her face at the back of this class now, a timid, dumpy, cross-eyed little thing. She'd taught so many Ethel Slaters in her time. She was barely a few years older than the children she'd missed today. They were rough, they were tough, most of them, all with bleak futures, but could any one of them throw a baby at a wall? Of course not. So how could Ethel? Linda had watched her break down and weep, wilt and collapse, shout out and be hauled back down. She was a victim, surely, but never a killer. And Linda had taken against Mr Cox with his gimmicks and shocks of a cracked skull and gory images, and warmed to Mr Joyce's kindliness.

Linda pulled open the door to the scullery after feeding her cat, picked out a couple of eggs from the bowl, paused in thought, then took a third and the block of cheddar wrapped in wax paper. It had been a long and difficult day, but it was a Wednesday, so it was still an omelette, and she deserved some cheese in it. She hadn't had chance to do a proper shop for over a week now, and the stone shelf in the scullery was low on stock. That worried her too. She'd asked her brother Philip and his two boys round for tea this Sunday coming. The boys always wanted the same: Yorkshire puddings, sausages, and onion gravy. She wanted to make amends with her brother. They'd grown apart when Linda was struggling to care for Dad at home, but then he did have his two sons to look after alone since their mother had died. She knew his life wasn't as easy as hers. She would have to get up early on Saturday morning and stock up.

Linda cracked the eggs into a saucepan and left it to sit on the stove. She wanted to read through her notes before she sat down to eat. The cat followed her into her back sitting room and hunched on the rug in front of the hearth. She knelt to put a match to the gas fire, then peered at his ulcer and tried to tell herself that it could be getting smaller. The curtains in here were always left open so the little potted cyclamen on the windowsill would get the most of any early spring sunshine from the garden. She pulled out the leaf from the card table, glanced through the black window and saw the reflected face of a tired, gaunt woman with a sprawling cat behind her, and spread out some pages. This time last night she had been convinced about Ethel. But not any longer.

She started with the notes she'd written that afternoon as Ethel Slater and Dr Samuels had given their evidence. Ethel's story had been believable, until Mr Cox had unpicked Dr Samuels' account of the bruise. Even though she had never given birth herself, Linda could picture the baby's drop head-first onto the floor in Ethel's bedroom, and then found dead in bed where his mother had slept. Ethel's showing in the witness box had the ring of truth about it, and her outbursts at Inspector Harrison from the dock had been gut reactions shouted from the heart.

Linda had made a dozen or so comments about the police inspector's evidence but then drawn a line across the page and written 'Nonsense' in the margin. She found it impossible to believe that Ethel had used the words the policeman had written down or read the confession through afterwards, even if the story was true. And she could see that Ethel had turned down offers of adoption with the best intentions, and the idea of abortion had never crossed her mind. It was easy to see too that the women from the terrace and the pub in Rochdale were hiding behind their own secrets and lies, but they had said enough about Ethel to persuade Linda that she was innocent. And then there was the mystery of Ethel's father. One of them was lying. If her father really was out overnight when the baby died, why would Ethel lie for him? And if he had spent the night in his own bed, then surely the postman's knock would have woken him too and he'd have had plenty of time in Ethel's absence with the teddy over the road to grab her baby from the bed or the drawer and hurl it across the room?

The medical evidence was key. The rest didn't make much of a difference. It was the crack in the skull and the bruise on the forehead that really mattered. She'd followed Dr Samuels' reasoning that a fracture would have bled, but then it was surely not a coincidence that the crack was just below the bruise and just above the brain haemorrhage. That was maybe too much to swallow.

She drew the bulbous outline of a pear at the top of the page, then added a thin little stalk and a curly leaf sprouting from the top, and shaded a few bits in with her pencil. Everything hinged on the bruise. She could see it in her mind's eye, dark reds and paler browns, ripening and softening in different shaded areas at the same time. All one pear, all one injury, Dr Samuels had said, until she'd been forced to describe a fresh red area at the edge, the first part that would have started to turn brown from an injury four days before.

Linda laid her pencil down, revolved the cyclamen pot a half circle, peered at her own frown looking back at her through the window, and turned to watch her sleeping cat. She was confused, undecided, but then she knew she always would be. That was exactly the point, though, wasn't it? If there was no way of knowing for certain, one injury or two, if science didn't have all the answers, then Ethel should get the benefit of the doubt, and be freed.

She took the few steps back to the kitchen, whisked the eggs in the pan, cut a wedge of cheese off the block and popped it into her mouth, then took up her notes and pencil again. This pear needed shading right round the edge, didn't it, she reckoned, if this was her bruise turning brown? It was all too difficult for this time of night. She could make an omelette without thinking. She'd best eat it while standing up here in the kitchen, leave her plate and pans in the sink till the morning, turn the gas fire off, and make her way upstairs.

*

'Blast!' she whispered into the darkness.

She turned her bedside lamp straight back on again.

She'd started to make a shopping list for Philip and the boys on Sunday but was too tired even for that and had just flicked off the lamp.

A gentle thud onto the blanket at the end of the bed had reminded her, and she looked up into a pair of wide, inscrutable eyes, a pink dry nose, long stiff whiskers, furry ginger cheeks, and an ulcer.

It was too late to bathe it, and the water in the kettle would be stone cold by now anyway.

She grabbed hold of him by the scruff of the neck and stared at his ulcer again. There was a dry, red scab in the middle where he'd rubbed it again, but there was definitely some new smooth skin round it.

It was healing, no doubt about it.

From around the edges first.

She turned the light back off again but knew she wouldn't sleep.

There was far too much to worry about: whether Barker's cat would scrap with her Tommy again, that she would kill her cyclamen plant, whether she'd remember to get everything for Philip and the boys on Sunday, the teaching her children were missing, how ulcers and bruises healed, whether Ray Cooper would browbeat them all in the jury room, and that by this time tomorrow they could have convicted a young woman for a crime her father might have committed or that might have never even existed.

Thirty

For all her faults and personal failings, and there were many her husband could list, Mrs Weaver was well organised and ran their home and their lives to perfection. The judge had left his suitcase open on his bed for his wife to pack for the cruise and arrived early at the office to bundle his final few effects into his briefcase. He hid the sherry bottle and the tumbler at the bottom under some papers, dropped the key to his wall cabinet onto the desk, lifted his robe from the hook, and then took hold of the handle on the door into court. He stopped then turned to the room for a last lingering look at his empire. He felt pride in his achievements. He'd served justice well, he thought. No regrets.

Ethel grasped the rail in the dock when his door swung open. The court dutifully rose to their feet, then fell back to their seats in a silent wave as the judge entered and took his own chair. All eyes settled on him as he flicked back and forth through the pages of his notebook. This hadn't been the most taxing case he'd ever had to deal with, but one or two interesting characters had lined up in the witness box. He might have a few words to say about some of them, not least the honesty of the policeman and the competence of his old friend Dr Lawson, if the verdict was the right one and if he had the time and inclination.

'Mr Cox,' he raised his head and said at long last, 'I gather we have heard all the evidence in this case now. Would you care to make a short closing speech to the jury?'

Mr Cox was on his feet already.

'I would, Your Honour. Let's begin with the accused, Miss Ethel Slater. A girl of seventeen, an aimless young woman, who seduced the boy next door. A schemer, she wanted to trap a husband but not to have his baby. That was the last thing she wanted. The father of their unborn child soon abandoned her. She turned down all offers of adoption but tried to have her baby aborted. She failed in this, as in most things she tried, so made plans to execute her baby at birth and dispose of the body. She was disturbed in this first attempt but succeeded when he was not yet a week old. Taunted by the man who had jilted her, she threw the baby at her bedroom wall for the second time. And then to verify it all, ladies and gentlemen, we have her confession, signed when the crime was fresh in her mind. What more do we need?

'Nothing. But we have some unreliable witnesses; that's what we've got. What is most revealing about their evidence is what they try not to tell us. Olive Songhirst, who wrote to Rochdale to arrange an abortion but is afraid of revealing her own dark secrets; Annie Lofthouse, who had more children than she knew what to do with and wouldn't help her own niece have one of her own; and Agnes Sathersthwaite, who lives next door to a family she detests and admits she may have heard the baby's head hit the wall once when he was born and again as he died.

'There we have it, ladies and gentlemen, the case for the prosecution. The killing of the baby that nobody ever loved. And you have everything you need to come to a just decision. We have the motive, revenge; we have the crime scene, a bloodbath in her room; and we have the cause of death, brain haemorrhage with two separate bruises that even Dr Samuels cannot deny. He was the baby that Ethel Slater never wanted. Do your duty. Say guilty. Convict this woman of murder.'

That was mercifully short, thought the judge. If Mr Joyce was as speedy, with luck he would be home in time for lunch.

'Mr Joyce,' the judge said, 'are you able to offer some words in defence of your client?'

'Yes, strong words, Your Honour. Because we have none of the evidence Mr Cox would have you believe. No motive, because this baby was all his mother ever wanted; no crime scene, only blood on the floor from a natural childbirth; and no violent cause of death, only one healing bruise when the baby was injured by a fall at birth and then signs of innocent overlaying in his exhausted mother's bed.

'Put aside all the slurs against Ethel Slater. Ignore what Mr Cox wants you to think the neighbours have tried to hide. Listen to what they did say instead. Olive Songhirst would have adopted this baby, not have it aborted; Mrs

Sathersthwaite doted on this baby – they both did; and Annie Lofthouse took Ethel into her home out of the kindness of her heart. And concentrate on two things, the medical evidence and the confession.

'The bruise on the scalp is the key to your decision. One accidental injury, like a pear ripening in a fruit bowl, or two separate blows to William's head. Ask yourselves this. Who should I believe? Dr Lawson, who is certain about everything and questions nothing? Or Dr Samuels, who questions everything and is certain of only one thing? That we cannot be sure the baby was injured twice. There you have it, members of the jury. If she cannot be certain, then neither can you. There is reasonable doubt.

'And then there is Miss Slater's confession. A false confession. I ask you to dismiss it from your minds. Think, put yourself in her shoes in that police station at midnight. A woman who has just found her baby dead and spent all day in a room waiting to explain her story. To anybody who might make things right. She's frightened, she's lonely, she's had enough of life. Ethel Slater was riddled with guilt, guilt that her baby had died, guilt she had left her mother to fend for herself, but not guilty of murder. She was guilty of not keeping safe the only thing that was really her own. No wonder she confessed. She would sign anything to get herself home, whatever it cost. Members of the jury, don't let the cost be her life. Reject this confession as meaningless words. Not guilty must be your verdict.'

*

Justice Weaver stifled a yawn and looked up.

'Ladies and gentlemen of the jury,' he said, fixing them in his gaze, 'you've listened very patiently over the past two days to all the evidence we shall hear on this grave and disturbing matter. Ethel Slater stands before you charged with the callous murder of her newborn baby. Your duty now is to think very carefully, then decide whether she wilfully committed two assaults, or whether her baby died by a tragic accident. You must decide whether she is guilty as charged or innocent. And my task now is to explain to you how to get to your verdict.

'Let's start with what we do know about Miss Slater. And then we'll ask what we don't know.'

Ethel looked to the jury, then to Mr Joyce. He'll say something to help me, surely, she thought, he knows I didn't do anything to hurt my baby. He looked back at her too, but all he could see was lank hair and a frozen, cross-eyed stare. There was nothing he could say or do now that would make any difference.

The judge continued. 'Now, members of the jury, Miss Slater has confessed to this crime, and you may well consider that to be the strongest piece of evidence against her. She has signed in her own hand a statement she made to Inspector Harrison, which concludes in its final sentence, "*I'm sorry, I didn't mean to kill my baby.*" The inspector, a police officer of long standing, has told us that he read out this statement to Miss Slater and that she signed it willingly. You may decide she said she'd killed her baby, but you've heard her say in court now that she denies it. You must balance this in your minds and come to your own conclusion.

'What else do we know about Ethel Slater? She is unmarried and lives with her parents. She lives a simple life, you might say. She struck up some sort of casual sexual relationship with the boy next door, Mr Edward Sathersthwaite. And fatefully she lost her virginity and fell pregnant on the same encounter.'

That's about the long and the short of it, thought Mr Cox.

I'd object to this, thought Mr Joyce, if I had the chance; it might be true but it's hardly fair. A loose woman, confirmed in the minds of some.

'Now,' said Justice Weaver, 'Miss Slater made few plans for her baby, and you might ask yourselves why not. She chose to have the baby in her parents' house, although she had the chance to go to a special home for unmarried mothers. And she declined the offer to have him adopted. In fact, she refused all help. Why? Perhaps she was frightened, perhaps she was feckless, or perhaps she did not want the baby at all.

'But, and this you must consider, why would a mother want to kill her baby? It is your duty to consider a motive. Revenge, says Mr Cox. To thwart the father. But no, says Mr Joyce, there is no motive, because there is no intention to harm her baby. She wanted to keep this baby all to herself.

'I take you now to the medical evidence, the heart of the matter. Dr Lawson is clear that baby William received two deliberate severe blows to the head, the first just after he was born and the second fatal one some days later caused a skull fracture and a brain haemorrhage. And, members of the jury, if you believe her father's statement that he was not at home, the only person who could have caused those injuries was Ethel Slater. Were there deliberate assaults intended to kill her baby? That is for you to decide.

'But Dr Lawson is absolutely wrong, says Dr Samuels. He is clearly mistaken; he has not even considered an alternative explanation. There are not two bruises on the head, she says, only one, when baby William fell to the floor as he was born. And there is no skull fracture, she tells you, only a crack where his skull bones grew together. And that he suffered an accidental bleed over his brain when his exhausted mother rolled on top of him during her sleep. Dr Samuels is experienced in these matters and has also told the court that she has witnessed this tragic story on more than one occasion.

'There you have it. You must weigh up all these options. Remember this – rely on witnesses only if you think that what they say is honest and accurate. Take your time, and return to this room when you are all agreed. And if there is no doubt in your minds that Miss Slater caused these injuries with the intention of harming her baby, you must find her guilty as charged. But if you consider that there is a reasonable chance that this baby died by accidental smothering, then you must find Miss Slater innocent of murder.'

With these final words he thanked the jury for their attention, half smiled at them, then closed his notebook and pushed it away from him. He rose to his feet, bowed his head to the barristers, and made for the door.

Thirty-One

'Enid, love, are you one sugar or two?' Nancy asked. 'Henry? Sorry, I should know by now, I know, but I forget you all as soon as I get 'ome. I've remembered you're weak, Reg, and you're not much milk, Albert.'

The jury had met for the very last time round this table. Today meant business. Justice Weaver had told them they must come to a verdict, '*Upon which you are all agreed*'. Ethel's future lay in their hands: either to be sent back down from the dock to the cell or walk out of the building to fresh air and freedom. The clerk of the court had followed them along the corridor from the courtroom and into the jury room pushing a large urn of tea and twelve cups and saucers on a trolley.

Nancy, a woman of late middle age with a wiry frame and pinched features that her husband put down to a lifetime of ceaseless and useless domestic activity, had taken it upon herself to set out the cups and pour the tea. She slid a battered old biscuit tin out into the middle of the table.

'And I've made us this to keep us goin', she added. 'We might be 'ere for a while. There's plenty to go round, and an extra chunk for you, Frank. I reckon you need fattenin' up.'

Nancy laughed at herself and Frank smiled back. George prised the lid off, pushed around the lumps of treacle toffee, took out the biggest for himself, then licked his finger and picked another for Ted sitting next to him.

Ray had had more than enough already. He pushed his cup of tea away without taking a sip.

'You stupid old woman,' he said. 'We're not here to have a bleedin' tea party.'

Nancy wilted onto her chair next to him without another word.

'There's no need for that, Mr Cooper,' Linda said.

She faced Ray Cooper from the opposite end of the table and fixed him in the eye.

An uneasy silence fell. They sat in an airless room with twelve chairs round an uncomfortably large table, a wooden floor, and a fusty smell, its monotony relieved only by a portrait on the wall of King George seated on the throne in coronation robes. The jury had already spent time in here while the barristers got on with their tedious legal arguments in their chambers and courtroom. They thought the barristers were clever men, especially when they couldn't understand what they meant. And most of them had done their best to listen to everything the witnesses had to say, even if it hadn't all made sense.

The jury was eight men and four women, and they chose to sit on the same chair on every visit to the room. They had struck up casual friendships: Henry with George and Ted, Pearl with Albert and Reg, and Nancy with Enid and Frank. But Jack had kept himself to himself, and Linda had chosen to sit at the end of the table furthest from Ray. She had tried her hardest to weigh up all the evidence, and winced like the rest of them at the sight or sound of injuries to a baby, but she understood one thing very clearly. She disliked Ray Cooper much more than she distrusted Ethel Slater in the dock.

'Look,' continued Ray, 'I don't know why we're bothering. We all know she's done it, and I've better things to do. I say we get the clerk back in here and call it a day.'

He pushed back his chair with a scrape along the floor and stood up to collect his coat.

'I'll tell him we're decided,' he said. 'Guilty. As sin. And I'm ready to give the verdict.'

'You can't go yet,' said Linda. She had grown more irritated as the trial had gone on with Ray Cooper's sneers and nasty views. Time to do battle. 'We've only just sat down,' she told him. 'And anyway, we might not all think she's guilty.'

She gathered her handbag up off the floor, then took out her wad of small brown envelopes and the sharpened stub of a pencil.

'I say,' she said, 'everybody writes down what they think, guilty or innocent, on one of these bits of paper, and we take it from there.'

'I'm with Ray,' Jack said. 'I've heard enough. Nowt will change my mind and I've a business to run.'

'Well, I'm with Linda, if you must know.' Nancy had found her voice again. 'I reckon it's only right we know where we all stand.'

'Good, that's decided then,' agreed Linda.

She scattered all the envelopes bar one for herself across the tabletop, and wrote '*innocent*' on her own. She turned it round for everyone to read and passed the pencil with a smile to the woman on her left. Pearl, Albert, and Reg kept their verdicts face down on the table, but then the pencil stuck at Frank. He fiddled with his bit of paper, put the tip of the lead to his lips, paused again, glanced furtively at Ray, looked down at his lap, and passed the stub on to his left. Enid and Nancy noted their verdicts and hid them face down, and Ray wrote '*guilty*' and slapped his slip down face up. Henry and George kept their verdicts from view and Ted wrote '*INNOCENT*' in big capitals and set his envelope on the biscuit-tin lid to face Ray. Jack said, 'Guilty, no doubt at all,' and stuck up his thumb to Ray at the far end of the table. Linda wrote down '*Guilty*' on Jack's envelope to save him the trouble and laid it on the table beside hers.

'Frank,' said Linda, 'you've abstained. Do you want to say anything before we do a count? We've all got to agree one way or the other at the end of the day.'

'I don't think I can do this,' he said. 'I think she's guilty, but just suppose we get it wrong?'

Ray Cooper had never liked the look of Frank; the Town Hall crawled with his sort. He seemed to have some brass, but he was a weed to be ground underfoot and he thought too much.

'Have some guts, ' Ray said. 'Be a man. Just say what you think is right.'

'Well, I will, then, seein' as you ask,' continued Frank.

He looked over the table at Ted's weather-beaten face and shock of white hair and his '*Innocent*' label balanced on the biscuit-tin lid. He admired the man's quiet belief in himself, his need to say so little, his certainty.

'The judge said we should say guilty only if there's no reasonable possibility it was an accident. His words exactly, and there is. The possibility of an accident, I mean. And if we say she's innocent and she's not, then we let a killer go free to have another baby, and she might do the same again. But if we say she's guilty, and we're wrong, which I reckon is worse, then it's two lives wasted and it should only be one. There's nothing more wrong than that, is there? And to cap it all, I'm not sure her father didn't kill the poor little scrap. He didn't stand a chance, one way or another.'

Far too difficult for me, thought Ray. He'd had a quiet word with Jack yesterday evening, and they had agreed that Ethel was guilty. The baby was dead, no room for doubt there, and it was no great loss if its mother went the same way as well. Plus, but he'd not told Jack this, he'd been dealt his own life sentence looking after his spastic daughter Joyce, so why shouldn't Ethel Slater get one too?

'She's signed a bleedin' confession, for God's sake,' Jack said. 'What more do you need? She's just a slapper; she eyes up young Sathersthwaite next door for a way out, lands him, and kills the kid to get her own back when he wants nowt to do with her anymore. They're both scum. He's told her to sling her 'ook, so she plans to drop it with no-one else there, chuck it at the wall, then stuff it in a shoebox. End of. But the old hag next door sticks her oar in. Then her lad gets wind of it and sends her a teddy bear to rub it in 'cos he's an evil bastard too, and she loses it. Does the job proper this time. All makes sense to me.'

'Stop!' interrupted Linda. 'We'll count these verdicts first.'

She pushed her own verdict and Jack's back into the middle of the table, gathered all the rest into a little heap face down, shuffled them around as if they were so many dominoes, then turned them over slowly one by one. The pile of guilties beat the pile of innocents.

'That's Frank's don't-know-yet,' she said, and slid his envelope back over to him. 'Six of us say guilty, and five of us say innocent.'

'Well, I suppose I'd best speak up for her to kick off,' said Reg. 'Don't anyone go believin' that Inspector Harrison for a minute. She never said what he's written down. She couldn't. They were his words, you can see that a mile off. Her brief was dead right. She's far too dim to use his big fancy words.'

'But she signed it, though,' said Jack. 'Maybe she didn't use them words exactly, but he's read it out to her, and she's agreed, it's a fair cop, that's what happened, as near as damn it, and owned up.'

'You haven't spent a night in clink, have you, Jack?' asked Reg. 'Like I have. I got banged up in Millgarth nick after takin' a good kickin' in The Black Bull in Horsforth. They kept me sat on an 'ard chair in a dark, freezin' room all night with a busted nose till the mornin'. I'd come round and sobered up, but I just had to get out o' there. I'd not broken any law, but I'd 'ave signed me own death warrant if they'd put it in front of me. They're bastards, the police. They just want the likes of Ethel Slater and me banged up and signed off. Harrison's sure in his own mind that she killed the baby, don't get me wrong, but he couldn't give a shit really, as long as he gets a confession. She's never read a word of what he's scribbled down. Or listened to him readin' it out.'

Reg is wrong about one thing at least, thought Jack. He knew just what to expect from the plods. They were all dodgy in his book. He'd had no problem buying a few of them off with the odd pack of cigarettes when they came nosing round his warehouse stacked with stolen army surplus.

'And another thing,' said Jack, 'I reckon Mrs Sathersthwaite is feedin' us a right cock-an'-bull story as well. She can't know it was Ethel Slater thumpin' on the wall, and not the baby's head landin'. There's no way she could tell; she was half asleep. Finds the baby on the floor, in a bad way. I'll buy that, but comes round. Come on, course it's in a bad way, Jesus Christ. It's just been chucked at a wall. And Slater tries to sell us all this bullshit about havin' a baby standin' up! My missus was flat out in bed. I mean, pull the other one.'

'I had my first standin' up,' said Nancy. 'It was our Edward. He was a couple of weeks early, and we weren't expectin' him yet. Tom was out on site, an' there was nobody else at home when me waters went. I tried lyin' down like you do, but it was much easier standin' and leanin' agen the kitchen sink. Me labour pain eased like that, and it all went fine. I mean, it was a long time ago now. It was even easier the next time, I can tell you. I knew what to expect then. We 'ad five kids all told, and I lose count of how many grandkids since. If only she'd trusted the old dear next door sooner, we wouldn't all be 'ere now. And I don't know what this teddy-bear nonsense is all about, Jack. Of course her aunty in Rochdale has made it and posted it. I'd 'ave done just the same. She's no more killed her baby than any of us in this room. It's barmy. She just doesn't 'ave it in her. It's as simple as that.

'Anyway, that's what I think, I've said me piece now,' said Nancy. She pushed the biscuit tin back in Frank's direction and added a drop more tea to her cup.

'I had a mare foal standin' up once,' Ted said. 'It was a good few years back now, me own fault really.'

'What?' said George. 'Come again.'

Ted hadn't given much away about himself, but George knew that he farmed a few hundred acres north of Leeds for a living and reared pigs. He liked to talk about the wettest spring and the driest summer he'd ever known, but this was the first time George had heard Ted say anything that might make a difference.

'She foaled onto t'stockyard floor. She were crowning in the barn on her side when I left her. I walked down to muck out her stable, and by t'time I got back she'd climbed onto her legs somehow and tottered out into t'yard. Yer can 'ave no end of trouble with 'orses. They can push out a foal within fifteen minutes start to finish. I really shouldn't 'ave left her. A mare can get very jittery birthin' of a foal and up and down on their 'ind legs, up and down, restless like. Cows are a lot easier, I allus say. I can't be callin' out a veterinary every time I 'ave a mare in foal. Anyway, it's cracked its 'ead in the drop onto the slabs and was dead within an hour. This young lass in court's done just the same. She's nowt but a kid herself. It's dropped head-first onto floorboards as 'ard as stockyard slabs, and it's a wonder it's ended up with nowt worse than a bruise. Farmin's all I know about, nowt else, but I reckon she's pupped on 'er 'ind legs. That's the long and the short of it, if you ask me.'

'Blimey,' said George. 'You're a dark 'orse yourself. If you're right, that explains the bruise on 'is scalp then?'

'And the mess on the bedroom floor,' added Ted. 'Cord an' afterbirth 'as to come away too. It could 'ave delivered straight after, 'specially if she's pupped standin' up or crouched on all fours.'

'The splash of blood on the wall an' all?' George asked. 'I reckon.'

'Alright then, I'll give you that, Ted,' George continued. 'You don't say much, do you? But I suppose that's farmers for you, stuck in a field by yourself all day. It's not 'cos you've nowt to say, though. Seems to me you know what you're talking about. It doesn't explain the second bruise, though, does it, old boy?'

'It doesn't need to,' interrupted Linda. 'Maybe there's only one bruise, not one on top of another. The doctors can't agree on that. Two together just doesn't make much sense to me at all. Just suppose she'd thrown her teddy bear twice, what's the chances of the wall hittin' his head in the same place? And Dr Samuels thinks there was only one bruise, just that it was ripening, like a pear.'

'Those two doctors 'aven't got a clue,' said Ray. 'They're talkin' out of their arses if you ask me. If they can't agree, we've no chance.'

'Ray, that's just it, and we are asking you,' said Linda. 'If they can't agree, Ethel should get the benefit of the doubt. That's Frank's point. You didn't look at the photos of the post-mortem, did you?'

'Too true, no, I did not,' said Ray. 'They're disgustin'. If doctors who get paid a bomb to look at these things can't do their jobs right an' won't agree, then we're sunk. They must be weird, anyway, to do a job like that. She's cracked this baby on the 'ead, and who cares if it's once or twice? She's guilty whichever way you want to look at it.'

'Well, I did 'ave a good look at 'em,' Linda continued. 'That bruise was a pattern of all shades of different colours, all mixed up together. And Dr Samuels said it could be one bruise changing, sort of ripening. A pear doesn't ripen all at the same time, she said, you get yellow bits and brown bits and hard bits and soft bits all together. But it's all one pear, that's what she's saying. I've really thought about this, and it stacks up for me. I think if we can all agree that it might, just might, be one bruise, and then we listen to Ted, we can't say she's guilty. Admit it to yourself, Ray, Dr Samuels could be right.'

'It's very stuffy in 'ere,' said Pearl. 'Can we have a break, please, Ray?'

'Yes, we're allowed,' said Linda. 'But we're not allowed to talk about all this outside this room.'

Ray snapped out of his daydream, tapped on his cigarette packet on the table, and raised a finger to Jack.

*

Ray and Jack skirted the door to the canteen and descended the polished marble staircase of the Assize Court, its enormous stained-glass dome suspending the massive chandelier and supported by stone arches, and reeking of old Victorian wealth. They sat together on the top step leading down from the portico to the cascading fountain in the town hall square. Ray took off his trilby, held a cigarette out to Jack, and struck a match for them both.

'There was plenty of brass around when they built this place,' Jack said. 'Statues, all these blokes watchin' what you're doin'. They give me the creeps. Put me in a ware'ouse any day.'

'I don't notice 'em anymore,' Ray returned. 'Place is full of toffs. I work upstairs next door.'

'Ray, listen,' said Jack. They both looked out across the people going about their lives in the square. 'I know we agreed last night that we couldn't hack it if she was found not guilty. Or at least you couldn't. But I'm a simple bloke, Ray, and to be honest I couldn't give a shit one way or the other. I can't say this in front of the old maids back inside, but I'm going to miss a big order if I'm not back at work to take a call later on. And no way we're goin' to shift missus lah-di-dah smarty pants Linda if we stick to our guns. Seems to me it's swingin' towards not guilty, and I'd go along wi' that just to get shut now. I've 'ad a gut full. What you reckon?'

'She did it, for fuck's sake,' said Ray.

'Maybe,' Jack said. 'So what? It's only a baby. I don't know what all the fuss is about.'

Ray took a couple of deep drags on his cigarette and ground the stub onto the step below.

'You know Joyce, my daughter, Jack?'

'No, can't say I do, but I'd 'eard she's a spastic. Why?'

Ray's eyelids snapped shut.

'She was starved of oxygen at birth, they reckon.'

'Shit, I'm sorry to hear that. I didn't know.'

'Cord tight round her neck.'

'Well, that's midwives not doin' their jobs for you.'

Ray picked his trilby off the step between them and brushed some imaginary specks of dust off the crown.

'She's my Joyce, Jack.'

He straightened out the hairs in the peacock feather in his hat.

'She was born at home, like Ethel Slater's baby. No midwife.'

'Fuck me! You couldn't get to unwrap it quick enough?'

'I was in the Blue Moon.'

'Christ!' Jack blurted. 'So it was your fault?'

Nobody had ever said it to his face before.

He looked up at the water tumbling down the fountain but was too choked to speak.

'But you blame Ethel Slater? Is that it?'

That hurt.

Ray turned to face Jack.

'Fuck you,' he said.

Quietly.

Jack was right.

On both counts.

'C'mon, Ray,' Jack said. 'Let's get back upstairs. Get job done. Yes?'

*

Nancy had cleared the crockery from the table by the time Ray and Jack returned to their chairs, and she was stacking the saucers in a pile and balancing the cups neatly on top of one another on the trolley. She was about to wheel it all back along the corridor to the clerk, with a polite request for another brew in an hour or so if he would be so kind, when Enid held the door open for her and whispered in her ear.

'What do you think, Nance?'

'Nay, lass.' Nancy kept her voice down. 'She's not done owt bad. You've just got to look at 'er. She's such a sad, cock-eyed, crooked little thing, she wouldn't say boo to a goose. She just wanted a baby to love and take care of, same as you an' me. She's never meant no 'arm to anybody in 'er life.'

'Ladies,' interrupted Linda from the far end of the table, 'can you two share it with the rest of us, please?'

'You say for me, will you, Nance?' Enid said as she took her seat.

'No, go on, Enid, you say it,' said Linda. 'We need your say too, please.'

'Well, all I know is that there was a girl a few doors down our street 'ad a baby that she found dead in 'er cot. A lovely girl, I allus thought. Her 'usband was away in North Africa or somewhere, but he'd been back on leave. There was folk as said it weren't his baby, but she told me it was, and I'd no reason to doubt 'er word. Anyway, there was them that thought she'd smothered it, an' t'poor lass could never come to terms with 'er loss, and at finish she put 'er 'ead in the gas oven. That's all I think, really.'

'Cruel.'

The room was stunned into silence by that one short word.

It was Ray who had spoken.

He was looking across the table to the two little stacks of envelopes.

Well, if timid Enid can pipe up, thought Pearl, then what's to stop me?

'Can I change me mind, please, Linda?' Pearl asked. 'I've listened to all this, and I'm not so sure anymore. I 'ad her down for wantin' rid of her baby when she turned down the mothers' 'ome and then took herself off to Rochdale, but she must 'ave been too far gone by then. I think I might 'ave 'ad it all wrong now. Ted and Linda 'ave made a lot of sense to me with the bruise.'

'An' her shoutin' out from the dock says a lot to me an' all,' Henry added. 'What with the bobby lyin' and her blurtin' out she never went to Rochdale to get an abortion at her aunty's. She meant "never" when she shouted it. Either she's tellin' the truth, or she's a bloody good liar.'

'But, ladies and gents, there's one big thing we're missin',' Albert said without looking up from the table. He'd been drawing circles round tiny matchstick men on one of Linda's envelopes. He took the last piece of toffee from the tin and laid the pencil back out on the lid.

'I did 'ave a good look at them photos, madam,' he said to Linda. 'An' there's a crack in the skull under a thumpin' big bruise over a clot on the brain. We've not explained them all lined up, 'ave we? She's clouted it. Wriggle out of that with one of your fancy theories.'

'No fancy theory,' said Ted. 'We can talk around all this till the cows come 'ome. She's overlaid it, plain and simple. First thing I thought of when she said she found it dead in 'er bed with some blood on it. Sows do it all the time if you don't keep sucklin' piglets away from 'er in a sow stall.

She can roll over onto 'er piglets soon as look at 'em. I've found 'em dead with flat 'eads and blood on their snouts many a time. Poor girl's given birth standin' up then fallen asleep exhausted on top of the little bugger, and there's nowt more to it. It stands to reason. She's guilty of nowt more than lovin' and trustin'.'

'I'm sure you're right,' said Linda. 'Anyone else want a say?'

'Not me,' Ray said. 'I said at the outset. I've heard more than enough. Let's get job done. We need a final vote.'

Thirty-Two

Ethel's warder turned his wrist to look at the time and sighed, then leant back against the wall of the cell and bit his nails. He'd chosen to sit opposite the doorway onto the stairwell back up to the dock, and told Ethel to lie out on the bench along the sidewall and face him. That way, he'd have a couple of seconds to react if she tried to make for the door.

He switched his vacant gaze off the bottom step every now and then to study Ethel's face, not to catch her attention but to watch her lazy eye, roaming and jerking in its socket. Ethel had come to know that people who didn't know her or like her did that. But she'd learnt not to care. Eddie's old playmate Tom Shaw from their days of childish games on the bombed-house rubble would just stop and stare at her eyes and say nothing. They were the times, though, when Eddie didn't even notice her face.

The wait was by far the hardest bit, the warder had told her, but he thought it would soon be over. The jury had a simple decision to make. Maybe so, but Ethel was scared that a much longer wait would follow. Winnie's reprieve had not come through. Her new-found friend had been taken from their shared cell to spend her last night alone, and Ethel's latest cellmate had said that Winnie had been hanged. Months, years, of torment brought to a swift, merciful end, her cellmate had said, and a noose would do the same for her. Ethel tried not to think about choking, but she could think of little else. And she promised herself to be brave when the time came, for her mother's sake, nobody else's, but she knew she wouldn't be. She lived in dread. But please God in His mercy might then let her hold her baby again. That was her only comfort.

But they must know she hadn't meant to kill her own baby. She had known at the time that couldn't be so, but now she could no longer be sure. Of anything. It was all so long ago and she'd heard so many men use their clever words and tell their painful stories. Perhaps all the lies were the truth, and much of the truth had become lies. Maybe her dream was the real world. Night after night she would watch the woman with cross eyes snatch a teddy bear from a blood-soaked bed and hurl him at the wall, only to jerk awake in beads of sweat and exhaustion.

And perhaps everybody else had seen her doing it too.

The jury would know what really happened and tell the judge one way or the other.

*

Ethel stared at the crawl of the hands of the silent clock on the wall and could see only her baby's face. But then a strip of light appeared at the foot of the door and flickered. She exchanged a glance with her warder at the sound of footfall in the courtroom above. The clerk descended the stairs and appeared in the doorway to tell him that the jury were ready to return. The warder stood up from his bench and gestured to Ethel to hold her arms out for the handcuffs, then pushed her back up the dark, steep stairwell towards the square of light in the dock.

'Court rise,' said the clerk.

Ethel turned her head up to the gallery behind her.

She saw a sea of blurred faces and hid her eyes with her hands.

'Stand,' the judge told her.

'Have you reached a verdict upon which you are all agreed?' the clerk asked Ray Cooper.

'Yes.'

'Do you find the defendant guilty or not guilty of murder?'

Ethel gaped down into the well of the court, but her eyes were misted and unable to focus on anything.

Or see the foreman turn to address the judge.

'Not guilty.'

But then the judge looked up and fixed her eyes with his.

'You are free to go,' he told her.

And peace be with you, he thought.

She threw her head back and screamed to the ceiling.

A visceral, anguished cry.

Only now was she free to start grieving for her lost baby.

And for her stolen innocence.

PART V

Rochdale, Tuesday 2nd June 1953

Thirty-Three

Ethel woke slowly to the familiar, soft snorts and gentle rattle of the dray in the street below her window. The drayman had come earlier than usual to deliver more barrels for the big day. She had not felt as alive as this since the day the gates had opened and the circus had come to town.

Because there was Frank.

'Mornin', Annie. I've got 'em extra treats today,' she called out as she passed the cellar door. She could hear the hollow rumbling of the empties rolling across the flags down below.

Frank had already pulled Noah and Miriam to a halt outside The Junction by the time Ethel got outside. They stood restless, massive and steaming, lifting and stamping a foot gently now and then, and swaying their heads slowly from side to side. She took hold of Noah's bridle and steadied him, looked inside his blinker into a big brown doleful eye, and held out an apple to his lips on the flat of her hand.

'Mornin', Frank,' she said. She ran her hand up and down Miriam's nose, then gave her an apple too. 'What a day for it, ey? I'd forgotten you were comin' this early.'

'Good mornin', sweet'art,' Frank replied. He lifted off his cap by the peak and repositioned it back on his head in a single swing of the arm. 'They 'ave a spring in their step when they know they're comin' to see you. You spoil 'em. You all shipshape an' ready in there?'

'You know our Annie. She's been plannin' this day for months.'

Frank took the two bridles out of Ethel's hands and slipped a nosebag of hay over each of his horses' heads, then moved aside to take a firm grip of the hook on the hatch and lift it open onto the pavement.

Rolling the full barrels down the ramp and hauling the empties back to the top was a three-man job. Frank lifted and dropped them over the side of the cart onto the leather stool at the kerb for Ethel to clip the chain round the rim. Then both taking the strain and playing out the rope between them, they lowered the weight of each barrel through the hatch and down the ramp. The cellar was Annie's job now that Albert had died. Out of sight down in the bowels of The Junction, she would give a shout when the empty was ready to drag back to the top. This was the task Ethel enjoyed more than any other at the pub: the polished brasses and rich, earthy smell of Noah and Miriam; the heave on the rope together; the neat row of barrels of best bitter stacked along the cellar wall. But it was Frank's nearness she craved most of all, to see the strength in his shoulders, the bristles of black hair at the back of his neck, the beads of sweat on his brow, and the warmth in his grin. And the bond that had grown between them. She'd told him her nightmare, and he'd doubted not one word. He had taken delivery from the postman one morning of the brown paper parcel of the teddy bear sent back from Leeds by Mr Joyce, and helped Ethel through her mother's and her baby's funerals.

'You back 'ere for the television later, Frank?' Ethel asked.

She held out half a carrot each for Noah and Miriam on her hand and gave their flanks a hefty pat goodbye.

'We've a few more drop-offs yet,' he replied, 'then I'm back. Not sure I'll watch it, though. Fancy do, not my cup o' tea. We've got The Grapes, so I'll be in the tap room.'

'You wouldn't get in the lounge anyway, Frank, don't think. Standin' room only.'

'Couldn't miss a darts match, Ethel. An' I'll let you into a secret, love. It's not only these 'orses gets a spring in their steps comin' to The Junction. You make me 'eart sing. You do know that, don't you?'

'Go away,' she told him. 'You're soft in the 'ead. And don't you be late.'

*

How to lay out the saloon and find the money for a television set had been Annie's biggest worries. Part of the problem was that she didn't know how many people to expect. If she could clear away the tables and stack them somehow in front of the fireplace, they could probably squeeze up to thirty people into the room. Jack had spent most of one afternoon finding the best place to pick up reception for the set, and he reckoned to get the clearest picture near the window in the corner as long as the drape curtains opposite the bar were pulled back. It would have to sit on a chair on top of a table so that people standing just inside the door at the back could get a view. And Jack would probably have to stay at the front to slap the box and fiddle with the antennae if they lost the picture. This all meant pushing the piano away from the corner in front of the stacked tables. Annie really couldn't be doing with folk standing up to get a drink during the ceremony, so Vera and herself could pass the plates of sandwiches and jellies out into the room from the bar. Once it was all over, they could move the chairs into the corridor or back to people's houses to leave a bit of a dance floor and somewhere to judge the fancy dress. Jack could then shift the tables back into their proper places for the evening session. They could leave the Union Jacks and the banner with the crown draped over the mantlepiece until they needed to light a fire later in the year. This all needed thinking through, sorted before the big day, nothing left to chance.

Annie wished her Albert had still been with her at The Junction to direct operations and take some of the strain, but he'd died getting out of the bath one Saturday afternoon, and it was not to be. Annie and Ethel got back home to the pub from the shops to find him. He had collapsed onto the bathroom carpet. He'd taken the plug out and the water must have drained away as he died. Annie had tried to pick him up and rouse him, but Ethel could see that he was long gone. Annie always needed somebody to fuss over, and thankfully Ethel had returned to The Junction after all her troubles were over. Annie knew, though, deep in her heart that, truth be told, she wasn't getting any younger. The mothering was switching the other way round and she couldn't do without her Ethel now. She was glad to see that Ethel was taking the reins at The Junction. And Annie had guessed that she was sweet on Frank.

Ethel missed her Uncle Albert too, but not as much as her mother. Her uncle had lived in the past, in his war years, and never felt the need to say much about the present. That's what Ethel liked about him so much; he was part of her own past, her carefree childhood visits to The Junction. Her mother had come with Ethel too to spend her final weeks at the pub after the trial and had slipped away in her bed with no fuss. She'd told her Ethel to find it in her heart to forgive her father for all his philandering; he was what he was, and she'd known that from the off, and they'd been happy enough in the early days; and you only have one dad.

Ethel and Annie had made the final touches to the planning on the day before the coronation. They decided between them that Ethel could manage the tap room by herself if Vera would help Annie out in the saloon. Frank and the darts teams would keep Ethel busy pulling pints, but they wouldn't need anything fancy, and she could carry the pies and peas in from the kitchen. Vera had said she would close her shop early and not open up on the day itself. All her regulars wanted to spend their time in The Junction anyway. She brought in bowls of mandarin orange jelly for the children, then made plates of boiled egg, fish paste, and corned beef sandwiches, and stacked them all in the larder overnight. She agreed to come in before opening time on coronation day and get to work again. Annie set out tumblers in four neat rows of ten at the end of the saloon bar near the door, and laid a bar towel over them overnight to keep out the dust. It would be a nice idea, Annie reckoned, to serve half a glass of Pomagne to each of her guests on arrival.

Little Bo Peep, a bobbie with a policeman's helmet, and a queen with papier mâché crown were the first to take their seats at the front with mums, dads, family, and friends in the rows behind. Annie had reserved the best chairs for children nearest the set. The sight of a new television staved off any stage fright they might have felt ahead of the fancy-dress competition. Barring one or two late-comers at the back of the saloon, all the chairs were taken, and the drinks served and the sandwiches passed out from the bar by the time the queen-in-waiting emerged from Buckingham Palace in the golden carriage. Jack kept the television reception alive and Vera waved her little flag back at the crowds down the Mall, while envious mums in the room sat in awe of a queen in an open carriage. Jack put his fingers into his mouth and whistled Ethel through from serving in the tap room in time to witness the glittering dress and train of a queen in procession up the steps to the Abbey. But then a respectful silence with hushed asides descended as a balding Archbishop of Canterbury placed the robes around Her Majesty's shoulders, the sceptres in her outstretched hands, and the crown on her head. What a shame it was raining for the thousands camped out along the return journey to the Palace and all the chiefs and dignitaries from foreign lands, mounted soldiers, and brass military bands. Once the Queen was back in her

Palace and waving from the balcony to her loyal subjects in
The Junction, Annie resumed her rightful position at the
piano and the throng rounded off their own celebrations
with a chorus of 'God Save the Queen'.

*

Not even the coronation of a new queen, however, could
postpone a darts match once it was in the calendar. And
for some of the team an excuse not to watch royal toffs
was a welcome distraction. The tap room was a tight
squeeze for twelve burly men, and within earshot of the
whoops and cheers in the saloon. The Junction usually
lost to The Grapes, and this match had gone the same
way towards the end of the coronation when the best
went off again.

'Frank,' said Ethel, 'you got a minute? I need an 'and,
and Jack's still in charge of the television set.'

Frank gave Ethel a nod and laid his darts down with
his pint on the windowsill.

Ethel came out through the gap at the end of the bar
and Frank followed her through the cellar door and down
the stone steps. He tried the light switch at the top, but the
bulb had blown, and they would have to manage by the
light shining in through the grate from the street. Ethel
took the spanner from the hook and released the nut at the
top of the empty barrel.

'Roll me over a best bitter, please, Frank,' she said.

Frank watched her draw out the pipe from the old
barrel and wipe it round with a cloth, then he reached for
a new one from the delivery that morning.

'Not that one, Frank. Oldest first. Along the back wall.'

'Right you are,' he said, and dragged a barrel by its lip across the slippery flags from the gap alongside the steps.

He leant on its rim while Ethel bent to loosen the nut.

'You've come on a fair bit, Ethel,' he said, 'since last time you were 'ere over Christmas.'

They both straightened up and faced one another across the barrel.

'I 'ave,' she replied. 'No two ways about it. I 'ad to. There was nowt left for me in the terrace.'

He dropped his gaze for a second then looked back up at her.

'Can I ask you summat sort of personal, Ethel? Summat I've been meanin' to ask.'

She lifted her left hand over her eye to get a sharper view of his face in shadow.

A trick she had learned of late.

'Yes.'

'Would you 'ave married Eddie Sath if he'd asked you?'

'I would that,' she said. 'Like a shot. I loved 'im. Since we were kids. I didn't want anybody else back then. Mind you, back then I didn't know there ever could be anybody else.'

'He missed his chance.'

They stood a moment in silence.

They both realised what each other had just said.

She dared to hope.

'Can I ask you summat else then?'

'Go on.'

'Can I kiss you, Ethel?'

'Frank,' she said, and took her hand down from her face, 'you've no need to ask.'

'EPILOGUE

35 Hob Moor Terrace
York
3 May 1960

Dear Ethel,

Aggie Sath walked over the moor from the old terrace a while ago and knocked on my door. She told me you run the junction now. I do hope this letter gets to you. I wrote to the junction once before a long time ago, but I don't know if you remember that. Mrs Sath told me you got married a while back and you've got a new baby girl. Lydia. I'm so pleased for you, Ethel, you deserve to be happy. I could never go back to the terrace after the trial and I live about a mile away now. I'd not seen anybody from back there till Mrs Sath came round. I hurt Charlie and he didn't deserve it but he forgave me and he's a train driver now. He takes the mail train out of the station first thing in the morning. He couldn't forgive Dennis, though, and set about him in the snicket. He broke your father's arm and he was in hospital for a while. He deserved a kicking, and so did I, but I never got one. Your father is by himself now in the old house. Mrs Sath says he had to get shut of his shop because nobody would buy anything. She sees him over the fence with his pigeons, but they don't speak. Mrs Sath lives alone as well. Her Eddie moved away too.

I can never make any sense of what happened to you, Ethel. There were people had it in for you and I don't know why. I think you were a soft target for cruel men. Please find it in your heart to forgive me, and your father if you can. You used to come over to tell me your secrets in my back kitchen, but I never told you mine. The long and the short of it is I only ever wanted a baby myself too, nothing more than that, but some things are meant not to be.

God love you,
Olive

ACKNOWLEDGEMENTS

My thanks to the neighbours in the street in York where I was a child, upon whose peculiarities many of the characters in this book are based. These people are all long gone, but they live on in my head. To His Honour Jeffrey Lewis for his advice on the legal system. To Jonathan Lamming for his advice on veterinary matters. And to the numerous friends in writing groups along the way, particularly Mark Connors, without whose upbeat encouragement and stinging criticism (meted out in equal measure), Ethel would never have got off the ground.

ABOUT THE AUTHOR

Phil Batman has known he wanted to be a pathologist for as long as he can remember. He completed his medical education at Cambridge University and then trained as a pathologist at St George's Hospital in London. He subsequently specialised in the investigation of suspicious deaths of babies. He became an expert in the medico-legal defence of some parents charged with their murder, felt the agonising doubts between innocence and guilt and witnessed miscarriage of justice. Phil lives in Ilkley, West Yorkshire.